CAPTIVE . . . OR CAPTIVATED?

"I told you before you could not escape," Fox whispered hotly. He held her firmly against the wall, his body tight against hers.

Jordan knew he spoke the truth. How could she escape from Fox? And how could her children ever depend on her again if she couldn't fight to get to them? Jordan trembled and, with a sob, she turned away, waiting for Fox's berating words.

But when the silence stretched on, she lifted her gaze, unprepared for the tenderness in the blue depths of his eyes. He lifted a finger to trace the path of a tear before his gaze swept over her face. Warmth spread through Jordan, sharpening her senses. The muscles in his strong chest pressed against her breasts, his powerful thighs crushed against her. And something more, something dangerous stirred inside her—something powerful that threatened to engulf her.

She dropped her gaze to his lips, lips that were so sensual, so entrancing. Lips that were slowly coming closer and closer. Jordan wanted to feel his kiss. His lips closed over hers, a startlingly gentle caress, a warm, wet brush of his lips. But with that simple touch, Jordan was swept away by the emotions raging inside her. Her world was spinning on its axis, and she clung to Fox as if he were the only thing keeping her from falling.

"I won't let you go, Jordan," he whispered against her lips. "Not this time."

CHAMPION OF THE HEART

LAUREL O'DONNELL

ZEBRA BOOKS
KENSINGTON PUBLISHING CORP.
http://www.zebrabooks.com

ZEBRA BOOKS are published by

Kensington Publishing Corp.
850 Third Avenue
New York, NY 10022

First Printing: June, 2001
10 9 8 7 6 5 4 3 2 1

Printed in the United States of America

To
Tracy Bernstein,
A great editor, a good friend.
Thanks for letting me write what is in my heart.
I wish you luck in all that you do.

And to
My partner, my love and my best friend—
My husband, Jack.

PROLOGUE

England, 1323

Dark demons cast by the dying fire in the hearth danced over the cold stone walls of the solar room. Lord Frederick Mercer sat on the bed, lifting his arm to tighten the straps of his plate armor. Beside him Michael shifted his position, bowing his blond head. Fox, five years older than Michael, paced the floor before the bed.

"I don't understand, Father." Fox Mercer looked at his father with confused eyes, his young face scowling in bewilderment. He was thirteen, but today he had enough pain in his heart and enough torment in his soul for a man five times his age. "Just tell the king who did it."

"I can't, Fox," Frederick Mercer said, bending to slip his booted foot into a spur. He was quiet for a moment, staring at his boot. "I can't." He reached for his other boot and slid it on.

Fox paced the drafty room, desperately searching for a way out of the terrifying predicament his father was in. For a brief, horrifying moment the shadows of the waning fire took on the shape of an executioner, his face masked in a dark hood, his thick arms clutching an enormous ax. Fox quickly looked away from the black silhouette on the wall. No one was worth this sort of protection, not with such disastrous consequences. Fox's gaze fell on his younger brother. Michael sat on his father's bed, his shoulders slumped, his head bowed. His brother's blond hair hung forward to obscure his face. Michael had been quiet for days now, unnaturally silent.

The chink of chain mail made Fox turn back to his father. As he looked at the man who raised him, who gave him a home, who always gave him hope for the future, he clenched his teeth, making his jaw ache with the effort. His small fingers clenched into fists so hard it made his arms shake. Why would his father give up everything to keep the identity of a murderer secret? Fox began to pace again. Back and forth, back and forth, fighting to keep his emotions in check, fighting to remain calm—just as his father had taught him.

But today this was a battle Fox would not win. He stopped and whirled to face his father. "Don't you care about what happens to us?" he asked in agony.

Lord Mercer straightened in his chair. "Of course I do. I care . . ." He took a deep breath. "I would do anything to protect you and Michael. Anything." He shook his head and resumed his preparations, standing and reaching for his belt. "I only wish I had killed the baron myself." He lifted haunted eyes to stare at Fox. "He was a horrible man, Fox." He turned to Michael on the bed beside him and tenderly stroked his hair. "A horrible man."

Fox scowled. "But I don't understand."

"You don't have to. We will not speak of it again." His father picked up his sword and gazed at it for a very long moment.

Fox couldn't stop the anger that burned in his chest. What kind of man was the murderer to remain silent while his father took the punishment for him? Had he no honor? Fox's jaw clenched. Whoever had murdered the baron would pay. It was a vow he was determined to keep, no matter how long it took him.

His father slid his sword into his sheath and then headed for the door.

Fox looked at Michael. His brother was staring at him with large eyes. They were the saddest eyes Fox had ever seen. He took his little brother's hand in his and squeezed it reassuringly. Together they left the room, shadowing their father as he moved down the corridors and through the stone tunnels that made up Castle Mercer's hallways, and then descended a dark spiral stairway to the Great Hall.

The noise coming from the Hall was a jumble of tones and timbers, some somber weeping and sad words of mourning, some dark laughter and sinister words of support. His family's doom waited in the room. Some of the gathered throng dreaded what was to come, while others approved and eagerly waited for the king's response. Fox's heart started pounding faster in his chest. His hand tightened around Michael's, his palm slick with nervous sweat.

His father did not hesitate at the room's threshold. He moved into the Great Hall with his customary strong stride, his head held high. Fox and Michael followed. Fox was careful to keep his eyes on his father's back. He didn't want to see the satisfied look in some of the gathered nobility's eyes. He didn't want to look at their disgust and their disapproval of the great man who walked proudly before him. They were all wrong in their merciless feelings for his father. All wrong.

Fox shifted his gaze to the front of the room. Normally, the raised platform situated there would hold the table for him and his family. But on this dark day, the table was gone. In its place was a row of seated people dressed in finery and velvets. One man drew his attention: King Edward of England. He was seated in an ornately decorated chair in the center of the row of nobles. He sat stiffly in the high-backed chair, surveying Fox's father with obvious disapproval, and absently rubbed his chin with long, slender fingers.

Fox's father stopped before the rise, bending one knee to the floor and bowing his head. Fox did the same, having to pull Michael down before the king.

A disgruntled snort came from the king, and Fox lifted his head slightly to see his reaction. The king studied his nails, announcing, "Rise, Mercer."

A murmur ran through the room. The King had not used Lord Mercer's rightful title.

Fox rose after his father, the insult and degradation not lost on him. Fox clenched his fist, careful not to hurt Michael.

The king waved a hand. Two men in chain mail came forward and took Fox's father's arm, leading him onto the rise. They turned him to face the crowd of nobles assembled in the room. A herald stepped down from the platform, clutching a rolled parchment. He was a thin man with a graying, manicured beard. The herald waited a moment for the room to become silent. Then he unrolled the parchment, cleared his throat, and read the king's decree.

"Frederick Mercer has been found guilty of official

corruption," the herald proclaimed, his voice echoing from one side of the Great Hall to the other.

Behind Mercer, the two knights lifted large metal hammers, and brought them smashing down at the back of his heels. His father's spurs cracked under the blows.

Fox stood immobile. Beside him, Michael sobbed and Fox felt the same anguish twisting his stomach and churning his throat. It took all his willpower to stand still and not rush to his father's aid.

Kchang! The grating, harsh sound of metal striking metal immediately filled the large room. The abrasive noise echoed from wall to wall, as if chasing the herald's ricocheting words. *Kchang!* The new blast of noise overtook the ghost of the previous metallic clang before it completely faded away.

With every strike, Fox willed his father's humiliation to stop, but it continued.

The herald looked back down at the unrolled parchment he held in his hands. "Frederick Mercer is stripped of his lands," he announced.

Murmurings spread like wildfire through the Great Hall.

Fox shifted his glance to King Edward, who lounged in his chair, calmly sipping a golden goblet full of ale, impervious to the destruction he was causing. He was an imposing man, large in presence, but slim in girth. He radiated power and authority with a mere glance and a gesture. Today, his eyes were dark, his expression calmly hiding his fierce anger, except for the grim set of his lips. The king scanned the mass of people in the Great Hall, as if searching for someone.

Why couldn't you tell him what he wants to know? Fox silently asked his father. Fox's jaw clenched with agony and anger. *Just tell him!* his mind screamed.

Kchang! The spurs finally broke away from the heel.

"His lands will be forfeit to Lord Vaughn," the herald droned.

Lord Vaughn! Evan's father. Fox's jaw clenched tighter. Evan. *My friend,* he thought bitterly.

On the platform, the two knights finally ceased their attack and stepped away from Lord Mercer. Each grabbed a fallen spur, one knight tossing a spur left and the other tossing a spur to the right.

Another knight clad in chain mail stepped forward with a sharp dagger.

Fox straightened instantly as the room became quiet, the murmuring dwindling into a prolonged stretch of complete silence.

The herald cleared his throat and repositioned the parchment in his hands. Finally, he read the last, chilling sentence written on the scroll. "Lord Frederick Mercer is no more."

Terror washed over Fox. Would the king allow his father to be killed? he wondered as the knight with the dagger ominously approached Frederick Mercer. The knight seized Mercer's leather belt, the belt that held his sword and scabbard about his waist, and raised the dagger. With a sharp, violent swipe, the knight cut the belt clean through. Frederick's sword fell to the floor with a loud, hollow clang. The knight picked up the sword, pulling it from its sheath, and lifted it high above his head.

Fox lunged forward.

But he was too late. The knight brought the weapon down, smashing the blunt part of the blade over his father's head with such force that the weapon broke in two. Frederick swayed under the brutal strike, dropping hard and fast to his knees. He swayed for a moment, his eyes nearly rolling into the back of his head, but he did not topple to the floor.

Fox reached out a hand to his father's elbow to steady him, but his father pulled angrily away from the offer of aid. He forced himself to stand erect as best he could, obviously struggling with the tremendous pain he was experiencing, his legs buckling under him as he stood. Blows of such force had killed lesser men. Blood trickled down his father's head, dripping over his left eye and splashing across his cheek. He steadied himself, bowed stiffly to the king, and turned to walk back down the aisle toward the large double doors that would free him from this public display of disgrace.

Fox watched him with a mixture of awe and humiliation. He recovered quickly and took Michael's hand, hurrying after his father.

The crowd gaped at Frederick Mercer as he moved down the aisle, most staring at him in disbelief, some even staring at him in awe for having the courage and strength to stand and walk from the room of his own accord. He had been a well-respected lord, a friend of many who were in the Great Hall. A brave, strong, honorable man. Now, he was a broken man—titleless, landless. A commoner. Lord Frederick Mercer was indeed no more.

Quiet descended over the room as he moved through it. Frederick kept his head high, his chin raised in defiance of their stares. Blood continued to drip down from his head and stain his face.

Fox moved solemnly behind his father. The room seemed to be in a haze from the embarrassment and utter devastation Fox felt swirling through him. Suddenly, something seized his hand. He glanced down to see small, feminine fingers clutching at his. He lifted his gaze to see a small angel. Her eyes were red-rimmed, her cheeks streaked with tears.

His look softened for a moment as he gazed at her.

Jordan Ruvane, one of the two best friends he had in the whole world. And the other was Evan Vaughn, he thought bitterly. He squeezed her hand once before moving after his father. Their hands slowly separated, their fingers sliding across each other until finally there was nothing but distance between them.

". . . The baron of Dalton was murdered. Stabbed."

"I hear Mercer knows who did it. But he won't say."

". . . Baron Magnus was one of the King's favorites."

Fox hurried past the gossiping nobles, hurried through the corridor toward the great double doors of the castle. He had to get out. He had to escape the superior looks, the haughty stares and whispers behind his back. *I don't give a damn what they think,* Fox told himself. But he couldn't stand the way they looked at him.

Just a day before, just hours before, the same people were his friends, his equals. Now they saw him as inferior. Fox clenched his teeth. He reached the doors only to find a downpour of rain slamming into the ground.

Fox halted. He couldn't go out. He took a step back and turned. Four nobles, two he recognized as Lord Hagen and Lord Lynch, were staring at him, whispering. Fox whirled and stormed out into the sheets of rain. He raced through the downpour, sloshing through large puddles and thick mud that clutched at his ankles, dashing through the inner and then the outer courtyard as the rainfall splattered his young body. The wards were mercifully empty. He continued across the lowered drawbridge and turned sharply to his right to run across the field that bordered Castle Mercer. The tall wet grass blew in the strong wind, slapping at his thighs. He could not see more than a few feet in front of him because of the torrents of rain, but he raced on. It was lucky he knew the way by heart. It was the only place he could go.

The last few days' events replayed in his thoughts as he ran. Lord Vaughn had magnanimously given his family two weeks to find somewhere else to stay and vacate the castle. But they had nowhere to go, nowhere to stay. His life was over. He could not be a squire or a knight. He would never be a lord. His future had been destroyed.

The roar of the river greeted him first. It was not the gentle caress it had been when he had visited it last, but a powerful rush of churning, whitecapped water. Its width had swelled to the very edges of the willow trees that dotted its banks, the fast-moving water pushing at the drooping branches that had sunk beneath its surface, making the trees appear alive.

Fox ran to two trees that grew very close to each other and pushed the heavy branches aside, stepping into the makeshift cave their branches had created. It was very dark in the cave today. So very dark and cold.

He sank down on the soft, wet moss, the chill from the ground quickly seeping through his already wet clothing, seeping into his very bones. He felt defeated. Alone.

Darkness settled over the land and over Fox's heart. And like the intense emotions and confusion that raged inside Fox, the storm continued to vent its fury outside the makeshift branch walls of Fox's secret hideaway.

"Fox?" someone called from outside the cave.

Fox knew the owner of the voice, but for a moment he thought he had imagined it.

"Fox?" She sounded a little more desperate.

Jordan. She shouldn't be here. She should be with the other nobles. "Leave me alone," he commanded softly. She didn't have to endure the pain he was going through. He buried his face between his hands.

"Fox," she almost sighed, ducking to move beneath the branches, stepping toward him. "I was hoping I'd find you here."

"I said leave me alone." His tone was stronger.

She fell to her knees, reaching out to him.

Fox pulled away from her touch, turning away from her. "You shouldn't be seen with me anymore," Fox whispered in a ragged and hoarse tone. "I'm a commoner now. A peasant. A nothing . . ."

"Do you think I care if you are titleless? Or if you have no lands? Would I have come out in this storm if I did? I don't care about any of that."

"Your father does," Fox retorted. "Your friends do."

Jordan reached out to clasp his hands. "You are my friend."

Despite the chill surrounding them, her hands were warm and soft.

"Not any longer." Fox ripped his hands away from her. She had to leave him for her own good. She could not be seen with him. It could bring the king's wrath on her and her family.

"Why are you doing this? I would never give up our friendship. You mean more to me . . ."

"Just go!"

Jordan shook her head. "Don't make me leave."

Her anguish tore at his young heart. He didn't want to hurt her. It took all his willpower not to apologize, not to let her be the friend he so desperately needed.

As the silence stretched, Fox thought it was over. She would leave him now. He lifted his gaze to her. Her dress was soaked. Her long brown hair hung over her shoulders, shining with rain. Her pale skin was speckled with raindrops. She looked like some fallen angel.

Her large eyes caught and held his attention. In them,

he swore he saw his salvation. He almost lifted his hand, almost reached out to her. But he couldn't draw her into his desperation. He clenched his hand, refusing to move it. She had to leave him.

But she didn't. "You think that by hurting me you will make this easier," Jordan said. "Well, I won't be forced away."

"Jordan," Fox whispered, fighting down his need, fighting the loneliness that engulfed him. He did need her. He would always need her. Fox suddenly leaned into her, embracing her tightly, pulling her close. "I don't want to lose you. You are all I have in the world now."

Jordan clung to him, squeezing his wet velvet tunic beneath her fingers. "You won't lose me, Fox. I'll always be with you. There will never be anyone else."

Fox pulled back slightly, his deep blue eyes sweeping her face, taking in every detail. Faithfulness shone from her blue eyes. He lifted a hand to brush his wet fingertips across her cheek.

Fox gave in to the complete and utter desolation he felt. He leaned forward, resting his forehead against her shoulder.

They held each other, the branches of the willow tree surrounding them, sheltering them, closing out the world and stopping time.

When the sun rose the next morning, Fox bounded from his room and raced to the inner ward. The night had brought him little solace and much restlessness. But of all the chaos in his life, he still had one privilege. He ignored the turned backs of his former friends, his former peers. Now they treated him no better than the dirt on the ground. But he didn't care. He didn't need them. He had the only friend that mattered. A true friend.

His gaze searched the throng of departing lords and ladies in the inner courtyard. Their tall headdresses and rich clothing were something he would not be able to afford anymore. But it didn't matter. He never liked the fashions anyway.

Then his gaze settled on the red lion emblazoned on a white flag, the Ruvane crest, clearly visible above the crowd. A bright smile blossomed on Fox's face, but then abruptly vanished as he saw the flag moving out of the castle, already beneath the outer portcullis. Fox raced after it, desperation swelling within his chest. Jordan was leaving! And without saying a word to him. Something horrible had happened. He could feel it in his very bones.

Fox desperately pushed his way through the knights, shouldering his way past one lord who shoved him rudely in the back. But Fox did not take his gaze from the departing flag. It drew farther and farther away, moving down the road toward the town. Fox tried to increase his pace, but the courtyard was too crowded with departing nobles, horses, and servants for him to move quickly. Finally, he burst through the crowd, breaking free of its confines, onto the drawbridge . . .

. . . only to see the Ruvane's flag picking up speed as it moved away from him down the road, flapping in the breeze.

"Jordan!" Fox screamed, but his voice was swallowed up by the wind. "Jordan!"

CHAPTER ONE

Ten years later

Jordan entered the small house, throwing her hood off her shoulders. Her cloak was damp from the misty rain that permeated the night air. She removed the cloak quickly and tossed it onto the table in the center of the room.

She stepped past the pan set at one end of the table. It had been put there weeks ago to catch the drips that fell from a hole in the thatched roof. For the past month, she had told Abagail to have it fixed, but she had never gotten around to it, and Jordan knew it was for good reason. The children were quite a handful. This time, she didn't comment on it as she moved to one of the two doors situated on the far wall.

An elderly woman with gray hair and wrinkled skin stepped before her. "Lady Jordan," she said, wringing her hands. Age spots freckled her loose skin, dotting the backs of her hands with spots of light and dark brown.

"How is she, Abagail?" Jordan demanded, her eyes on the door over the woman's shoulder.

"Maggie can wait for the moment," Abagail said. "I just checked on her."

Jordan looked down at Abagail for the first time that night. She had dark rings beneath her blue eyes, and her usually neatly wrapped bun had strands of gray hair poking out wildly from the back of her head. She reached over to a nearby table and handed Jordan a candle, jerking her head at the other door.

Jordan swiveled her gaze to the other door. It was slightly ajar, and in the darkness, Jordan saw four pairs of wide eyes watching her. She cast one longing look at the door over Abagail's shoulder before moving toward the other door.

Jordan heard little feet scampering through the room as she opened the door, blankets being whisked aside, small voices muttering to be quiet. A ray of light fell across the room from the candle Jordan held in her hand. The weak circle of light illuminated two large straw beds, one on each side of the small room. Forms huddled beneath the blankets. They were moving around far too much to be asleep.

Jordan entered the room and moved up to one of the beds, setting the candle down on a nearby table.

"Is Maggie going to die?" a small voice wondered.

The thought sent agony through Jordan's heart, but she masked her worry and turned to the other bed and the owner of that small voice. "No, Kara. Maggie is just very, very sick."

A thick set of dark curls emerged from beneath the

blanket, then Kara's big hazel eyes. "I know. That's what the physician said."

"Mistress Abagail said we can't see her," another, older voice complained.

Jordan turned her gaze to the first bed to meet the stare of a dark-haired boy. "And she's right, John. Maggie is too sick for visitors right now."

"When will she be better?" John asked, throwing the covers to his lap and sitting up.

Jordan sighed at John's question. She wished she knew the answer. "I don't know," she said quietly.

"But we heard the doctor say she needed herbs from far away."

Jordan nodded at Ana's statement, turning to address the blue-eyed eight year old in the opposite bed. "She does. Sir Evan is riding out to get them tonight. He should return by morning."

"What if he doesn't?" Jason wondered.

Jordan turned her gaze to the small boy beside John. He was usually so vibrant, but he seemed withdrawn now. "All right," Jordan said, trying to hide just how much Jason's question unnerved her. "That's enough questions for tonight." She moved to one of the beds, pulling the cover up over the two boys. "I'll be here all night." She bent to press kisses to John's and Jason's cheeks. Then she crossed the room to the other bed. "Don't worry about Maggie. I'll stay with her." Jordan pulled the blanket up to cover Ana and Kara, pausing to press a kiss to baby Emily's cheek, who was sleeping like a little angel, though the two year old had more of the devil in her. Jordan kissed Kara and Ana.

Kara pushed the blanket aside to show Jordan the straw mattress, and pointed to an empty spot on the mattress. "I'm saving Maggie's spot for her."

Jordan smiled down at her. "You do that, Kara," she said softly. "Keep it warm for her."

Jordan walked to the door.

"Lady Jordan!" Kara called, stopping Jordan. "The door."

"I know, Kara," she whispered. "I'll leave it open a little."

Jordan stepped from the room and set the candle down on a table, leaving the door open a crack to let some light spill into the room for the children. They so hated the dark, she knew, especially with what was happening to one of their friends. It made the dark that much darker, the quiet that much quieter. She could feel the anxiety and fear in her heart, too.

She stared at the other door for a moment, afraid of what she would find on the other side. She willed herself to be strong and took a deep breath before walking to the other door. She pushed the door open slowly, trying to be quiet. The old wood creaked despite her best efforts.

The room was dark, the only illumination coming from a candle that was in danger of going out at any moment. The sputtering flame cast sinister shadows on the wooden walls. To Jordan's overtired mind, they looked like hovering black ghosts waiting to claim the dead. She quickly forced that unpleasant thought away and stepped deeper into the room. In the corner was Abagail's bed, a comfortable straw mattress. But the figure on it was far too small to be Abagail.

Jordan hurried over to the mattress. Maggie was still and pale in the candlelight, her brown curls laying limply around her head. The edge of the thick wool blanket was folded beneath her small hands, as if she had not moved in a very long time.

Jordan knelt beside the mattress, taking the girl's tiny

hand into her own. Maggie was only four years old. She had her whole life ahead of her. It wasn't fair. Jordan brushed the hair back from Maggie's forehead and was shocked at how warm the little girl felt. Heat emanated from the girl's skin before Jordan even touched her.

Tears rushed into Jordan's eyes and she silently begged Evan to hurry.

Maggie's eyes fluttered and then opened to mere slits. "Lady Jordan," she managed to whisper, although it seemed to take all her strength to do so.

"Yes, Maggie," Jordan whispered. "It's me. Don't talk. Save your strength."

"I'm so cold," Maggie said.

Fear shriveled any glimmer of hope in Jordan's heart, and she climbed into bed with Maggie, pulling the child tightly against her, making sure that the blanket was wrapped around every inch of the little girl's body. She rubbed Maggie's hot forehead.

"I don't feel well," Maggie whispered.

"I know, sweetheart," Jordan soothed. She rubbed her cheek against Maggie's hot one. "I know."

Maggie's eyes slowly closed again.

Jordan's eyes again filled with tears. Maggie had been with her the longest. She had been abandoned at the castle as an infant, barely able to walk. She would have died if Jordan hadn't found her and nursed her back to health. She was the reason Jordan had convinced her father to give her the old run-down Johnson cottage to shelter the children who had no families. She worked a small patch of garden in the castle so they would have food to survive on and mended their clothing so they wouldn't be cold. They were the abandoned children. The children no one wanted except for her. Maggie had given Jordan's life a true purpose.

And now she was unable to help the poor girl. She could do nothing for her but hold her and hope Evan made it back in time. He had to get the herbs. The physician had said that only the herbs would save Maggie's life.

Maggie groaned softly.

"Shh," Jordan whispered. "It will be all right," she said as much to Maggie as to herself. "Everything will be fine."

CHAPTER TWO

The road was dark and empty. A layer of wispy fog floated across the dirt, glowing a ghostly pale yellow as it absorbed what little moonlight reached its shifting surface. A light mist of rain fell from the night sky, its droplets beginning to break up the patch of fog. The rain was not enough to drench Fox, just enough to annoy him and obscure his view of the road. He swiped a few drops of the cool mist from his forehead with his fingertips and looked further down the dirt road, peering out from his hiding place behind the leaves of a bush.

A form shifted at Fox's right. "How long are we going to wait in this weather?" a large man with red hair and a beard asked.

"As long as it takes," Fox replied. Fox glanced at the big man beside him. Fox couldn't even remember his real name, nor did he recall anyone ever telling him what it was. Everyone just knew him as Pick—an obvious name for a master pickpocket and lock picker. But the name fit, so Pick he was and Pick he would always be. The odd thing about the big man was that no one outside Fox's small band would ever believe that a man of such girth, with shoulders as wide as a horse and arms as thick as tree trunks, would have the subtlest touch Fox knew. The man could steal toys from a child and somehow the child wouldn't even notice.

"Maybe Frenchie heard the baker wrong," Pick suggested.

"Pick, you know gossip is one thing Frenchie doesn't get wrong," the man to Fox's left said, pushing his damp blond hair from his head. Beau had been known as Beauregard O'Connell, but Fox knew if he called him that to his face, he wouldn't have much of a face left. Beau was a good-looking man, younger than Fox, with hair down to his shoulders. The man had hawklike deep brown eyes that seemed to look right through people sometimes. But those keen eyes had saved Fox's men more than a few times, because Beau had the archery skills to go with them. Good aim and a quick, sure release had provided many an avenue of escape for Fox's band.

Pick chuckled low in his throat. "Not like his cookin', eh?"

"I still have that burned rabbit stewing in my gut," Beau complained. "My tongue wants to climb out of my mouth and hide in my ale mug every time he calls us for supper. The man wouldn't know how to use a spice if his life depended on it."

"Maybe that's why he's with us," Pick added, laughing. "An outcast cook for a bunch of outcasts."

"I don't think he was thrown out of Chandler Manor for his cooking, but he should have been," Beau remarked.

Fox ignored Pick and Beau's chatter. His eyes were

focused ahead on the empty road, waiting. The darkness seemed thicker now than just a few moments before. The sliver of moon trying to poke out from behind the clouds had disappeared completely. What little light it had been throwing down on the road now was gone. Even the fog seemed to have vanished. He had to rely on his other senses now. His ears were tuned to any noise, any sign of activity. This road was the only route they could take to get to Ruvane village, and that was where Frenchie had heard they were headed.

Silence greeted him. Too much silence. Then the rain grew heavier, the drops getting larger and larger, and the mist became a steady stream of falling water. Above them, thunder rumbled in the night sky, threatening a storm.

Nervousness churned in Fox's stomach. They had to come this way. *Damn them, they'd better come this way. There is too much at stake for them not to.* He impatiently wiped more rain from his eyes.

Suddenly, the tweet of a bird sounded above the falling rain, but it was no real call. Only an alert. Their target was coming up the road. Pick and Beau moved into action immediately. They disappeared into the forest around Fox, moving in opposite directions to surround the approaching merchant.

Fox listened again. The first alert was a sound for them to get prepared. Now would come the call of how many men were in the group. He heard one tweet, then another. Fox listened intently, but no further call came. Thunder grumbled in the sky, loud and angry. Two men? Fox wondered with amazement. Only two men? This would be too easy. He breathed a sigh of relief. For once in his life, something would be easy.

He listened to the pattering hum of the rain as it hit the leaves around him, his gaze focused on the road before him. He couldn't make out anything in the darkness. Then he heard it—the soft plod of horses in the thick mud of the road.

Fox's body stiffened in anticipation. Far off down the road, he could barely make out two silhouetted riders coming over the hill.

He slowly, silently slid his sword from its scabbard. The handle was wet from the rain, but Fox's palm gripped the leather hilt with confidence.

The two riders came closer.

Every muscle in Fox's body tensed as he stepped out into the middle of the road. Above, the clouds drifted across the sky and a slight gap appeared between them. Moonlight shone down through the gap, illuminating the road before Fox—and illuminating a cart being drawn behind the two riders, a cart filled with ten men at least. A chill raced up Fox's spine. Two men! That had been the signal! Only two men! Not two and ten! Fox's gaze darted to the bushes on the side of the road, but there was no sense in trying to hide. The riders had obviously seen him, and he needed what they were carrying. Needed it desperately.

And then the riders were before him, slowing their horses. Fox reached out and grabbed one of the horse's bridles. "Good evening, good sirs." Fox glanced at the men in the cart and breathed a soft sigh of relief. They were farmers, from the looks of them. Very tired farmers. They were all asleep, except for one old man who looked at him curiously.

"What do you want, knave?" one of the riders grumbled, keeping his head down out of the rain. "Out of the way. We are on our way to Ruvane village. The cart is full. We can carry no more."

Fox stepped up to the riders, having to look up through

the rain to see his face. "The rain must have soured your temperament," Fox responded.

"I'll sour you, you oaf." The man raised his fist.

Fox lifted his weapon in one fluid motion and rested the tip against the man's throat. "I think not."

Pick stepped out of the woods, moving to stand beside the second rider. He grinned up at the riders, his smile much more predatory than friendly.

The first rider slowly lowered his fist.

"What is it you want?" the second rider asked in a calmer voice. "We have no coin. Nothing worth taking." As he spoke, his hand dipped down toward the handle of a dagger jutting out from his saddlebag.

Fox swiveled his gaze slightly to the second rider. He wore a hood, no doubt to keep out the rain. "I want what you carry to Ruvane village."

"God's blood, man!" the first rider cried. "Do you know what you ask?"

Fox nodded. "I do. Now please hand over the bag." The first rider opened his mouth to object, but Fox pressed the blade against his throat. "Quickly."

"You can't ask us to! There is—"

"I can more than ask. I am demanding it."

Suddenly, a whooshing sound filled the air and a tuft of Pick's hair seemed to leap off his head. The second rider cried out in alarm as an arrow sunk into the dagger's wooden handle, a mere inch from his fingers groping for the blade! His horse started from the brunt of the impact, but the rider quickly brought him under control.

Beau stepped out of the woods, a second arrow nocked and ready to fire.

Pick bent down and picked up the chunk of his lopped-off hair. He touched his head, feeling the spot where the arrow had shaved his locks.

The first rider produced a pouch from his saddlebag and held it in his palm for a moment, as if weighing its value against the life of the other man. Finally, he held the bag out to Fox. Fox's hand closed around the bag and relief coursed through his body. "Thank you, sirs." He backed toward the cover of the forest.

"You're an insufferable maggot!" the first man hollered, shaking a fist at Fox. "You don't know what you've done!"

Fox ignored him and disappeared into the foliage. Pick and Beau quickly trailed him. He made his way through the woods, moving in and out of the trees, leaping fallen logs, looking over his shoulder to make sure they weren't being followed. He paused at a tall tree and yanked the string on the bag open. He worked the neck of the bag wide so that he could peer into the pouch. He smiled in relief when he saw the contents.

"Is it there?" Pick asked.

"Yes," Fox replied.

"Then we must hurry." Beau passed him, racing on.

Fox pulled the string closed and tightened it quickly, then looped it around the leather strap of his belt, patting the precious bag before racing deeper into the woods after his companions.

"Hey, wait for me," a voice called out.

Fox turned to see a young woman racing through the trees towards him. She was dressed in a leather tunic and leather breeches, her womanly figure clearly showing through the tight clothes. "Let's go, Scout," Fox called out to her.

Scout hurried to his side, moving nimbly through the trees, crashing through a small bush.

"Two men, eh?" Fox said.

"I saw them," Scout countered. "I just didn't want to panic you. They were all asleep anyway."

"Next time, just give me the numbers."

Scout scowled. "Yes, sir, *Lord* Mercer. As you command. Far be it from me to make a decision." Scout moved angrily away from him, joining Pick and Beau.

Fox frowned, cursing silently, but hurried on. His hand unconsciously moved to encircle the bag of precious herbs he had just taken from the riders. He needed them far more than anyone in Ruvane village could ever need them.

CHAPTER THREE

Jordan held Maggie tightly, doing her best to shield the young girl from the horror that was threatening to take her from the world. It was almost morning, and Evan wasn't back yet. Maggie's breathing was growing weaker and weaker, her small body laboring with each intake of air, her skin blotchy, far from its normal healthy coloring. The fever was slowly consuming her. Jordan wanted to tell Maggie to open her eyes, to give her just a glimpse of life, but Maggie needed every ounce of her strength, so she kept silent. She was afraid if she tried to wake the girl, Maggie wouldn't open her eyes at all.

Jordan's arms tightened around her. She couldn't lose her. Not after raising Maggie herself. She meant more to Jordan than . . . Tears rose in her eyes as she once again silently begged Evan to hurry. He should have been back hours ago. Where could he be?

She squeezed her eyes closed, wishing that somehow

she could take the sickness into herself, that somehow this tragedy could be hers to bear instead of Maggie's. Despite Jordan's best efforts to fight it back, a hot tear squeezed out of the corner of her eye and trailed down her cheek.

The sun's rays began to peek beneath the door and spread across the floor, drawing closer with the passing minutes. Jordan watched the light grow brighter and brighter, creep closer and closer. Usually, the sunlight cheered her and warmed her spirit, but today the light seemed unusually bright and glaring, bringing with it the hands of death.

Suddenly, the door was thrown open. For a brief, horrible moment, a black shape stood motionless in the doorway, taking on the ghastly appearance of Death, darkly robed and ominously quiet.

Jordan's hands tightened around Maggie.

Then the shape stepped forward. It was Evan. He entered the room and moved toward her.

Jordan felt such relief rush through her that her arms trembled as they held Maggie against her bosom. She sat up in the bed, holding Maggie against her chest. "Do you have the herbs?" she whispered in a voice dry with relief. "Has Abagail made a drink I can give to Maggie?" She looked at Evan, her eyes imploring him for answers.

But Evan was shaking his head at all of her questions. "No, Jordan."

"No?" Jordan asked in confusion. "Abagail hasn't made the drink yet? Tell her to hurry. Maggie is—"

"I don't have the herbs."

"What?" Jordan gasped weakly.

"The merchants were robbed before I reached them." Evan looked away from Jordan to stare at the floor.

"No," Jordan whispered, pulling Maggie tighter against her. "No."

"I'm sorry, Jordan."

Jordan looked down at Maggie's somber face. She stroked the little girl's pale cheeks with the backs of her fingers, moving some of her damp, brown locks away from her closed eyes. Her small, small hands were still clasped together, resting atop her tiny chest. Jordan wouldn't let her go without a battle. Jordan lifted her gaze to Evan, even as tears filled her eyes, blurring her vision. "There has to be something else we can do."

"I—I think we've tried everything."

"No. We have to think of something." But even as Jordan said the words, Maggie's breathing slowed. She pressed her cheek to the girl's head and looked at Evan through her blurry vision. "She's dying, Evan," Jordan whispered in agony.

Evan looked away.

"Maggie," Jordan sobbed, and pressed her cheek to the child's. "No," she begged. But even as she said the word, the girl's breathing stopped altogether and her body went limp. Her chest no longer rose and fell. Jordan pulled Maggie tightly to her, sobbing, pleading with the Almighty not to take her. Maggie was only a child, the daughter she didn't have yet. She couldn't die because of some silly herbs.

"Jordan," Evan called.

But Jordan refused to look up. She kept her eyes closed tightly, her fists wrapped in the girl's cotton dress. Her body shook with unspoken sorrow as she held Maggie.

"Jordan." Evan's voice was firmer, demanding her to look up.

Jordan didn't give a damn what he wanted. He had failed

to bring her the herbs that would have saved Maggie's life. It was his fault. It was all Evan's fault.

But she knew deep down it was not Evan's fault. It was her fault for letting the children play in the rain the other day. Everyone had warned her.

But the herbs would have saved Maggie's life. Who could have stolen them? And why? Why?

Someone grabbed her shoulder, shaking it gently. Jordan looked up to see Evan standing beside her. He jerked his head at the doorway. Jordan looked over Evan's shoulder to see the children standing in the doorway. Kara, Ana, and Jason were sobbing. John was holding Emily slightly behind them in the open door.

Jordan straightened and looked away to the dark wood wall to compose herself. It took her a long moment to blink back the tears and wipe her cheeks. She carefully laid Maggie on the bed, smoothing back her hair one last time. A well of grief opened inside her as she gazed at Maggie's still face, but she fought down the tears. She pulled the blanket over Maggie's head, saying a silent farewell.

She slowly turned to the children and rose from the bed. With each step she took toward them, their tears pulled at the fragile wall of protectiveness she had tried to throw up around her own emotions. She had to stay strong for them. She had to keep her composure. Their large eyes looked to her for a reason, their tears demanding an answer. She reached the door and stopped.

"You promised us Maggie would be all right," Ana said. "You promised."

Jordan knelt before them, pain and failure welling up inside her. She could feel the protective wall starting to crack. "I'm so sorry," she whispered.

Jordan knew she had to control her tears. She had to

be strong. She had to be. But when Kara threw her arms around Jordan's neck and cried into her shoulder, the wall shattered completely and Jordan could do nothing to prevent the wave of anguish that overflowed her senses. She hugged Kara tightly, sobbing.

All the other children threw their arms around her in a protective shelter of love and grief.

They wept for a long time together, holding each other, comforting each other as best they could. Thankfully, Evan had closed the door on Maggie's death, sealing out the image of her unnaturally still form.

Abagail clapped her hands. "It's time to eat, children," she said in her motherly voice.

Jordan looked up at her and stood. She dabbed a sleeve at the corners of her eyes. "Abagail is right," she agreed, gently taking Kara's shoulders and guiding her to her chair at the table. The rest of the children followed, taking seats at the wooden bench.

When the children were all seated at the table, eating in a strange brooding silence, Evan gently took Jordan's elbow to lead her to the side of the room.

"You have guests arriving at Castle Ruvane. You can't afford to dwell here much longer," Evan said.

"I will stay as long as I am needed," Jordan replied softly, her eyes taking in the way Ana bowed her head and wiped at her eyes.

"Jordan," Evan began sternly.

But Jordan's gaze had turned to the closed door, and the image of the young girl lying lifelessly inside filled her mind. Maggie. They had been so close to curing her. "I can't believe she's gone. Just yesterday morn I was playing hide and seek with her."

"Life is like that," Evan said, distracted. He glanced at the front door as if he had somewhere better to be.

"You can leave, Evan," Jordan said coldly, angrily. "Thank you for staying and thank you for your help with Maggie."

Evan's gaze shot to her as she began to move past him. "Don't be like that, Jordan. I did my best. I will capture the cur that stole those herbs and make him pay for what he did. You have my word on that."

Jordan faltered and turned to him. "You know who did it?" she asked, shocked.

Evan nodded. "The merchant saw him. Yes," Evan said stoically. "I know who did it."

"Who?" Jordan demanded, grabbing his arm tightly.

Evan shifted his blue gaze to her. There was such animosity in his gaze that for a moment Jordan was taken aback. Just by his stare, just by the hatred in his gaze, she knew who it was. And she couldn't believe it.

"The Black Fox," Evan said. "The Black Fox killed your Maggie."

CHAPTER FOUR

Jordan still couldn't believe it. Fox Mercer had been her friend long ago. Her very good friend. But then their friendship had fallen apart when his father's title and lands had been taken away from him. She had tried to write him letters to renew their friendship, but he had returned every letter unopened. They certainly were no longer friends, but she had never considered him an enemy. Now she knew better. He was an outlaw. An outcast. A thief.

And now she could add murderer to the list. Her anger mounted as she followed Evan toward Castle Ruvane, guiding her horse behind his. Fox had stolen the herbs that would have saved Maggie's life! Jordan's eyes narrowed slightly. A cold-blooded killer.

She knew Evan hated Fox. His face twisted and his lips drew back in a tight grimace every time he spoke his name. His eyes would narrow and his jaw would clench if Fox's name even came up in conversation. There was no love lost between the two former friends.

Fox had come to be most annoying to Evan, stealing and pillaging within Vaughn's borders. But Jordan saw the pattern of his robberies. He wasn't randomly stealing, as Evan thought. Fox was supplying his men, taking crops and food, pigs and horses. Only occasionally, when it was obvious that he was purposely antagonizing Evan, would he rob people of their coin. He was certainly not the most dangerous outlaw. Simply the most annoying.

But now his childish antics had killed someone dear to Jordan, had cost a young girl her life. It was time to put an end to it. Evan had been after Fox for the past year. Jordan had remained silent because of some long ago loyalty she had still felt for Fox. She had felt guilty about leaving him without saying good-bye. But she had tried to right her wrong, had written him countless letters, only to find each one of them refused again and again, returned unopened. Maggie's death had changed everything.

"I can help you capture the Black Fox," Jordan said quietly.

Evan turned to her, surprise lighting his eyes. He reined in his horse, halting the animal until they rode side by side. He almost laughed . . . until he saw the scowl on her brow. "You can't be serious, Jordan. You know nothing of his kind. You know nothing of criminals and robbers. Not to mention setting traps or . . ."

"But I know Fox."

"You *knew* Fox."

The condescending tone of Evan's voice annoyed her. "I can set a trap he will be unable to resist. I can get him to jump at the bait. Take my help or leave it, but I guarantee you Fox will come." She spurred her horse into a canter, moving down the road toward Castle Ruvane.

Evan hurried after her. "All right, Jordan! All right. I'll use whatever means I must to capture the Black Fox. I will listen to what you have to say."

Jordan groaned inwardly as she made her way through the crowded Great Hall of Castle Ruvane. She didn't enjoy being at the castle, especially not today. She didn't feel like wearing the heavily embroidered dress her maidservant, Therese, had chosen for her.

The image of lowering Maggie's casket into the ground still burned in the forefront of her memory. They had buried her in the town's cemetery on the western edge of the village before returning to the castle. She could still hear the clumps of dirt hitting the wooden box. And every so often she swore she could hear the soft echo of the other children crying, their small voices drifting in the wind.

She caught herself looking over her shoulder more than once, expecting to see John or Ana standing right behind her, tears streaming down their cheeks, their chests heaving with sobs. But every time she turned around, the road was empty and still. Deathly quiet.

Today, the castle was far from quiet. All the more reason she did not want to be there. The Great Hall was bustling and loud with raucous laughter from the knights attending her father's tournament. Many of the men had come from miles around; some had traveled for days, even weeks, just to attend. More seemed to be arriving every hour. The castle had quickly filled to capacity, and some of the knights had been forced to raise tents just outside the castle walls.

There seemed to be an unusual air of excitement about this particular tournament, but Jordan couldn't quite put her finger on why. There were still four days to go before the tournament officially began, and the knights were already practicing very hard for it. A few of the men had already been wounded in practice battles; one had been taken home on the back of a wagon, still unconscious from a serious blow to his head. She had asked her father about the level of excitement among the knights, but he had avoided giving her a straight answer, telling her that the thrill of battle simply had attracted many fine warriors. When she pressed him further, he just smiled and kept silent.

Jordan made her way toward the head table. It was positioned on a raised platform so it sat just above the other tables, its occupants looking down at everyone else. At the head table, she saw her father laughing with another well-known lord, Lord McColl. McColl was a small man, his black hair peppered with gray. His son sat beside him, a young, wiry lad who looked down at the other tables with envious eyes, studying the dozens upon dozens of knights gathering at Castle Ruvane for the tournament, obviously wishing to be one of them. Also at the head table was Evan. Thankfully, the only empty chair was between her father and Evan.

As she made her way past the lower tables, many knights bowed respectfully to her. Others stared furtively, while others ogled her quite brazenly. She was the hostess and smiled back at many, favoring none, mumbling greetings to them as she passed.

A brazen young lord leaped before her, startling her. He grabbed her hand in his and pointed to an empty seat beside him. "I have kept your seat warm, Lady Jordan. Please."

Jordan shook her head respectfully. "Thank you, good sir, but I will sit beside my father."

The young knight tried to pull her toward his table, and she could smell the strong scent of ale on his breath. She glanced at her father, whose eyes burned into the man. Jordan leaned close to him. "If you want to compete in the tournament, you had best release me at once."

The young man glanced over his shoulder at her father and quickly removed his hand from her. "I shall win the tournament in your honor," he whispered to her before returning to his seat.

Jordan frowned at the knight, then moved past him to the head table, raising the hem of her dress as she moved up the two steps. Every lord at the table greeted her with a slight bow. Then Jordan took her seat. Her father lifted her hand and pressed a kiss to it.

Before Jordan could even utter a word of greeting, her father stood. The musicians immediately ceased their playing and the din of conversation quickly lessened into muted whispers.

"I'd like to thank everyone for coming to participate in the tournament," her father said.

Murmurings erupted from one table and then laughter.

Her father continued, undaunted. "I know you've traveled far. There are gathered among us some of the most skilled knights in all the realm. As reward, the winner of the melee shall be granted a prize worthy of the most valiant and able of knights."

A prize? Jordan's father had mentioned nothing to her of a prize. She took a sip of the ale one of the serving women had placed before her.

"A prize worthy of the greatest knight or lord in all the lands."

What could it be? Jordan mused. Part of the Ruvane lands?

"The winner shall have my daughter Jordan's hand in marriage."

A murmuring spread like wildfire through the Great Hall. Then a hearty *huzzah!* rumbled through the chambers.

Jordan's stomach dropped. She could feel the color drain from her face, could feel her flesh turning from pink to white. Marriage? Prize? The idea was so sudden, so ludicrous, that she was having a difficult time comprehending it.

Jordan glanced at her father in disbelief. Had she heard him right? When he retook his seat, she shook her head slightly as if trying to clear it.

All of these men had gathered at Castle Ruvane for her? She glanced down at the dress she was wearing, the revealing glimmer of her breasts, the open curl of fabric at her shoulders. No wonder Therese had insisted she wear this garment. She was dressed like a trophy, sparkling and shiny for all to see.

Her father patted her hand comfortingly. "You are well beyond the marrying age," he said softly and leaned close to her. "Besides, Evan is the best knight in all the lands. You have nothing to worry about."

Jordan glanced at Evan. He smiled brightly at her. "You knew we would marry," he said simply.

Jordan frowned in worry and returned her gaze to her father. She searched for something to say, some way out of this ridiculous position she found herself in. "But why this way? Why as a prize? Why not just betroth us?"

The rumble of laughter that churned in her father's throat confused her. "It was how I won your mother's hand, may she rest in peace. I hope you will find the same happiness we had." He squeezed her hand tightly. "We must honor tradition. It has brought me great fortune, and I expect it to do the same for you."

"But, father," Jordan said weakly, "what if Evan doesn't win?"

"He is the best knight in all of England," her father replied with assurance. "How could he not win?"

Jordan sat motionless for a moment. Then she tentatively lifted her gaze to survey all of the men gathered in the room. Some were old and gray, some were bearded and gruff, some were young and full of vitality. Suddenly, her apprehension overwhelmed her.

Her father kissed her cheek and whispered, "You must feel honored that all these men have come here to compete for your hand."

Jordan harumphed. "Not so. They've all come for the blood sport," she whispered.

Her father scowled slightly in disapproval. "You're showing that rebellious spirit again."

Jordan picked up the dagger she used for slicing her meat. "Which none of the men know about."

Her father chuckled. "It's lucky for you that Evan knows all about it. When you are married, it won't come as a surprise to him that his wife has a will of her own."

Jordan peered at Evan to find him in earnest conversation with Lord McColl. Again, the thought rose in her mind: *What if Evan doesn't win? What if some fat, lazy slob wins my hand? Or some vicious evil lord?*

"Jordan," her father whispered.

She turned her attention to him to see that his gaze was on her hand. She realized suddenly that she was playing with the dagger, moving it in a full circle around her hand, maneuvering it expertly over her fingers and under her palm, repeating the move again and again. She stopped instantly, grabbing the dagger by its handle. She shrugged helplessly at her father.

Her father sighed. "You have nothing to fear, dear heart. Vaughn is the best knight in the lands. He will win the tournament and your hand."

A deep frown creased her brow. Jordan only wished this entire tournament was at an end.

"You need not worry. I will not let any harm come to you."

Jordan lifted her gaze to her father. Slowly, a smile crossed her lips and she threw her arms around him, hugging him tightly. "I know," she whispered. "I know."

Her words came out strong, but she still could not shake the feeling this tournament was going to change her life in ways she had never imagined.

CHAPTER FIVE

Jordan had found it hard to concentrate and even harder to get the villagers to take her seriously. All they had wanted to do was gossip about the tournament and how she felt about being the grand prize.

"All those men fighting over you," she remembered a farmer's wife declaring, her eyes aglow with jealousy. "They'll be all sweaty and dirty, grunting like pigs, smashing at each other like savages. And then they get to take you home . . ." Jordan remembered the woman waving her hand before her face, fanning her reddening cheeks. "It's so exciting."

Jordan ground her teeth, bringing herself out of the memory. That was why it had taken three days to put the plan into action. She had been getting the same kind of response from everyone. No one was concerned about capturing some rogue bandit. But finally she had managed to convince several farmers to participate in her plan.

Now, she had only one obstacle. Jordan faced Evan with her hands on her hips. "I'm going with you."

"No, you are not!" Evan said, facing her in the hallway of Castle Vaughn.

"Yes, I am!" she insisted. "It was my idea, my plan. I got the villagers to cooperate."

Evan scowled at her. "It's too dangerous. There is no way I'm going to let you come."

"You can't stop me," Jordan said, her eyebrows furrowing, her arms crossing stubbornly.

"Damn it, Jordan, I should be practicing for the tournament today, not chasing down some damned fool. I'm already giving you more than I should."

Jordan scowled. "You're not giving me anything, Evan. This isn't for me. This is for Maggie." Jordan looked hard at Evan. "And I'm going!"

"All right! All right!" Evan conceded, throwing up his hands in defeat. "You are so stubborn!"

Jordan set her chin defiantly and glared at him.

Evan shook his head. "Fine," he finally relented. "But you have to stay well away from the battle. On the hill on the north side of the farm."

Jordan nodded in agreement, fighting down her obvious enthusiasm. She had thought it would have been more difficult to convince Evan to let her accompany him.

"But if your father finds out, I'm saying it was your idea," Evan warned. He grumbled something about women and moved past her into the inner ward of the castle, calling for the stable boy to saddle another horse.

Jordan had to move quickly to follow Evan. She raced after him, skirting a dog that ran in front of her, and trailed him beneath the inner gatehouse and into the outer ward, where Jordan saw exactly why Evan was letting her go with him without much of a fight.

Two rows of armored knights sat atop large battle horses, twelve men in all. Each was bedecked with the Vaughn insignia, a crested black dragon over a red background, on their tunics over their breastplates, swords secured in their scabbards, shields fastened to their backs. Some of them had crossbows strapped to their saddlebags, quivers filled with arrows tied next to them. It looked more like he was heading off to a small war than going to capture an outlaw.

Evan paused and Jordan slammed into his back. She pulled back quickly, mumbling an apology.

Evan spoke curtly to a tall man with blond hair. He cast a sour glance at Jordan and then moved toward his horse.

When the man walked away, Jordan wondered, "Are you expecting an army?"

"Just being cautious," Evan said and started toward his horse at the front of the line. "Jordan, Captain Pavia will stay with you on the hill. You are not to leave his side, understood?"

Jordan nodded and pulled herself up into the saddle. She looked again at the knights awaiting Evan's command to proceed.

Fox didn't have a chance.

She had convinced a few of the Mercer village farmers to cooperate with her in spreading a rumor, one she knew a hungry renegade outlaw would be unable to resist. Murderer or not, he still had to eat and feed his men. She and her father had taken care of the villagers in the years after Castle Mercer's downfall. They trusted her.

"Let's bag us a Fox," Evan announced.

* * *

Fox was desperate. Six sheep. They could eat them and use their wool for clothing. The animals were invaluable to him. He lay absolutely still in the high grass on the outskirts of the farm.

The farm had been still for hours. He had a cramp in his calf, but he dared not move for fear of alerting the farmer that he was there. The fading sun was still hot, making a trickle of sweat slide down his neck beneath his tunic. Night would arrive soon, and then he would strike. He had kept a keen watch on the farm for several hours, counting the men and women going in and out to work the fields and tend to the other livestock. So far, he had seen only three men and two women. And one of the men he had seen earlier rode off on a horse and had not returned.

He shifted his stare to the other side of the farm. Somewhere hidden amongst the thick copse of trees was Beau.

Something prickled the back of Fox's neck, making his hair stand on end. He scanned the clearing below him for a moment, carefully taking in the large barn behind the farmer's house, the empty path from the farmer's house up the rise to the top of the hill. There were more trees at the top of the hill, and it was here that his gaze came to rest.

Something was wrong. He couldn't see anything. It was just a feeling, one he had had many times before—a gut feeling that never deceived him.

A slight breeze stirred the grass around him, but he remained as still as a statue, staring at the trees on the top of the hill. But there was no movement.

Maybe he was wrong. Maybe this was the one time he was mistaken.

And then something flashed in his eyes, blinding him for an instant. Then it was gone. It was as hot and bright as sunlight. Someone was up there! Was it armor? The brilliant flash shone again in his eyes.

Fox scowled. It was no thing of nature. Someone was there. But who? Was it a secret rendezvous with a lover?

Or was it a trap?

Fox glared at the trees, his gaze piercing through the leaves. Something moved, shifted. And then Fox made out the shape of a horse through the branches. The flash blinded him again and he had to look away.

He cursed silently as he turned his gaze toward Beau. He had to warn him to stay put until he found out whether it was a trap or not.

Suddenly, the front gate of the barn opened and a man led out six sheep. Fox's jaw clenched and he looked carefully at the man, trying to see beneath the brown tunic and breeches and the straw hat. He didn't recognize the man as one of the two remaining old farmers. Had he been in the barn the entire time?

The man led the sheep to a fresh growth of grass, then quickly returned to the barn, leaving the animals alone in the field. The man was hunched, but there was definitely something amiss about his movements; they were not as slow as an old man's. It was something that could have easily been overlooked. It was something Beau would not see.

And sure enough, Fox turned to the copse of trees to see his friend emerging from his hiding spot. Fox cursed silently.

As soon as Beau reached the sheep, the barn gate exploded open and a squadron of armed knights charged out.

Fox's eyes grew wide as he watched them overtake

Beau. His fingers curled into tight fists and he ground his teeth together hard. With every fiber of his being, he wanted to fight beside Beau. His hand moved to his sword, but he did not grab the handle. He knew he could not outfight a dozen men. To even attempt to do so would spell disaster for them both.

He cursed silently as they disarmed Beau and shoved him to his knees. One of the men dismounted and approached Beau. He was tall, with blond hair. Every one of Fox's muscles bunched. Could it be? Fox wondered. His hand immediately curled around the handle of his sword. His teeth clenched even tighter. He couldn't make out the man's features clearly, but in his gut he knew he was looking at his old friend. Evan Vaughn.

Suddenly, Evan backhanded Beau, sending his friend face first into the dirt.

Fox's muscles bunched, and he started to rise. Disaster or no, no one struck his friend and walked away. But the sound of a horse halted any impetuous action. He shifted his gaze to see a horse charging down the slope where the blinding light had originated.

The rider was a woman! Her long brown hair waved behind her like a flag as she rode hard toward Beau. She reined in her horse between Beau and Evan and exchanged obviously heated words with the latter, dismounting before him. A sliver of light speared at his eyes again and he realized the glinting glare was coming from a silver medallion the woman was wearing about her neck. It glimmered and glistened as she moved.

Fox watched the woman with a growing fascination. Even from this distance, he could tell she was beautiful. Her hair was full and hung about her shoulders like a pile of illustrious satin. Was she in charge of these savages? She must have been the one he had seen in the trees on the hill.

Suddenly, he froze as the woman turned to stare in his direction. Had she seen him? Would she give his location away? His muscles tensed, ready to flee, although he knew he could never outrun men on horses. He waited for the men to turn toward him.

They never came. They tied a rope around Beau's wrists and Evan held it as he mounted his horse. Beau walked behind the horse as the squadron began to move up the hill. Fox knew they were going to take him to Castle Vaughn. He would have to get to the others quickly. He didn't know how long they would let Beau live if they discovered he was one of Fox's men.

Maybe they already know, a voice inside him warned. Fox's insides trembled. He had to get Beau free as soon as possible.

The woman looked away from his direction and quickly moved to Evan's side, grabbing at the reins of his horse, pulling the animal in a different direction. She pointed to her left, motioning with great insistence that Evan follow her. Evan appeared to argue with her for a moment, then threw up his hands in defeat. He turned his horse and headed in the direction the woman had pointed.

Toward Castle Ruvane.

Fox's breath tightened in his chest. Where were they taking Beau now? And then realization engulfed him in a chilling blast of insight. He knew who the woman was. He knew why there had been an instant fascination with her. He found himself staring with very mixed emotions at Jordan Ruvane.

* * *

Evan fumed from atop his horse. "I can't believe the Black Fox wasn't there himself! I won't believe he only sent one of his men!"

Jordan wasn't listening to Evan's tirade. Fox had to have been there somewhere. But why hadn't he shown himself? Did his men mean nothing to him? Had he somehow suspected a trap?

Jordan glanced down at her hand, realizing she was playing with her necklace. It was a nervous habit she seemed to have acquired ever since stories of the Black Fox had reached her ears. She looked down at the necklace. It was a gift of ornate silver and rubies from Evan.

They were on the road to Castle Ruvane, leading their one prisoner back to her home. She cast a glance over her shoulder at the man. His blond hair lifted in the breeze, but his eyes remained downcast.

Jordan reined in her horse and let the squadron of soldiers move past her until the prisoner was beside her. "He was there, wasn't he?" she asked him.

The only movement on his face was a twitch at the corner of his mouth.

"How could he leave a friend to be taken?" she wondered, trying to goad him into some sort of response. "What kind of friend is that?"

"A better one you'll never find, lady," the man retorted, a strange smile twisting his lips.

Jordan had known that . . . years ago. She pushed aside the old feelings of loyalty that suddenly threatened to surge forth. She had a loyalty to Maggie.

Jordan locked gazes with the man for a long moment. She was certain Fox had been there. Positive. He must have detected their trap!

Evan rode over to her. "Jordan," he chastised, "you shouldn't speak to such a man. It's below you."

Jordan cast a glance at the blond man, at Fox's man. At least they could question him and find out where Fox's stronghold was. At least one of Fox's men had been captured. The Black Fox would be next.

CHAPTER SIX

''Show us, Lady Jordan,'' John begged. He swiped a strand of his dark hair away from his eyes. ''Please, you promised.''

Jordan smiled at John, nodding her head softly. ''I will.'' She glanced over at Jason. ''But Jason has to eat all of his carrots first.''

Kara groaned. ''Oh, no, we'll be here forever and a day.'' The other children moaned right along with her.

Jason looked up at everyone and grinned, then proceeded to stuff five of the smallest carrots into his mouth, chewing loudly. He looked over to Jordan. ''Done,'' he said around a mouthful of the orange vegetables.

Jordan smiled at him. Jason was a notoriously finicky eater, most often barely taking more than two bites of food at a meal. Jordan sometimes couldn't help but wonder how he kept up his energy with his eating habits.

They had come to a clearing near the cottage for a

picnic, something they tried to do at least once a week. Jordan looked at the empty spot on the blanket, the untouched food on the nearby plate. Kara had insisted that Jordan set a place for Maggie, though John had tried to explain to them that Maggie was never coming back. "But she'll always be here in our hearts. Right, Lady Jordan?" Ana asked, touching her chest.

Jordan missed Maggie terribly. All of the children missed her, too, but none as much as Ana. They had been great friends, Ana always watching over Maggie like a mother hen, never squabbling. Their favorite game had been sisters. They would dress up in old remnants that Jordan had brought for them from the castle and pretend they were sisters, doing the gardening and washing the dishes together. It made their chores more fun.

But now Ana wouldn't touch the dress-up clothes. She wouldn't even look at them.

Emily squirmed in Jordan's lap, and she looked down at the girl. She was chewing on some lavender. Jordan gently took it from the girl. When she screamed in protest, Jordan handed her a carrot instead. The child munched happily on the root.

Emily was certainly growing. Jordan remembered the first time John had brought her to the house. He said her parents had been killed by outlaws. He had found her on the road near their bodies, sitting in the mud, just crying and crying. She had been terribly skinny, dirty, and pale, and it looked as if one of the outlaws had hit her on the cheek and bruised her face. Jordan remembered the outrage she felt when she first saw her. That had been over a year ago. Now, at the age of two, Emily was bright-eyed and beautiful, even a bit on the plump side. Content was a word that came to Jordan's mind. Little Emily seemed very content. She stared at Jordan with large brown eyes and unabashed love.

"All right," John said. "Jason's finished."

Jordan turned to the older boy. "Yes, he is," Jordan agreed. "Good boy." She rubbed his stomach. "It might actually be full in there today."

Jason grinned.

Jordan set Emily on the blanket and rose to her feet, glancing around the clearing.

"Over there," John said, pointing to a large tree nearby. "See that big green patch of moss? Can you hit that?"

Jordan followed his gaze to the tree, seeing the green smattering of growth John was referring to. The tree was about fifty feet away, the patch of moss about two feet wide. It would be difficult to hit, but she thought she could do it. She nodded to the gathered children. Then she hiked up her skirt so it came to above her knees.

Kara giggled.

"Remember what I told you, Kara. This isn't appropriate behavior for a lady, and I would never do it before adults. And I don't want you to try this until you've been practicing for two years."

"I remember," Kara said earnestly.

Jordan locked gazes with the other children. "That goes for all of you, too."

They all promised.

"It took me a long time to learn to do this," Jordan told them. She lifted her skirt higher and removed a dagger from a hidden sheath strapped to her thigh. She stared at it for a long moment. Its black handle was in sharp contrast to the polished silver blade. She took care every night to polish the blade and sharpen it. She had never used it on a person, but she felt more secure that it was there. It gave her confidence and made her feel safe, especially on those late nights when she came to visit the children. The roads were often very dark and ominous and she occasionally traveled them alone, despite everyone's warning her not to.

She lifted her gaze to see the bright eyes of the children shining expectantly at her. John gazed at her with rapt anticipation.

Jordan cast a glance across the clearing at the old tree. In one quick move, she pulled the skirts of her dress up between her legs and kicked herself over onto her hand, cartwheeling in the direction of the tree. As her body came round, she flung the dagger at the tree and cleanly caught herself with the other hand, then continued to cartwheel and land squarely back on her feet. The movement was very fluid, very precise, very difficult to do. But Jordan had been practicing it nearly every day for years and it had come to be second nature to her now.

Jordan knew by the gasps and exclamations from the children that she had hit the target square in the center . . . as she had the last time she had shown them the move. And the time before that. She never missed a target the children gave her. Not anymore. She didn't want them to be disappointed in her.

Jordan adjusted her skirt. Kara threw her arms around her legs and beamed a radiant smile up at her. "You're the greatest, Lady Jordan!"

Jordan scooped Kara up and brushed a kiss against the girl's cheek. "Thank you, my lady."

Kara giggled and Jordan set her back on the ground.

Ana stood and walked toward the tree where Jordan's dagger was lodged firmly in the thick bark. Jordan followed her to pry the blade free. She flipped it over in her hands.

Ana lifted her blue eyes to Jordan. Jordan could see the sadness in her gentle face. ''Who will teach us when you are gone?'' the little girl wondered.

''Gone?'' Jordan echoed, confused. ''I'm not leaving, Ana.''

Ana scowled and looked away. ''The tournament is tomorrow, is it not?''

And then Jordan understood the source of Ana's sadness. Her heart ached for the agony the girl must be experiencing. To be abandoned by her mother and father and then to think she was losing the only person who had been a constant in her life since then would be very painful. Jordan knelt in the grass and took one of Ana's hands into hers. ''Ana, look at me,'' Jordan whispered. When the girl lifted those crystal blue eyes to her, Jordan wanted to cry for the worry so clearly evident in her expression. ''I will never leave you.''

Ana looked away again. ''But the tournament . . . you are to be wed to the victor.''

''That's right, yes,'' Jordan said. ''And who is the bravest knight in all the lands?''

''Sir Evan,'' Ana grumbled.

''And who is the strongest knight in all the lands?''

''Sir Evan,'' Ana mumbled.

''Then who will win the tournament?''

A begrudging grin stretched Ana's lips. ''Sir Evan.''

''And where are Sir Evan's lands?''

''They border the Ruvane lands,'' Ana said in a monotone voice, as if she had been told this over and over again. And she had.

Jordan pulled Ana into her hold, wrapping the girl in a tight embrace. ''I will never leave you, Ana,'' Jordan whispered. ''Ever.''

Ana lifted her stare to meet Jordan's. ''Swear?''

Jordan nodded earnestly.

Ana held out the smallest finger on her hand. "Pinkie swear?"

Jordan smiled a big smile. She wrapped her smallest finger around Ana's. "Pinkie swear." She squeezed Ana tightly. "It will take more than a marriage to keep me away from you." As she held Ana, she opened her eyes to see John glancing sideways at Kara. Kara was bowing her head, kicking a spot of weeds with her bare toe.

"What is it?" Jordan asked.

"Nothing," Kara quickly said.

John bowed his head, refusing to meet her gaze.

Confusion washed over Jordan. "John?"

Though he scowled, John would not lift his eyes to her.

When Jordan moved up to him, his scowl increased, his lips tightening to keep some secret in. Jordan placed a hand on his shoulder. "You can tell me anything."

"John," Ana hissed.

Jordan turned to Ana. "Tell me."

"They said you lied to us about Maggie and now you would lie about leaving us, too," Jason said.

John and Ana turned to the young boy. "Jason!" they said in unison.

Shocked, Jordan glanced at Jason, then Ana, and then John.

"You did promise nothing would happen to Maggie," Kara said tentatively. "And now she's gone."

For a moment, Jordan could not move, could not breathe. Their lack of trust hurt her. "I did all I could for Maggie."

John looked at Ana.

Guilt welled up inside Jordan. She had promised. And

Maggie was dead. "I'll never leave you," Jordan proclaimed. "I'd join a convent before I left you."

Kara giggled.

"You have to believe me," Jordan said. "I won't leave you."

But when she looked at Ana's blue eyes, she saw disbelief shining there. Jordan swung her gaze to John. He was looking at her with hope, but she could see the doubt in his gaze. How could they believe her? They were abandoned children, cast away by the very persons they loved most in the world. Why should they believe her?

Jordan clenched her jaw. She would prove to them she wasn't going to leave. Determination filled her.

Emily walked up to Jordan and took her hand, smiling at her.

"I won't leave you," Jordan said with resolve. "Not ever."

CHAPTER SEVEN

The sun glimmered brightly in the mid-morning sky. Jordan stood on the platform that overlooked the battlefield, nervously surveying the gathered crowd of armored knights. The day of the tournament had arrived so quickly. It seemed just hours ago that she had watched the men shine their armor and polish their blades, and now here she stood before them all as their prize. The spoils of the victor. Several knights had already ridden or walked up to her, expressing their undying love and devotion to her.

Jordan scoffed to herself. They didn't even know her. How could they love her?

An uneasy feeling churned her emotions, settling in the pit of her stomach. Many of the men were young and impetuous, barely beginning to shave the stubble that peppered their jaw, but others had the look of a dangerous savage burning in their dark faces. Jordan scanned the large field, looking for Evan, but she could not find him amidst the glistening, gleaming metal. The yard itself had to be widened to accommodate all the knights who had come to win Jordan's hand in the tournament. Apprehension grew stronger inside Jordan. How could she even hope Evan would win against all these knights? There must have been fifty visiting warriors, Jordan realized, if not more.

The platform was packed with other nobles, all anxiously awaiting the start of the tournament. A noblewoman stepped up to Jordan, a woman she didn't recognize. The woman wore a green dress, heavily embroidered with leaves. "This is so exciting," the woman said. "All of these men fighting to claim you." She waved her hand over her face, fanning the heat flushing into her cheeks. "If only I could be so lucky."

Lucky? Jordan felt nothing of the kind, only an impending dread. Something horrible was going to happen today. She knew it. She could feel it clawing at her spine.

The noblewoman next to her waved coyly at several of the knights who looked Jordan's way. Appalled, Jordan looked at her, catching the woman's gaze. "Well, they all can't have you," the woman explained. "I'd be happy to settle for second place."

Jordan turned at the sound of approaching hoofbeats, seeing Evan approaching. She had never felt more relieved to see him than she did today. But beneath that relief, uneasiness still stirred inside her. She desperately wanted Evan to win today, but her thoughts carried her beyond just today, to the future. To a very uncertain future. Would she be happy with him? In his arms? Would his lips feel right when they pressed up against hers?

A nervous excitement stirred deep in places that were unfamiliar to her. Would she be making love to this man tomorrow night after his victory, after their wedding celebration? Was it nervous excitement or just plain fear? She didn't know. The war of emotions was leaving her thoughts foggy and muddled.

"Greetings, my lady," Evan said, beaming her a confident smile. "And I do mean *my* lady, for today I shall be victorious and claim you as my prize."

Prize. Is that what I am to all these men? Jordan again wondered. *Just a prize. Not a woman, not a companion. A thing to be won. A trophy to hang on the mantel over a burning fireplace. A decoration to show off to one's fellow warriors.*

"Are you feeling all right, Jordan?" Evan asked, a scowl of concern shadowing his brow.

"Yes." Jordan tried to muster a smile, but failed miserably.

"You seem troubled."

"I . . . I'm just worried, Evan," Jordan told him. She looked out across the meadow, where knights filled both sides of the field. A wide space remained open in the middle on which to fight. One knight on the left side of the meadow was dressed in his ceremonial armor, with fancy etchings on the silver and an elaborate ducklike figure atop his helmet. His white steed pawed the ground in anticipation. Many others mirrored the elaborately adorned knight, all dressed in their best armor.

But there were others as well, others without so much obvious wealth. Some did not even have a horse. One knight was dressed in nothing fancier than brown leather armor, clutching a large ax. There were many more like him, their weapons just as deadly, the lethal intent in their eyes just as sharp and ferocious. And they had all come to win her. To fight, perhaps even to kill for her.

The reality of what was happening flooded over her, a

wave of dizziness splashing across her. Were all of these men willing to kill to claim her and her dowry? Was she worth dying for?

"Jordan?" Evan was staring in alarm at her.

She tried to force a smile to her lips, but could not summon even the illusion of calmness. "There are so many men, Evan."

Evan grinned at her. "Ha. Don't be afraid, Jordan. I will be victorious today. There are none on this battlefield I fear. Lord Graves is a great warrior, but I have plans for him. I'll put him into the ground he is so aptly named after."

Suddenly, a trumpet sounded and Jordan turned her head to see her father climbing the stairs of the platform, a group of older men trailing behind him. He came to stand beside her, clasped her hand, and squeezed it briefly, smiling warmly at her before releasing her fingers. Then he turned and his gaze swept the field, taking in the assemblage of battle-ready combatants. A grin of satisfaction touched his lips. "Welcome to the tournament!" he called.

"Huzzah!" the gathered throng of warriors shouted, dozens of glistening weapons thrusting skyward. "Hail to Lord Ruvane!" filled the field. "Hail to Lady Jordan!"

The peasants surrounding the field erupted into gleeful shouts. "Huzzah!"

The crowd of onlookers was massive; it looked as if villeins from every neighboring village had gathered here today.

Jordan turned back to Evan to wish him luck, but he was gone, already moving into his place among the knights. She looked back to her father.

Lord Ruvane let the excited cheers fade away, let the crowd calm for a moment, before continuing. "I know the greatest warrior in all of England has come to visit us today. I know he is out there amongst you fine men."

Again, the men erupted into excited cheers, all of them claiming to be that man.

Lord Ruvane turned to face Jordan, taking her hand into his. She smiled nervously at him and he smiled back. "This is how your mother and I met, Jordan. This is how our love began. This is where fate led us to bringing you into the world. You know you are my greatest joy. I only want a lifetime of happiness for you."

"I know, Father," Jordan said softly.

"Don't be afraid, child," he reassured her. "Today will be magical. Today will be a day you will treasure for the rest of your life, as I treasure the day your mother came into my life."

Jordan nodded softly to her father.

Lord Ruvane released her hand again and turned to face the crowd of fighters anxiously awaiting the signal to begin. He nodded to Jordan.

Jordan hesitated, but only for a mere moment, suddenly wishing she could be with the children . . . or anywhere else. But the day was here and there was no turning back now, no way to deny what fate had in store for her.

She lifted a yellow cloth high in the air.

Beside her, the noblewoman gasped in anticipation. The sound of swords being drawn echoed through the field. Horses whinnied, their hooves clawing at the dirt. Men gripped their weapons tightly, shifted their shields, preparing to do battle.

And then there was utter stillness. Even the mutterings of the gathered crowd dwindled into whispers, then faded into complete silence.

For the first time, Jordan saw a knight she hadn't noticed before. He was clad in black armor from head to foot and rode a magnificent black stallion. He clutched a mighty blade in one hand, an unadorned black shield in the other. His face was hidden beneath his black visor, but even from this distance Jordan could feel his gaze boring into her. A tingle of foreboding shot up her spine.

"Jordan," her father whispered to her, pulling her thoughts away from the mysterious dark knight.

Jordan dropped the cloth, and the yard exploded with action as the two sides rushed at each other with a loud war cry that threatened to break open the sky and bring a crash of lightning to the meadow. The wooden platform rumbled and shook beneath Jordan's feet as the armor-clad men raced to meet their opponents. The charges ended in an explosion of metal against metal as swords clashed and rising shields met striking axes.

Jordan couldn't help the feeling of dread that snaked through her body as the warriors battled. But even with her misgivings, the battle was tremendous and exciting to watch. All around her, the nobles screamed and yelled. The villeins standing around the fenced-off field cheered on their favorites, cursing as a favored knight fell but then quickly choosing another to encourage with shouts of support.

In the first minutes, many men fell and disappeared into the sea of armor. Jordan scanned the field for Evan, looking for the black dragon of the Vaughn crest amidst all the other family crests. A knight with a purple plume on his helmet crossed swords with a knight who had a large dent in his. A man with no armor and blood running over a large gash in his head was being helped from the field. Her gaze swept past them.

It stopped cold as she found the black-armored knight feverishly wielding his sword. The metal blade glinted hotly in the sunlight, striking down man after man. He was relentless in his attacks. Was he the Lord Graves Evan had mentioned? She didn't know for sure. All she was certain of was that he was a magnificent fighter, his every strike efficient and deadly accurate.

Jordan forced her gaze past him to the other end of the field, continuing her search for Evan. But she couldn't see him. For a moment, panic welled in her stomach. Had he been unhorsed already? What if he had been defeated? What if he had been hurt?

"Look at him fight," the noblewoman beside her said.

Jordan pulled herself out of her growing panic. "Who?"

"Sir Evan." The woman pointed across the field.

Jordan followed her direction. It took her only a moment to find Evan in his silver plate mail, slashing down every opponent he came into contact with. Relief surged through Jordan.

"He is a very competent fighter," the woman said.

Jordan nodded her head, keeping her gaze on Evan, as if her will alone would help him win the battle.

By midday, over half of the men had been beaten and taken from the field. One man had been seriously injured when an ax-wielding opponent had sliced through his armor. Another had a crippling sword cut on the back of his thigh. Seven had been knocked unconscious.

Four had been killed.

Now the field was emptier, but the fighting continued.

Jordan's nerves were clenched so tight she could not sit down. Her shoulders ached from the tension that surged across them. She was clutching her skirts so hard that her hands ached and her knuckles turned white. She was so worried for Evan. His thrusts and swings were not as hard nor as precise. He was tiring. But he was still one of the few men left on horseback.

Another man dressed in bronze armor drew Jordan's gaze. He fought valiantly on the ground, disarming opponents with masterful strikes. He had lost his helm in the battle and his face was smeared with grime and dirt. Evan made his way toward the man, striking down one opponent as he spurred his horse forward. The bronze-armored man turned as he heard Evan's charge. He raised his weapon to block the strike, but Evan's blow was mighty, the speed of the horse adding extra power to his swing. Evan's blade smashed his opponent's sword back, sending the man's own blade into his neck. He fell hard to the ground, blood spurting from his fatal wound.

Shock flared through Jordan. The move was horribly brutal, as well as unchivalrous. It was dishonorable for a knight on horseback to strike a man on the ground in a tournament.

Around the field, many onlookers hissed and booed at Evan, expressing their disapproval.

"That was cowardly," the noblewoman muttered. She looked away from Evan, finding another knight to give favor to.

Evan swung his horse around looking for another man, but the field was nearly empty, the tournament almost at an end. His gaze came to the last remaining rival on the field.

Jordan followed his gaze to find a man sitting on his horse at the opposite end of the field. It was the black-armored knight, with no tunic, no crest of allegiance to indicate who he was or where he had come from. He sat strangely still in his saddle. Then he dismounted and swatted his horse's flank, sending it running to safety.

Jordan frowned.

"Take the challenge, Vaughn!" someone shouted nearby.

"Fight him with honor!" another voice cried.

Evan's horse pranced nervously as Evan surveyed this final adversary. He turned to look at Jordan. Would he attack the black knight from horseback? Jordan found herself scowling fiercely, displeasure evident in her slanted eyebrows.

And then Evan dismounted, sending his animal galloping away. He stepped forward, raising his sword as he moved.

After a brief second, the black knight moved forward. He lifted his sword high in the air to meet Evan. The metal clanged loudly, sparks flying from their striking weapons with the force of their attack. Again and again their swords met, each blow quick and powerful. Both men appeared to have suddenly been re-energized by this final confrontation, their strength surging back into their bodies.

Who was he? Jordan wondered as the black knight deflected all of Evan's attacks. He stood bravely against Evan, matching him skill for skill. Why did he wear no crest? Jordan's heart pounded and her hands played nervously with her necklace. This black knight was the best Evan had come up against.

The black knight raised his weapon and brought it quickly around to the side, hitting Evan in the arm. The plate mail deflected the blow, but Evan teetered for a moment. Then he slipped and went down on one knee.

Jordan gasped. She didn't realize she was holding her breath until he recovered quickly and rose to his feet again to meet his opponent's swing.

Her father exhaled in relief, too. She glanced at him to find him nodding his head, as if he were looking at a son to find him exactly what he expected.

The black knight pursued Evan relentlessly.

Evan turned on the knight, ramming his sword against his plate armor. But it bounced harmlessly off. Evan brought his sword around again, smashing the black knight's helm. The black knight appeared dazed and stumbled back.

For a moment, Jordan thought it was over. Her heart beat wildly in her chest.

Evan lifted his weapon high for the final attack.

Suddenly, the black knight came to life, shoving his gauntleted hand into Evan's chest. Evan tumbled backward and hit the ground in a cloud of dust, his sword flying away from him.

Jordan's mouth dropped open as the black knight moved to Evan, lifting his sword high in the air, meaning to plunge it deep into Evan.

"No!" Jordan shouted, taking the first step down the platform.

The black knight halted at her call and glanced up at her.

Jordan saw searing blue eyes gaze at her for a long moment from beneath his black visor.

Evan struggled to twist and turn to find his weapon. But the weight of his armor kept him pinned to the ground. The black knight turned back to Evan.

"No!" Jordan cried out again. He was going to kill Evan. Instinctively, she lifted her skirt and grabbed her dagger, throwing it across the field. It flew fast and straight, lodging into the gap at the underside of the knight's left arm.

He staggered back from Evan, lowering his sword, and clutched at his arm.

"Jordan," her father chastised angrily.

Horrified, Jordan watched as her dagger did little to

stop the black knight. He gripped his sword in two hands and moved toward Evan again.

With a wave from her father, four men rushed onto the field to restrain the black knight, pulling him away from Evan.

Jordan jerked forward to move to Evan's side. But her father grabbed her arm, restraining her.

"Come forward, black knight," her father said.

Jordan struggled for a moment, then turned to her father in shock. That's when the realization hit her. This man, this black knight, had beaten Evan!

The black knight shrugged himself free of the men holding him and stepped toward the viewing platform, holding his left arm.

Jordan turned to him. Complete dread washed through her.

"Well done, sir," her father called out in greeting. "You have done well this day."

The black knight halted directly before the platform. Behind him, the four men finished helping Evan to his feet. He ripped off his helmet, hollering, "Unmask, sir, so I can see who beat the best fighter in all of England!"

"Yes," Lord Ruvane agreed. "Remove your helm so we may welcome you into our family."

No! Jordan thought, her insides twisting. *This can't be!*

For a long moment, the black knight did not move.

Silence blanketed the entire field.

"Remove your helm," Lord Ruvane insisted.

A grumbling grew and spread amongst the spectators, who were moving forward, edging closer to the platform to see the winner.

The black knight sheathed his sword and then reached up with his right hand to pull the helm from the back of his head. As he lowered it away from him, his face slowly emerged into view. Wet hair, dark as coal; blue sapphire eyes, hard as rock; an aquiline nose; lips thin and set in defiance; and a strong, square chin.

Jordan knew him immediately. She gasped in shock and her heart skipped a beat in her chest. "Fox."

His intense gaze swiveled to her, pinning her to her spot, a searing torch igniting her body.

His name was echoed around the platform and fence by everyone who had gathered, but no voice echoed louder than Evan's. "The Black Fox!" he raged.

"I have won Lady Jordan's hand fairly." Fox's voice, thick with bitterness, rose above the outburst.

Evan marched up to him. "Have you lost your mind, Mercer?" Evan proclaimed. "You can't have her."

"Did you really think I would allow my daughter to marry an outlaw?" Lord Ruvane asked Fox in disbelief.

"Guards!" Evan called, stepping toward Fox and placing the tip of his weapon at Fox's throat. "You are under arrest, Fox Mercer."

Men in chain mail and tunics bearing the Ruvane crest rushed onto the field, surrounding him.

Fox stood his ground, not even trying to escape. His gaze swiveled to Jordan again. Accusation burned in his eyes.

Her shock disappeared, quickly replaced by her own anger. He should be imprisoned! He should be locked away forever for stealing the herbs that would have saved Maggie's life. She lifted her chin slightly and narrowed her gaze. What did he have to accuse her of? She should be looking at him with disdain. "Take this murderer to the dungeon," she spat.

The murmuring rose again.

"I declare Sir Evan the winner of the tournament and

of my daughter's hand in marriage,'' Lord Ruvane exclaimed.

But there was no loud cheer from any of the onlookers. Just murmurings of confusion and awe and shock that the Black Fox had been captured.

''You heard the lady. Take him to the dungeon,'' Evan ordered.

The guards roughly seized hold of Fox's arms. His black helm fell to the ground, and Evan kicked it aside as the men marched their prisoner toward Castle Ruvane.

CHAPTER EIGHT

"I can't believe he would dare to show his face here!" Jordan marched back and forth across the solar, her fists clenched tightly at her sides.

Evan leaned back in his chair and let her rant, a grin on his lips.

"What could he have hoped to accomplish?"

"Your hand in marriage," Evan supplied, graciously.

"Ha!" Jordan exclaimed in disbelief. "I would not marry him if he were the last man in all of England!" She drummed her fingers on her lower lip. "He's a wanted outlaw, a thief, and a killer. But he is not stupid. He knew there was no chance for him to win my hand in marriage. So why come here?"

"Jordan," Evan mused, "Fox never was very smart. I never thought so."

Jordan turned to look at Evan. "You used to be good friends."

"Jordan, that was a lifetime ago. And truthfully, *you* used to be friends with him. I just tolerated his presence because I thought you liked him."

I did like him, Jordan thought, remembering their childhood friendship. *I liked him very much.* What had happened to the boy she had so admired? What had happened to the young man she had almost believed herself to be falling in love with? What had frozen his heart and turned his soul to ice?

"What if he came to defeat you?" she mused. "His old *friend?*"

Evan stiffened.

But Jordan continued, not noticing the insult she had delivered. She waved her hand wildly about in the air. "It makes no difference why he came." She scowled darkly. "The only thing that matters is that because of him, Maggie died."

Evan slouched slightly in the chair. "Well, we have him now. He will cause us no more misery. He will pay for his crimes, and pay dearly. He'll be doing no more stealing."

"Yes," Jordan said quietly. But her mind refused to stop thinking about those eyes that had stared at her from the battlefield. They were not the eyes of a cold-blooded killer. They were not the eyes of a man who would take the life of a child to extract some sort of twisted revenge. Then why had he done it? Why had he stolen the herbs? Was it truly to get back at her? And if it was, did that then, in some macabre twist of fate, make Maggie's death her fault? Guilt churned in her heart, even though she knew she could not realistically blame herself for the little girl's death.

Suddenly, the door opened and her father entered like

a storm cloud. His fierce scowl warned Jordan of his temper. "Jordan," he rumbled.

Jordan knew better than to let her own temper show when he was so enraged. "Yes, Father."

He held out a dagger to her. "I believe this is yours."

Jordan took the dagger from his hands. She studied it for a moment. "Thank you, Father."

"Do not thank me yet, child," he warned. "Your interference in the tournament was a disgrace."

"He was going to kill Evan!" she objected.

A frown marred Evan's brow, and he straightened in his chair. "I can defend myself."

"Imagine, my own daughter throwing a dagger in the midst of a battle," her father said, pacing. "And because of it, a man is wounded."

"A criminal is wounded!" Jordan corrected.

"Still, it is man's work, not woman's, to wield weapons." Lord Ruvane puffed out his chest. "You will go and mend his wound."

"What?" Jordan gasped.

Evan rose. "I'll go with Jordan."

Lord Ruvane held out a hand to him, stopping him. "No. Jordan must learn the consequences of her actions. She will go alone down into the dungeon, amidst the robbers and thieves."

"Mend his wound?" Jordan objected. "But, Father . . ."

"He is a criminal!" Evan joined her defense. "To send her unprotected . . ."

Lord Ruvane waved his hand in dismissal. "Mercer is chained to the wall. What can he do to her? Besides, there is a man guarding the dungeon. She will be in no danger."

Jordan glared at her father for a long moment, disbelief etched in her brow. "Father, you can't—"

"Your behavior was unacceptable. You will do as I say."

Jordan turned from her father to Evan, beseeching him with her eyes. Grudgingly, he dropped his gaze, his jaw tight.

Aghast, Jordan whirled from the room. *Mend Fox's wound!* The man who was the cause of Maggie's death. *Maybe I can put poison in his wound. Or mayhap I can tie the bindings so tight that his arm will fall off.*

Mend Fox's wound, indeed!

Jordan stood at the top of the spiraling stairs and looked down into the darkness. She held a basin of water and some cloth. It wasn't tainted with poison, as she would have liked, but the bitterness in her mouth might as well have been poison.

A sudden memory flashed into her mind. She remembered standing at the top of the stairs, terrified by the patch of blackness that seemed to descend into eternity below her. "Don't be afraid, Jordan," Fox had whispered to her. He had grabbed her hand, holding her fingers tight. "You never have to be afraid when I'm with you."

Strange she should remember that now.

She descended into the dank, dark bowels of the castle, a chill climbing her spine despite his comforting voice still echoing in her ears. He wasn't with her today, and he would never be with her again. Never as a friend.

She moved deeper into the darkness. Around her, the air seemed to thicken with a chill dampness. This was no place for a lady, especially one on the verge of marriage. But her father's word was law. She clutched the basin as a sort of shield.

She moved carefully down the spiraling stairway, careful not to slosh the water on her dress. At the bottom of the stairs, the bottom of the castle, the bottom of the world, she continued on to the guard's post. Her protector. Her guardian in case one of those foul vagabonds tried to touch her. But what she found caused her even more dismay.

The guard was slumped over the table, snoring loudly, an empty cup of ale still gripped loosely in his hand. Jordan stared for a moment, her mouth open. She turned back toward the stairs, to her father. But then she halted. It would serve him right to know he sent her here unprotected. She could just imagine the shock on his face, the horror.

Besides, he would still send her back down, and she would have to carry this basin of water all the way back. She just wanted to get this unpleasant task over with and get out of the dungeon.

She moved up to the guard and took a candle from the table. Then, balancing the basin in one hand and the candle in the other, the cloth tucked beneath her chin, she muttered a curse and walked into the darkness of the dungeon hallway. She moved to the door and peaked through the barred windows. Jordan knew there were two other prisoners in the dungeon right now, but she could see no one in the gloomy interior. The candle cast its light only a few feet into the dungeon's belly.

Jordan put the basin and candle down and slid the heavy bolt aside. The loud grating sound reverberated through the dungeon. She glanced back toward the guard's post, hoping it would wake the man up. But the guard did not appear. Only his snoring echoed down the hallway after her.

Jordan grimaced and eased the door open. It squeaked

on rusted hinges. She bent to retrieve the basin and candle before stepping into the room.

The light from the candle flickered in the large room, casting more light into the dark room as it spread out wider. One room served as the dungeon for all. Several pairs of manacles hung empty on the wall. Dark corners hid a myriad of unseen evils.

As her vision adjusted more to the gloom, Jordan made out a hunched form huddled against the far wall. His knees were raised, his arms resting atop them. His head was down, and his thick black locks cascaded in waves over his arms. He was chained to the wall, the thick metal manacles surrounding his wrists.

Slowly, his head lifted until his blue eyes locked on hers. There was a hard edge to them, a predatory look in them. They narrowed slightly.

Fox, part of her wanted to call out, but she pushed that soft side away and kept silent.

"Come to stare at your rightful future husband?" he wondered.

She opened her mouth to reply, to deny his accusation, but then promptly closed it. That was exactly what she was doing. Staring. But not at a man she would even dare to consider as a future husband. The very thought of Fox trying to claim her as his wife sent an odd flush racing through her veins.

Finally, Jordan shook her head, the strange sensation quickly turning to heated anger. "I'm here to mend your wound." Jordan moved to Fox's side, angrily placing the basin and candle at his feet. Some of the water sloshed from the bowl.

"Alone?" Fox asked, genuinely surprised.

Jordan knelt beside him, lifting furious eyes to lock

with his. "I don't need my father to protect me from you." She dropped one of the cloths into the water.

When she looked up again, she saw he had been stripped of his armor. His wound was bound by a dirty cloth and his shirt had been ripped and hung open to reveal a portion of his chest. A strong chest. She could see the muscles and the ridges of his stomach.

Fox chuckled deeply. "Perhaps you need someone to protect you from yourself."

Jordan snapped her gaze up to his. His deep blue eyes shone with a dark knowledge, and his lip was quirked to one side. His impudence irritated her. Jordan grimaced and reached for his arm. When her hand closed over his skin, she was surprised at the strength that rippled beneath her touch. She couldn't help but run her hand across his smooth muscle until she touched the sticky cloth that bound his wound. Slowly, Jordan unwrapped the cloth and threw it onto the floor.

She gasped at seeing the wound. Blood still oozed from the red, irritated cut near his upper elbow. Without taking her eyes from his wound, she reached into the water and pulled out the cloth. Gently, she touched the clean water to the wound, washing it with soft strokes.

"Unchain me, Jordan."

She turned to him. Had he truly asked that of her? She stared into his eyes, eyes so intense that she almost reached for the manacles. *Am I mad?* she wondered. *What's come over me?* She jerked back, dumping a cloth in the water of the basin.

"This is dangerous work. Have you no one else to tend me?"

He was mocking her! Jordan lifted her gaze to him. His eyes were a cool blue in the candlelight, centered on her with amusement. His cheeks were clean shaven, and she could see the muscle in his jaw working.

She realized quite suddenly that she was rather close to him. As if in response, she felt a jolt through her body. Her gaze shifted to his lips. Sensual, inviting. She had always liked Fox's lips, had often found them mesmerizing when he spoke. And even after their long years of separation, she still found her gaze hypnotized by them.

She shook herself and dipped the cloth into the water to clean it of blood. "It is a punishment."

"Punishment?"

"I threw the dagger," she said quietly, keeping her concentration on her work. But she couldn't help the guilt that surged through her. She had done this. She had caused him this injury, and it probably hurt like the devil. She finished wiping the cloth along his skin, cleaning it of blood.

A frown darkened Fox's brow. "It would take more than your dagger to kill me."

Shocked, Jordan sat back. She studied his dark face, the sudden anger that thinned his lips. She had certainly not meant to kill him, although at that moment the thought was not altogether unpleasant. She should have wanted to kill him for what he did to Maggie. But she would have been just as happy to see him locked up. She picked up the clean cloth and began to wrap it around his wounded arm. "Why did you steal those herbs?"

He lifted his head even higher to face her squarely, revealing more of himself to her. She saw a strong, square jaw, and angry but still very sensual lips. "It's none of your damned business," he retorted.

Jordan's mouth fell open, her eyes rounding in surprise at the vicious tone in Fox's voice. She snapped her mouth closed and her eyes narrowed. "They were meant for me. I sent Evan to hurry the merchant. I needed—"

"I don't care why you needed them."

Jordan pulled the cloth tight around his wound and was rewarded by a gritting of his teeth. "You uncaring, unfeeling cur. Do you know the consequences of your actions?"

"The question should be, do I care?"

Jordan rose before him, her blood boiling at his callous retort. "You heartless bastard!" She wanted to stomp on his toes or kick some sense into him. She moved closer, leaning down near him to give him the full force of her anger. "A child died because of you," she spat.

For a brief moment, Fox sat motionless, a quick spark of dismay and disbelief flashing across his eyes. Then he looked away from her, his face once again disappearing into the dark shadows of the dungeon. "One less noble child makes no difference to me," he muttered.

Jordan brought her hand around and slapped his cheek soundly. "A child is a child, noble or not. And her death is on your hands." Jordan closed her mouth, and her lips thinned in a tight line. Maggie hadn't been a noble, just an abandoned girl. And Jordan had loved her dearly. "That is something I will never forgive you for." Jordan grabbed the basin and candle and whirled for the door. "I hope you rot in here."

The cell door slammed hard with a resounding clang, the bolt slamming back into place.

Fox gritted his teeth, listening to Jordan's footsteps fading into the distance. Why should he care about what the herbs meant to Jordan? Why should he care what happened to anyone besides his people? Had his actions really caused the death of this girl?

Fox cursed silently and pushed the dark, unpleasant possibilities from his mind. *I can't let myself care,* he thought. *These are my enemies. All of them. Every noble man, woman, and child who lives on Ruvane lands or Vaughn lands and the lands stolen from my father. Every one.*

"She's a whirlwind," a voice from the opposite wall said.

Fox didn't reply. To see Jordan standing before him looking so damned beautiful . . . It would have been easier if the years had turned her into an ugly wretch. At least it would have been more fair. But life wasn't fair. He'd learned that a long time ago. He knew he made his own luck.

And his own luck should be coming any moment now—if they stuck to the original plan and if nothing had happened to them. If no guard had recognized them . . .

Fox leaned back against the cold wall, running his hands through his black hair, the chains that bound him clanking as they moved. His arm throbbed. She had made the cloth too tight. But no matter. *This little venture has cost me more than I thought. The dogs have stripped me of my armor and my horse. Ah well,* he thought. *I will get them back.*

"At least this cell has good scenery," the voice added. "Some of the stones are quite colorful."

And I did find Beau, Fox thought, as the man chained opposite him continued to let his mouth run on and on. His friend was worth all the horses and armor in the kingdom. Now they needed to escape.

Suddenly, the sound of the bolt being drawn again filled the cell. The door swung open. For a moment, Fox was blinded by the light of a torch from the hallway. He put up a hand to protect his eyes to see who was entering.

The doorway was suddenly blocked by the bulky shape of a large man, a man rippling with muscles.

A grin stretched across Fox's face. He stood up. "I was just wondering when you might show up, Pick."

The large man shrugged helplessly before he suddenly lurched into the cell. He landed on his knees before Fox. Four guards followed him in. One guard kicked the big man in the ribs, making the burly man grunt. "Get over there, you big ox."

The other guards stood alertly in the doorway, watching Pick move slowly toward the dungeon wall.

Pick smiled at Fox as the guard clapped manacles over his wrists. "Apparently so was Vaughn."

The guard stepped away from Pick, joining the others at the door. "Sweet dreams," the guard said. The other guards laughed as they left the cell, closing the door, sealing them in darkness.

"Nice to see you, Pick," Beau greeted.

"I'm sure you think so," Pick answered shortly, rubbing his side. "But I could have done without a few of these bruises."

"It's kind of chilly down here," Beau said. "I hope you brought us some blankets."

Pick grunted.

"All right," Beau said. "Now what, Fox? I don't think this was part of your master plan, was it? Ol' Pick here was supposed to get us out, not join us, wasn't he?" Beau turned to look at Pick. "Not that I don't enjoy your company, big man . . ."

Fox waited until the ugly sound of the laughing guards faded into the distance before turning to his large friend. "It's time, Pick," Fox said softly.

Pick nodded his head and reached into his mouth. He pulled out a thin piece of metal that had been held in place in a large gap in his back teeth and held it up before him.

The sliver of metal was barely visible to Fox in the murky gloom. But the sound of metal against metal as Pick slid it into the lock on the manacles was clearly audible in the darkness.

CHAPTER NINE

Jordan shook the water from her velvet dress. It would dry. But she had been so angry returning to her room that she had spilled the water over the front of her dress.

She had changed into a white velvet gown with gold trim and left her hair down, a headband of gold around her head. She was braiding her long locks as she moved down the stairs when suddenly she heard the cry.

"Fire!"

Jordan dropped her hands from her hair, lifting her eyes to the hallway below her.

"Fire!" A shout sounded through the inner courtyard. "Fire!"

Immediately, she bolted down the stairs, running as fast as she could. She whipped around the corner . . .

. . . and almost slammed into a wall of flesh. She lifted her eyes for a hurried apology, but stopped dead. Fox stood before her!

Fox! But how . . . What in heaven's name was he doing out of the dungeon? Jordan opened her mouth in shock, to call out for help. But Fox's eyes darkened and he grabbed her arm, pulling her to him, slapping his palm across her mouth, silencing any cry of alarm she had been about to make. "It doesn't look like you'll get your wish," he growled. "The Black Fox rots in no man's dungeon."

Jordan struggled in Fox's grip. There was a fire in the castle. She had to help!

Fox pulled her toward the door, his hand tight across her mouth. Jordan struggled harder, trying to wrench herself free. Fox only tightened his grip, moving his hold down her arm to around her waist.

As they paused near the doors, two monks appeared from the Great Hall.

Jordan's eyes widened at their appearance. Her chance for escape! She lifted her foot and brought it down sharply on Fox's. He barely noticed, just shot her an aggravated look and pulled her even tighter to him.

The monks approached them quickly. Jordan's heart leaped for joy. Surely they would help her. Surely they could see Fox was holding her against her wishes. They would free her and Fox would be returned to the dungeon. She doubled her efforts to escape, twisting and turning in Fox's hold.

But as the monks neared, they slowed, and any sense of hope diminished from Jordan's thoughts, then completely vanished as the monks pulled three brown robes from the confines of their clothing and tossed one to a red-haired man who quickly donned it, and one to Beau, who also put it on.

These were no monks! They were friends of Fox! They were helping him escape.

"What are you going to do with her?" one of the

monks asked. A female voice, Jordan realized. "We don't have another robe."

Fox quickly pointed to a rope tied around another monk's waist, cinching the robe. "Give me that."

The monk untied the rope from around his waist and held it out to Fox. Fox took it and pulled Jordan's hands roughly behind her back, binding them firmly.

Instantly, Jordan opened her mouth to cry out, but one of the monks shoved a wad of cloth into her mouth, again silencing her.

Fox took the final robe and tossed it over Jordan's shoulders, lifting the hood to hide her face.

Jordan's mind screamed, but her cries were muffled by the ragged cloth threatening to suffocate her. She thrashed wildly in Fox's arms, but his grip was firm and unwielding.

Fox roughly dragged her out the door, moving silently through the inner ward. "Just stay near me," he ordered the other monks. The monks followed his command, keeping Fox in the middle of them all, hiding him as best they could.

Jordan glanced quickly over at the roar she heard behind her to see that the blacksmith's roof was ablaze with fire. The hood over her head blocked most of her view, but she could still see servants and guards scrambling everywhere, everyone working urgently together, moving buckets of water quickly hand to hand to combat the spreading flames.

The five hooded monks moved unnoticed beneath the inner gatehouse and into the outer courtyard. Five horses were saddled and waiting at the side of the courtyard near the stables. The group walked to the horses and mounted.

Fox lifted Jordan onto his horse. She tried to slide away, but he swung up into the saddle behind her, dragging her up. She tried to spit out the gag in her mouth and finally managed to free herself of it. But her cries died beneath the roar of the flames and shouts of the castle occupants desperately trying to douse the growing fire.

Fox covered her mouth again and seized the reins. He spurred the animal toward the outer gatehouse. Toward freedom.

Fox glanced back in the direction of Castle Ruvane. The towering structure was almost out of sight, nothing more than a small blemish on the horizon. The road behind them was empty. It didn't seem as if they were being followed. He glanced at Scout. She shook her head, confirming his sentiment.

They weren't being followed. The guards must have been too busy with the fire Smithy had started to notice their escape. Jordan shifted her position slightly in the saddle before him and Fox's gaze was drawn to her. The hood blew off of Jordan's head and a strand of her hair flew free of the confines of her braid. The wind whipped it back against his face. It rubbed his cheek as though it was a caress. Fox lifted a hand to push the hair from his face, but he caught the surprisingly soft lock in his palm. He gazed at it a long moment before opening his palm to free it.

He lifted his gaze to the back of Jordan's head. *The lack of pursuit won't last long,* he thought. *Not once Ruvane finds out I have his daughter.*

Fox groaned softly. That was the last thing he needed, to bring down Ruvane's wrath on his friends. Why did she have to come out of the stairway then? *Why did you feel compelled to bring her with you?* another voice inside him wondered. *You should have just left her there.*

But now that she is here, what am I going to do with her? he silently mused.

"What are you going to do with her?"

They had stopped to give the horses a rest, and Fox had allowed Jordan to dismount. Her legs were cramped and achy from the long ride. The other monks had long since shed their disguises, discarding the robes. And now Jordan felt all of their eyes on her as they awaited Fox's reply to the big man's question. She bowed her head, refusing to look at them. At least Fox had not found the dagger hidden at her thigh. But the weapon brought her little comfort. She couldn't use it against all of them, no matter how good her aim had become. And besides, her wrists were still bound behind her back.

"Just let her go," Beau offered. "She'd be more trouble than she's worth."

Yes, Jordan encouraged silently, lifting her gaze to lock with Fox's. *Let me go. I have to get back to the children. There is no one to make sure they get food. No one to visit them, to take care of them. Abagail is there, yes, but she doesn't know where to get the food, much less how to pay for it.* They needed her. She had no time to waste with these . . . murderers.

"I don't want another woman in our home. One is quite enough," the old man with whiskers said.

"What's that supposed to mean?" the solitary woman in Fox's pack of rogues asked.

"Let her go, Fox," the tall man added. "We don't need the trouble."

Fox sighed and his gaze bored into her.

Hope surged through her, but she dared not say a word.

She knew whatever she told him, he would do the opposite. *Let me go,* she prayed.

"You want me to cut her free?" the tall man asked and stepped toward Jordan.

"No," Fox whispered. "She stays. We could use the ransom."

"Ransom?" Beau echoed. "That could take days. Even weeks. What are we supposed to do with her in the meantime?"

"No," Jordan whispered. Panic constricted her chest. She had to do something. She had to do something fast. The children needed her. She couldn't be away from them for more than a few days, let alone a few weeks!

They all stood watching her, tired from the long ride. None of them seemed to be on edge, or even very alert. This would be her only chance. Desperate, scared, she spun around and elbowed one of the horses in the flank with her bound hands, screaming at the horse, frightening it enough so it reared and kicked wildly. Startled, the gathered band of thieves moved quickly back from the upset animal.

Jordan whirled and raced off into the dark, thick forest, disappearing into the night.

Fox and company all stood for a long, quiet moment, watching Jordan run into the trees.

Fox glanced at Beau. Beau shook his head. "I'm seeing to my horse," he said and moved to the horse Jordan had set into motion. He rubbed the animal's mane, calming the beast with easy strokes. Then he sat down, placing his hands behind his head.

Fox's gaze shifted to Pick.

Pick smiled and shook his head. "You're the one who wants to ransom her. You go and get her."

Scout notched an arrow and pointed it at Jordan's retreating back. "I'll bring her down."

Fox cursed silently. "No, no, no. I'll get her." He pushed Scout's bow aside and watched Jordan for a moment. Did she truly think to escape him with her arms tied and her long dress hindering her movement? Fox sighed heavily and walked into the forest after her. Even in the darkness, he could see her shadow moving ahead of him. His large strides easily kept her in view. The thick undergrowth tugged at her dress, slowing her pace to nothing more than a brisk walk.

Where did she think she was going?

Then she tripped over a branch and fell, face forward to the ground.

As Fox reached her side, she was sliding her hands beneath her feet so they were tied in front of her instead of in back. He grabbed her, pulling her to her feet.

"Let go of me!" Jordan snapped. She twisted out of his grip, and Fox suddenly found himself staring down the tip of a dagger.

Slowly, a grin spread across his lips. What did she hope to do with that?

Jordan held the dagger firmly before her with her bound hands. Suddenly, she thrust the dagger at him and he took a quick step back, easily avoiding the strike. "Are you actually trying to kill me, Jordan?" he asked, incredulous.

"Get back," she whispered.

"You won't get away."

Jordan took a step backward. "We'll just see about that."

Fox watched her with a growing fascination, watched the way the moonlight made a halo around her magnificently curvaceous body. Time had been very friendly to Jordan Ruvane. Very friendly indeed. She took more steps back, away from him. Fox knew he couldn't lose her. He would never hear the end of the jabs and ridicule from his friends.

He took a step toward her, but she suddenly leaped away from him, twisting her body in midair, doing a sideways somersault over a fallen log. With her hands bound! It was one of the most amazing maneuvers he had ever seen. Then, almost immediately, he felt a sharp tug at his clothing and heard a loud thunk near his stomach. He glanced down to find his tunic pinned to the tree behind him by what could only have been *her* dagger. Amazement washed through him. How had she . . .

It didn't matter now. He had to stop her. He quickly reached up and pried the dagger loose with sharp back and forth motions, then lurched forward to give chase.

But she was gone, the trees hiding her like a blanket. Fox cursed silently. He gritted his teeth and froze, forcing his breathing to slow. Calm. He had to remain calm. He closed his eyes. Silence. Then, from in front of him to the right, he could hear her, moving through the leaves and branches. Running.

He vaulted into action, ducking tree branches, leaping over fallen logs, bursting through underbrush. Then he paused again. Instantly, he heard her—this time closer.

His heart raced as he continued his pursuit. He would catch her, he had no doubt. But rage rose in his heart that she would dare to even try to escape. He had expected her to be frightened and docile, but she was proving to be more stubborn and brave than he had anticipated.

Fox closed quickly on her and reached out for her, but she dodged left and he grabbed nothing but air. He cursed silently and adjusted his path. She was directly in front of him now. He reached out again and grabbed her shoulder, trying to halt her. "Jordan!" he shouted, his tone insisting that she stop.

Jordan yanked free so hard that she was propelled forward onto her hands and knees. She skidded slightly from the impetus and finally came to a stop on the muddy forest floor.

Fox halted beside her, breathing hard. He stared at her lowered head. Strands of her brown hair had come free from her braid and curled around her cheeks. She was breathing hard as well, her back rising and falling with each hard-earned mouth of air. Fox shook his head. Stubborn little . . .

"Why are you doing this, Fox?"

Fox straightened. The tenderness and confusion in her voice pulled at what remained of his heart for a moment. But only for a moment. He grabbed her arm in a fierce grip and pulled her to her feet, then whirled and headed back toward his horse, dragging her roughly in tow.

He hadn't taken but two steps when Jordan stumbled. He looked back at her and realized she was limping. Her skirt was ripped from her knee down, and a slight trickle of blood trailed down her left leg. *Serves her right for running from me,* he told himself.

Part of him wanted to stop and make sure she was all right, but he refused to listen to that weaker voice inside him. He wanted nothing to do with her. The only value her life had was the ransom she would bring. He yanked her forward, his hand tight around her upper arm. She stumbled, but this time he didn't stop. He pulled her sharply along behind him without even a glance back.

Finally, he broke through the bushes to where the others were waiting. Fox released Jordan in the middle of the group, roughly shoving her away from him. "We waste no more time. Let's move."

The others nodded at him. "Took you long enough," Beau chided Fox. Scout had a dark scowl on her face as she turned to mount her horse.

Fox turned back to Jordan and grabbed her waist, intending to lift her onto the horse. Out of the corner of his eye, he caught sight of her face and faltered. Strands of curling locks hung damply to her cheek. He swiveled his gaze to study her face. Her lips were full and pouty. The lower one actually jutted out slightly as if at any moment she was going to cry. Her cheeks were slightly red—whether from exertion or embarrassment or anger, Fox didn't know. Her large blue eyes were sad and full of tears. The years had changed her so much. She was a beautiful . . .

He shook himself mentally. She was a spoiled woman who was going to burst into tears at any moment. Well, he didn't have time for a weeping, wailing woman. He leaned close to her to lift her.

"Take your hands off me this moment, Mercer," she commanded.

There had been no tears in her voice, no quivering tone. He pulled back to look at her. The tears glinted in her eyes, but now he was sure they were tears of fear, of uncertainty. And suddenly, irrationally, he wanted to wipe away her fear.

The thought was fleeting and he shoved it from his mind instantly as though it had scorched his brain. He narrowed his eyes. "The Fox you knew doesn't exist anymore. He has been dead for a long time. I am the Black Fox."

"Call yourself what you will. But I will call you a

barbarian. A thief. A criminal. A murderer. You hide in the dark like a coward.''

''I am not a coward,'' he growled.

''No? Then what do you call a man who steals a woman from her home to ransom?''

''A desperate man,'' Fox snarled. He lifted her up onto the horse and quickly mounted behind her, holding her tight against him so she couldn't escape.

''I loathe you,'' she said with all the vehemence that coursed through her slender body.

''As you should,'' Fox replied and spurred his horse forward toward Castle Mercer.

CHAPTER TEN

Jordan trembled in the saddle as she stared at the crumbling ruins of what used to be Castle Mercer. She knew the castle had fallen into disrepair over the years, but she was surprised at the extent of its decay.

The morning sun was just beginning to rise on the horizon. Its reddish light drenched the collapsed walls and cracked stones in a bloodred glow. For a moment, she felt as if she were looking at some fallen stone giant, its numerous wounds spilling blood everywhere she could see, staining the half-erect walls with the red-smeared memories of a hard-fought battle. A chilling breeze seemed to float forth from the empty castle interior, whistling soft, eerie whispers to her as the slight wind circled round her.

Jordan shivered and goosebumps peppered her arms. She wanted to rub the chill away, rub her hands up and down her arms, but her bound wrists prevented her from doing so.

As they crossed the drawbridge, the planks creaked and moaned, and Jordan thought for certain the rotted boards wouldn't support their weight. At one point in the middle of the bridge, a gaping hole showed the brown, murky moat below. The water was dark, its surface overgrown with decayed plant life.

The horse continued on, moving beneath the rusted portcullis. Jordan glanced up as the animal brought her under the raised metal spikes. Teeth. That's what they were. Huge, metal teeth waiting to take a bite out of any unsuspecting visitor. She quickly looked away.

Inside the outer ward, the houses, which had once been home to thriving merchants and villagers, stood empty, some without doors, some with collapsed thatched roofs. Weeds had overrun the outer courtyard, climbing their way around the houses and up the castle walls, encompassing the cracked and crumbling stone in a tapestry of varied greens and browns.

Her wrists chafed, the tight ropes digging into her flesh, the binds seeming to grow tighter and tighter the deeper they moved into the castle. Again she shivered, but this time it wasn't from any chill wind. She knew the source of the dread snaking up along her spine. It was this place, Castle Mercer.

Its eerie tales had spooked nearby villagers for a decade.

As they approached the inner ward, Jordan noticed that not only were both the inner and outer wards empty, but so were the walkways. Wind blew eerily across the vacant battlements. The only soldiers guarding the castle were the ghosts from long ago.

Indeed, she had heard many rumors and much gossip about the ghosts of Castle Mercer. Many a villager had seen specters patrolling the gatehouses at night. No one would dare to step foot into the crumbling castle for fear of being swept away into the afterlife. She glanced up at the rising sun. At least it was almost daytime. Most ghosts didn't come out during the day. At least, she hoped they didn't.

Fox halted the horses in the middle of the inner courtyard. Jordan remained seated for a long time, glancing around the courtyard for any sign of dark demons. Castle Mercer was supposed to have been vacant for years. Evan had told her many times that no one lived at Castle Mercer anymore. Every year, he sent a man out to make sure none of the villagers had taken up residence there. But the villagers were far too scared to go anywhere near the castle, especially after the year the man Evan had sent returned with a horrifying story of floating ghosts and terrifying footsteps. Evan had to find another man to send every year after that—and most refused to return to the castle a second year.

Jordan knew Evan would not look in Castle Mercer for her. It was a perfect spot for Fox to keep her. Evan was convinced it was empty. The villagers were terrified.

And then there were the ghosts.

Movement behind her caught her eye and she whirled to see a little girl trailing in the distance behind them with a large branch of leaves, dusting the ground, wiping away any sign that someone had entered the castle.

At the feel of hands around her waist, Jordan startled, pulling back in the saddle, stifling her scream. She looked down to find that Fox had already dismounted and was reaching to ease her from the horse. Jordan cursed herself for letting her imagination run away with her. Ghosts. There were no such things. She was constantly telling the children that, yet here she was letting herself get spooked by old stories and foolish flights of fancy.

She pushed Fox's hands away and slid from the saddle. She nearly fell to the ground, but leaned into the horse's side to keep her balance. Her gaze darted to the darkened doorway of the nearby blacksmith's shop. Had something moved in there? For a fleeting moment, she thought she saw a flash of white pass the doorway. She quickly looked away, again cursing her imagination. *I'm just tired,* she rationalized. *Just tired.*

Fox put a hand to her lower back and ushered her up the two steps to the keep. She offered no resistance. One side of the great double doors hung from one of its hinges, leaning heavily against the other. There was just enough room for one person to enter. Fox pushed her gently through the opening.

Jordan stopped instantly when she entered the dark keep. There were no torches on the walls, and only a bare sliver of light from outside penetrated the dark hallway. She involuntarily took a step back, wanting to get out of the murky gloom, but Fox bumped into her as he entered the keep behind her, stopping her movement.

He gently pushed her a step forward, but Jordan tried to retreat again, afraid to move ahead. In the black interior of the decaying building, she thought she heard someone moan.

Fox's chuckle sounded in her ear, but Jordan refused to move. He took hold of her arm and guided her down the hallway, pulling her forward.

Jordan remained close to Fox, her gaze flickering from one shadow to the next. Her fingers closed over his tunic, holding it tightly in her fist, a beacon to this world.

Her eyes grew used to the darkness, but the images that reached her made it feel as if she were living a nightmare. Shadows seemed to slither around her, their black tendrils weaving and shifting in the darkness. More disturbing sounds reached her ears. Footsteps. For a moment she thought someone was walking right behind them, but when she turned to look she could see nothing but more eerie shadows. It took her another moment to realize she was hearing Fox's footsteps and hers echoing around them off the cracked stone walls.

They moved past the double doors of what used to be the Great Hall. A shaft of rising sun shone in through the open entrance and down the hallway, allowing her a glimpse into the room. She stopped walking, forcing Fox to pause. She was grateful for the momentary ray of sunlight. The Hall was empty, a mere shadow of its former grandeur. There were no rushes on the floor, and several cracked wooden benches lay overturned not far from the entrance.

Jordan remembered the many times she had seen this cavernous room bursting with life and energy. She glanced to her right and remembered the time a juggling bear and its master had come to Castle Mercer. They had stood right near the wall where she was. The bear had been wearing a silly red hat, but had been an impressive juggler, bouncing the balls off his big black snout. And over there, deeper in the room to her left, she remembered the impressive ice sculptures that had filled the room during a feast Fox's father had hosted.

But now the room was barren. Even her pleasant memories did nothing to cover the emptiness she felt at the sight of it. This was no longer the place she remembered from her childhood.

And Fox Mercer was no longer the boy she had once called friend.

Suddenly, a bang sounded from somewhere deeper in

the castle. Jordan jumped and faltered, moving closer to Fox. The noise sounded again. A wooden shutter banging in the wind, perhaps.

Fox continued down the hallway passed the Great Hall, pulling Jordan along behind him. He turned a corner and Jordan almost screamed as a stark figure crossed the hall in front of them. It had long white hair and was wearing a long, flowing white robe. It was gone as quickly as it had emerged.

Fox stepped forward, seemingly oblivious to the specter that had just crossed their path, but Jordan's feet wouldn't move. "This castle is haunted," Jordan whispered.

"Only with old memories."

Jordan lifted her eyes to Fox. In the gloom, he was but a darkened silhouette in the hallway, a mere ghost himself.

Again he moved forward, pulling her with him.

But Jordan couldn't get her feet to take a step.

"Afraid?" Fox asked, mockingly.

Was it her chattering teeth that gave her away? Her shivering hands? Or the goosebumps shooting up and down her flesh? Jordan didn't respond, but her feet magically began to move again. She stayed close to Fox. He was not afraid of these phantoms and their ghostly noises, and he was the only protection she had.

As they moved through the hall, Jordan saw no more traces of the ghostly apparition. It had simply . . . vanished.

They turned another corner and another, moving deeper into the castle, deeper into the darkness. She tried to remember where she was in the castle from her many childhood visits, but her mind refused to cooperate. She felt lost. Fox paused at the bottom of a set of narrow stairs. He had to pry Jordan's fingers from his arm to get her to let go of him. He stepped up into the darkness and vanished. For a moment, Jordan panicked. She rushed forward and tripped over the first stair, tumbling forward into Fox's back. He quickly reached out a hand to steady her.

"Patience," Fox said.

"Don't leave me," Jordan hissed. "Not here."

"There's not enough room for both of us in the stairway. You know that."

And she did, suddenly remembering the layout of the castle. These stairs led up to the second floor, to the bedrooms. She had used them dozens of times without incident. But today they seemed to lead to danger, to an unknown fate.

"Give me your hand," he instructed.

Jordan reached out to him with her bound hands and he found her fingers, closing his hand over hers. Strangely, she felt more secure. He began to move up the stairs. Jordan followed, carefully, a step at a time.

"Careful," he said softly, "this stair is broken."

Jordan stepped over the chipped slab of rock, and within seconds they emerged into the second level corridor.

Far in the distance, light cast an eerie glow on the stones in the hallway. They moved toward the light and Jordan found herself clinging to Fox's arm. Another ghost? But the light looked more like sunlight.

As they neared, she could see that the light came from an open doorway. Fox moved to the doorway of the room and paused.

Jordan stared into the room. She had known this room long ago. It was his mother's old room. But the bed was gone. The beautiful decorative chest was gone. Everything she remembered being in the room was gone. A large window facing the northern wall was open, allowing the morning sunlight to enter the room. A wooden table with benches on either side was positioned near the window. Jordan's gaze was captured by the cold, dead hearth on the eastern side of the room. One chair was positioned before it. The walls were bare, except for one ripped, frayed tapestry she didn't remember, and the floor was uncovered and cold.

A great hound lumbered up to them. He sniffed Fox and passed him without incident. He stuck his wet muzzle into Jordan's white dress, sniffed, and growled slightly. Jordan took a step away from the dog.

Fox pulled her toward the hearth, and the great hound followed them like a guard, snarling softly.

Jordan cast a glance over her shoulder at the dog.

Fox turned toward the door. "Prepare the north tower," he instructed.

Jordan turned to see a short, stocky man with gray hair standing silently at the room's threshold. He nodded and moved off. The room filled with the other members of Fox's band. Beau, the one who had been their prisoner at Castle Ruvane, entered and took a seat on one of the benches, the tall one with red hair and beard followed him. The woman crossed the room to the window, leaning back on the ledge with her arms crossed.

The north tower? In all the time that she had been at Castle Mercer, she didn't think she had ever been to the north tower.

Jordan twisted her wrists, trying to shift the ropes, but her movement only seemed to tighten her bonds.

Fox stared at her thoughtfully. He had changed. She almost didn't recognize him. He had a growth of stubble covering his square chin. His nose was strong and straight, not the pug little nose of the boy she remembered. His eyes were dark and brooding.

But as she looked closer, she could see they were still the eyes she remembered. They were the only thing that remained of the boy she once knew. But this man, this grown Fox, was very handsome. If he weren't a criminal, she would have acknowledged the fact that he might be pleasing to be with.

But he killed Maggie, a voice inside her reminded. She looked away from him, mentally chiding herself for her stray thoughts.

"We have to keep her hidden," Fox said. "I don't want him to know she is here."

All eyes were once again on her. She lifted her chin slightly.

Beau smiled slightly before saying, "Fox, you can't keep her hidden forever."

"Just until I receive the ransom," Fox said.

The sun had risen higher and was now starting to fill the room, vanquishing the shadows. Jordan's confidence grew stronger as the sunlight grew brighter. Evan would find her. He would not rest until she was safely back with him.

In his arms. *Yes,* a voice reminded her. *And in his bed.* She pushed the thought away. She had to get out of here. She had to keep her thoughts focused on figuring out how to escape.

"It could be months," Beau said softly. "You can't keep her locked up in the tower that long."

"Not long," Fox said. "Just until I receive the ransom."

Jordan gritted her teeth. They were speaking of her as though she weren't standing directly in front of them. "Evan will pay any ransom you demand," she said imperiously.

Fox smiled.

Jordan's heart skipped a beat and her confidence died beneath the radiance of his grin.

"That's what I'm counting on," Fox said.

Jordan turned away from him to face the hearth and realized for the first time that the chair was occupied by an elderly man. Another of Fox's band? Jordan stepped forward. His long hair was completely white, his hand wrapped around a mug that rested on top of his knee. He wore an old, faded white velvet jupon.

Something was familiar about the man, but Jordan couldn't place what it was. She stepped around the chair, moving between the hearth and the man. Old blue eyes lifted to her, tired eyes, weary eyes that looked empty. Jordan scowled slightly. He looked like a man already dead.

Suddenly, something lit in his eyes, transforming them from a blank stare to an excited gaze. He stood slowly from his chair.

Jordan took a step back, fearful of this walking dead creature before her. But something about the old man kept her bolted to the spot. Something . . . very familiar.

It took Jordan a long moment to understand. The white hair and ancient, old wrinkled skin had confused her. He had aged almost double the ten years she had last seen him. "Lord Mercer?" she gasped as recognition blossomed inside her.

"Father," Fox called, moving forward quickly. He took a hold of Jordan's arm, pulling her away from Frederick. "I didn't see you here. I'm sorry to have disturbed you."

"Wait!" The voice that spoke was old, crackling with the effort to muster up such an outburst.

Frederick Mercer stepped slowly up to Jordan. He gazed deeply into her eyes.

Jordan didn't know what she should do. It had been another lifetime since she had seen Lord Mercer.

Then Frederick extended his hand to her, palm up.

Jordan swallowed hard and glanced sideways at Fox. But, slowly, hesitantly, she lifted her bound hands and placed one of them in his.

Frederick accepted her hand without any emotion. He stared at her hands for a long moment.

Just as Jordan was beginning to feel restless and confused in the prolonged silence, Frederick lifted his gaze to Fox. "What is the meaning of this?" he asked his son.

Fox looked at Jordan in confusion, then back at his father.

"The ropes, boy," his father hissed. "Why is she tied?"

Fox sputtered. "She is . . . she is our enemy!"

"Remove these ropes immediately."

"She is Jordan Ruvane. She is our enemy!" Fox repeated.

"Rubbish! She is a guest!"

"Guest!" Fox exploded. "She is not a guest! She is a noble!"

"Of course she is. Would we invite any less into the castle?" Frederick asked. He turned to Jordan. "You'll have to excuse him, Lady Jordan. He's been out of sorts lately."

Fox ground his teeth, his body stiffening. He signaled the woman in his band with a wave of his hand.

The woman came forward and cut the rope from Jordan's wrists with a savage chop from her blade.

Jordan rubbed her free hands, massaging the circulation back into them. Red welts encircled her tender wrists.

Frederick placed his hand out and Jordan didn't hesitate this time in taking it. She lay her hand on his arm and he moved toward the hallway. "Welcome to Castle Mercer,

Lady Jordan. Let me show you the changes I have instigated from the last time you visited."

Bewildered, Jordan glanced back over her shoulder at Fox, but he just looked at her angrily as Frederick led her from the room.

CHAPTER ELEVEN

"Lord Bentley, meet the Lady Jordan," Lord Mercer introduced.

Jordan stared into the empty hallway, aghast. No one stood before her. No one was in the entire castle! Who was he introducing her to?

Lord Mercer laughed. "She is quite shy today," he said.

He had been introducing her to and speaking with invisible persons all morning. He even chastised a fictional servant for spilling the clean linen. Jordan didn't know what to make of him. Part of her was frightened of him and part of her was deathly worried for his well-being.

Lord Mercer turned his gaze to her. "How thoughtless of me," he said to Jordan, still cognizant enough to see the distress on her face. "You must be weary from your journey," he continued, somehow misreading her alarm for fatigue. He barely lifted a hand when the woman who had been following them all morning suddenly appeared at their side. "See my lady to her room," Lord Mercer commanded.

The thin woman grunted and grabbed Jordan's arm. "This way," she snarled.

Jordan did not have time to object, for the woman all but propelled her down the hallway. Every time Jordan faltered, hearing a moan or seeing a movement in the shadows, the woman urged her on with a none too gentle shove. They moved down long, dark hallways that held silent demons waiting for the night, past huge spider webs that hung from gaping black doors. Jordan briefly thought of trying to escape, but she didn't know which way led to the doors of the keep.

The woman urged Jordan through a dark archway, and she almost tripped on the stairs before her. She touched the cold, moist, grimy walls to help guide her, but pulled back once as her fingers brushed something large and hairy. The woman behind her gave her an impatient push, forcing her on, the shove almost knocking her to her hands and knees.

The stairs seemed to spiral up around and around forever. Jordan wondered how far up they were going, wondered *where* they were going. And then she remembered what Fox had said and she knew where she was being led. To the north tower.

And then, as if the castle had some magical glimpse into her thoughts, a door appeared at the top of the stairs.

The woman stepped before Jordan and shoved the door open. She mockingly bowed and spoke with sarcasm. "Your room, m'lady."

Jordan hesitated, peering cautiously into the dark room. The woman seized Jordan's arm and hurled her into the room. This time, Jordan did land on her hands and knees on the cold floor. She glanced back at the door as it closed, her eyes widening in alarm as the woman sealed her in the darkness.

Jordan rose quickly, taking a step toward the door.

"I hope you enjoyed your tour," a dark voice said.

She whirled, her fearful gaze scanning the dark shadows that seemed to come alive before her very eyes. Jordan pressed her back to the door.

A flint was struck, and glistening gold light flared across a clean-shaven face with rugged contoured cheeks. A candle was lit and the light pushed the shadowy demons back to reveal the man who had been hidden in their murky depths.

Fox.

Jordan gasped as he lifted his gaze to her. His eyes were a stark blue in the blackness. He turned toward her and stepped forward. The darkness fell from his shoulders like a cape as he moved further into the candlelight. His hair hung to his shoulders and the light captured it, caressing it like a merchant handling expensive velvet. He was gorgeous, easily the most handsome man she had ever seen.

"Fox," she whispered softly, his name a mere caress against her lips. *What in heaven's name are you doing?* she wondered, chastising herself. *He is a killer. Maggie's killer.* She mentally shook herself. *You must remember that he stole what could have saved her life. And he didn't give a damn about the consequences!* Jordan rose slightly before him. "Why have you taken me?"

He stepped close to her. "Remove your dress."

Jordan pulled back, stunned. "I beg your pardon."

"I said to remove your dress." He turned away from her to a small table and fiddled with something she could not see. She heard the sound of dripping water.

Amazed, angry, and affronted, Jordan crossed her arms, refusing to do anything of the kind.

Fox turned back to her, a dripping towel in his hand. He raised an eyebrow at her defiance. "I've seen many women in many states of undress. One more is not likely to affect me."

Still, Jordan did not move. "I am perfectly capable of bathing myself."

Fox looked down at the towel and back up to Jordan. He chuckled softly. "Water is a precious commodity here in Castle Mercer. It is not used to bathe. And if it were, I would not allow it to be used on the likes of . . . your kind."

Jordan scowled at his rudeness. "Then why must I undress?" she demanded.

Fox took a step closer, and then another until he towered above her, his brooding stare unnerving, his tall stature intimidating. But Jordan stubbornly held her ground. "If wounds are not properly seen to, they could become infected. I saw a cut on your knee and I wanted to make sure there were no others."

His concern seemed genuine, but Jordan had quickly learned not to trust this man who now called himself the Black Fox. "I can see to my wounds myself," she said, refusing to give in to his intimidation. "It wouldn't be fitting for you to touch me in such an intimate way."

Something darkened in Fox's eyes. "Only a servant is not allowed to touch a noble."

Jordan began to shake her head. "That isn't—"

Fox took a step closer. "I am no servant of the Ruvanes, Jordan," he hissed. "Just a victim."

Jordan withdrew. "I didn't mean—"

"And whether I decide to touch you or not is my choice," he whispered.

Fox was so close that Jordan could feel the heat of his words on her cheek. Her mind screamed to respond, to reply to his whispered challenge. But her throat had suddenly become dry, her mind empty of stinging retorts. The only image on her mind was that of the way his sensual lips formed every word.

He dropped the towel into her hands. "See to your own wounds, then." He turned his back on her and headed for the door.

Humiliated by her response to his closeness, by the sudden and inexplicable sensation of drowning in the deep blue waters of his eyes, Jordan struggled to find a stinging retort. But all she could come up with was, "Evan and my father will pay any amount of coin for my safe return!"

Fox paused at the door. Finally, he turned. "I am not asking for coin. At first, that possibility had entered my mind. But I know of a much more suitable ransom."

Confusion washed over Jordan. No coin?

"I am asking for the return of my lands and my father's title."

Aghast, Jordan pushed herself from the wall. "My father doesn't have the power to restore your title. Only the king can do that!"

Fox stared calmly at her, unaffected by her outburst. "Then it looks like your stay shall be a long one." His hand reached for the door handle.

The children! No. She couldn't remain captive. "No!" Jordan gasped. She lunged forward, desperation overcoming all apprehension. She grabbed Fox's hand. "You can't keep me. I have responsibilities!"

His eyes narrowed and he yanked his hand free of her grip. "Your responsibilities will wait until I get my title and lands returned."

The children would be alone! No food, no one to comfort them. They would think she had left, too. Another promise broken. Panic and fierce anger burned through Jordan like a lightning bolt. Tears of desperation rose in her eyes as Fox turned to leave. She would not abandon them. Impulsively, desperately, Jordan rushed forward, shoving him aside.

Her shove did little more than if she had tried to move a stone wall. He whirled on her as she attempted to flee the room and caught her arm, hauling her back inside.

But Jordan did not stop her struggles. She stomped on his foot, while twisting her arm to free herself.

Fox's teeth clenched tight and he pushed her against the wall, capturing both her hands in his and pushing them above her head, pinning her against the cold stone. "I will not tolerate your attempts to escape."

Jordan didn't hear him. She didn't want to. All she knew was that the children would be alone and she had to reach them. She kicked at him again and landed a blow to his shin.

They struggled, but deep down Jordan knew she could not escape by force. But she didn't know what else to do. She continued to struggle in Fox's hold.

Fox pushed his body tight to hers.

Awareness flooded through Jordan and she stopped immediately. She could feel every inch of his body, from his hard chest to his hips, all pressed very intimately to her.

Jordan studied his face, her breathing and her heart racing from the attempted escape. He had the deepest, bluest eyes she had ever seen, so crystal clear that they reminded her of a gem. His nose was straight and his lips were sensual . . . and so close to her own.

What was happening to her? Suddenly, she renewed

her fight, embarrassed at the feelings and thoughts he aroused in her.

He pressed tighter until she had to succumb.

His blue eyes scanned her face as if he could see every aspect of her soul. His gaze dropped to her lips and lingered like a caress.

Suddenly, abruptly, he released her and stepped away from her, then stormed to the door.

"I will do everything in my power to get away from you," she vowed. "Everything."

But Fox did not stop. He slammed the door hard, making her jump slightly.

Frustrated by her lack of control, furious at Fox for his apathy at her plight, Jordan paced the room. It was unacceptable that Fox was asking her father for titles and lands. She didn't have the time to waste sitting here in Castle Mercer when the children had no one to watch over them. Who would comfort Ana when she had her nightmares? Who would make sure Jason didn't feed his vegetables to the hens? Who would leave the bedroom door open for Kara?

Abagail was getting old now. It took all her efforts to keep up with the children for just a day. How could she do it for weeks and months at a time? How would they get food?

Jordan could not remain here. She had to get back to the children. She would not forsake them again.

She had to escape.

CHAPTER TWELVE

Beau pushed the white garment across the table toward Pick, who sat at the other end. ''I did it last night,'' he said.

Pick caught the white garment and lifted it, tossing it back at Beau. ''Scout did it last night. At least it's not raining.''

Beau caught the material and looked hopefully at Smithy sitting across the table from him.

Smithy shook his head. ''Don't even ask,'' he said gruffly and rose, moving from the room.

A small girl shuffled in, skipping over to snatch a piece of the rock-hard bread that was sitting on the sole table in the room.

Beau looked at her, studying her scraggly hair, her ripped dress. Perhaps if she were older *she* could patrol the walkways. He sighed and shook his head, glancing at the fabric in his hands.

"I'll do it," Beau heard a voice call out.

Beau glanced up to see Fox moving toward them across the room. A relieved grin lit Beau's face. "I knew I could count on your self-torturing soul." Beau tossed the white material into Fox's outstretched hand.

"Where have you been all day?" Pick wondered, banging a piece of bread against the scarred wooden table until a chewable piece broke off.

"Delivering a message to Vaughn," Fox replied, removing Scout's bow and arrow from his shoulder and placing it on the table.

"I didn't know your aim was that accurate," Pick said around a mouthful of bread.

"It didn't have to be. I just shot the arrow into the Great Hall during the evening meal." Fox slipped the white garment over his head. "With any luck it hit Vaughn."

Beau exchanged a glance with Pick, then turned to their leader. "You know, Fox," he said, "I still don't understand why you got yourself captured to free me. Don't misunderstand me, I'm honored, but wouldn't it have been better if only Pick had gotten captured? What you did was pretty risky."

Pick chuckled at Beau. "There goes your conscience again. It had nothing to do with rescuing you."

"Of course it did," Beau corrected his big friend. "Right, Fox? You got yourself captured at the tournament as a big plot to rescue me, right?"

But Fox was studying the white cloak that fell to the floor in long folds.

"Right?" Doubt had edged its way into Beau's voice.

Fox lifted the white hood and pulled it over his face. His body became completely shrouded in white fabric, his face barely visible in the dark shadow the hood threw across his face.

"Tell him, Fox," Pick encouraged. "Tell him why you went to Castle Ruvane at all."

"Guilt?" Beau suggested. "For not helping me fight the soldiers? For letting them capture me without so much as a 'Hey, let my best man go, you dogs, or I'll destroy you all'?"

"No," Fox answered immediately from deep within the hooded cloak. "I wanted to kill Vaughn."

Silence stretched in the room.

"You could have taken a bit longer to come up with the answer," Beau complained. "It's nice to know where I stand in the order of things."

"The tournament was the perfect cover to face Vaughn," Pick explained. "It was the perfect opportunity to finish that bastard off. Hell, it would have even been legal."

"So what the devil happened?" Beau asked. "Why isn't the man dead?"

Pick and Beau lifted their gazes to Fox, but he wasn't looking at them anymore. Fox was looking up toward the north tower. "Jordan happened."

Yes, Jordan happened.

Fox strolled down the walkways of the castle, careful to avoid the loosened boards above the outer gatehouse stairway. It was one of the many traps they had set all over Castle Mercer . . . just in case.

God's blood, but how had it come to this? He had thought never to lay eyes on her again. And yet there she was in the north tower. His prisoner. His to do with as he wished.

His gaze shifted again to the tall spiral of stone that

jutted out of the northern corner of the keep's roof. One slit crosslike window had been carved in the stone for the archers to use as defense many, many years ago. The window was dark, and no light would come from the room because of the large tapestry he had hung over the window. He had allowed Jordan only one small candle, her only light in the gloomy room. Even giving her that made him slightly apprehensive, but he knew no light would seep from beneath the tapestry. If it did, it would be a beacon to all looking for her.

A pang of guilt speared his chest. She was alone in that tower. Alone in a foreign place, scared. He should at least make sure she was all right.

The hell you say! he scolded himself, bridling at his thought. *She is my prisoner. She is my enemy.*

She is so damned soft and she smells of fresh lavender. And her eyes were so large and blue and innocent that he felt all his sins and all his flaws being washed away by the purity of those eyes when he was in her presence.

Purity? She was as guilty as he! She had abandoned him all those years ago, left him alone to become what he was. A few nights alone in that tower would not hurt her.

He moved along the walkways again, the white robe making him nothing more than a specter in the moonlight. He and his friends had learned long ago that the villagers believed Castle Mercer was empty and haunted. So they had created their own ghost, making certain he would be visible to any who dared come near the castle at night, letting the myth grow stronger and stronger. They did everything in their power to enhance the villagers' belief in the otherworldly phantoms rumored to have taken up residence in Castle Mercer. It added another level of defense to their security precautions. They hadn't seen a villager near the castle at night for months, if not years.

But Fox didn't think their little illusion would stop Vaughn's men.

Fox rolled his arm slightly. His wound ached tonight. It was healing nicely, but if he continued to have to subdue Jordan by force, it would open again.

Fox chanced a glance up at the northern tower. He wished he could subdue her soft lips in a different way. In the darkness that surrounded the tower, he saw a brief flare of light. Something waved back and forth and then fell, burning as it tumbled to the ground. Fire.

Fire! He raced across the walkways toward the keep. What was she doing? He ran down the steps and through the inner courtyard. Another piece of burning material fell from the slit cross, its flame lighting up the night. He cursed as he pushed his way through the small opening of the keep and ran down the hallway.

Was she trying to burn down his home? Fox dashed up the spiral stairway, winding around and around. Or was she trying to alert someone to her whereabouts, as he had feared?

Either way, he had to stop her.

Jordan ripped off another piece of her dress and held it over the flame of the candle. When it ignited, she moved to the window, pushing the tapestry aside. The window was so small that she could stick only her arm out of it. She moved the burning cloth back and forth, waving it like a flag, until the fire scorched her fingers and she had to drop the fabric.

She then reached down and gathered her skirts in her

hands. She was about to rip off another strand when the door exploded open.

A ghostly specter stood before her all in white, fire burning from his eyes.

CHAPTER THIRTEEN

Jordan scrambled back, moving away from the demon as he entered the room, knocking over a table in her panic and spilling the basin of water across the floor. *The legends are true!* her mind screamed. *This castle is haunted! And the ghosts are coming for me!*

"What do you think you're doing?" Fox roared.

From her prone position on the floor, Jordan stared up at the apparition hovering before her, but then quickly noticed that this "ghost" was wearing brown leather boots and it had a voice uncannily similar to a voice she had come to know very well over the last day. Jordan's fear faded as she realized Fox stood before her. She climbed unsteadily to her feet.

"Doing?" she finally manage to echo, still trembling from the mental picture of the demon who had crashed through the door in his hurry to get to her.

Fox threw back his hood, and his gaze shifted from

her to the window and then to the candle. He turned back to her, piercing her with an accusing stare.

Jordan followed his stare, and then lifted her chin in defiance. "Did you expect me to sit around like a helpless damsel and wait to be rescued?"

His eyes narrowed and he approached her, moving swiftly until he stood just before her. "I see my mistake now."

Jordan backed away from him until her back came up against a wall. Heat radiated from his body as he drew nearer.

He grabbed her wrist. "I should have bound you from the beginning."

Jordan gaped at him, her mouth dropping in shock. She twisted her wrist in a vain attempt to free herself.

"Is that what you want?" he demanded, pulling her closer until she was mere inches from him. "Do you want to be gagged and tied?"

Jordan struggled, pulling at her arm, pushing against his chest.

In one swift move, he twisted her arm around to her back, bringing her face closer to his. "Is it?" he demanded.

His eyes burned with rage, his lips pulling back in a feral snarl, revealing tightly clenched teeth.

Jordan stopped her struggles, instantly aware of his closeness. It was inappropriate. It was uncomfortable. It was . . .

Her eyes drifted down to his lips. Sensual lips that called to her. And for a moment, she forgot everything except how close his lips were. How would they feel pressed against hers? She lifted her eyes to his and lost herself in them, floating in those deep pools of clear blue.

Fox released her arm slightly and placed a hand to her back, pulling her even closer to him. His eyes swept her face. Each look, each caress, sent warmth spiraling down to her stomach.

Jordan felt a heat flame to life inside her. What was happening? What was this feeling? It was so . . . comfortable and anticipatory. It was a feeling she didn't want to stop, one that needed more.

Then Fox suddenly stepped back. It was as if a wall had been erected, forcibly thrust between them.

Jordan felt lost for a moment, disoriented.

Fox took another step back. He scowled slightly and dropped his gaze, looking just as baffled as she felt. "I will not bind you this time." He struggled to recover his composure as best he could.

Jordan wanted to say something to him, but she felt unsure and awkward. Any words she uttered now would sound foolish.

He grabbed the candle from the table. "But you will give me your word you will not attempt something so foolhardy again."

Jordan stared at him as he waited for her response. How could she give him what he wanted? How could she tell him she would not try to escape when she knew she had to reach the children? "I will not attempt something so foolhardy again," she repeated. *Because next time it will be more than just an attempt. Next time I will succeed.*

Fox's eyes narrowed. He studied her for a long moment.

Jordan lifted her chin.

"You want to return to Vaughn that much?"

Jordan thought she heard a note of absolute amazement in his tone, but she couldn't be sure. She wasn't exactly sure how to answer. It wasn't Evan she needed to return to, but she did not want to tell Fox that. She did not want to give him any more information to use against her.

Her hesitation was enough of an answer for Fox. His jaw clenched and he blew out the candle. "Then you are not to be trusted," he said from within the darkness.

His footsteps moved toward the door. Fear crept through her as the thick blackness surrounded her. "Fox," she called out, afraid to take a step away from the wall and yet afraid to remain standing where she was in the utter darkness.

His steps hesitated, finally faltering.

"Is the castle really haunted?" she asked in nothing short of a whisper.

Silence stretched in the room until Jordan thought she heard the groan of an ancient ghost moaning right beside her. In the distance, she swore she heard metal clanking. The wooden floor creaked nearby. Then a waft of air brushed against the hairs on her neck. Or was that the breath of a spirit?

"Only by my memories," Fox finally said softly, sadly. Then, the door opened and he was gone, sealing her in the darkness.

"Lands and titles! God's blood, does he believe I am the king?" Evan roared, pacing the small stone room in Castle Ruvane. Weathered parchments bound in leather filled the shelves in the room. A candle burned on a plate on a small table near the bookshelves.

"Give him the lands, Evan," James Ruvane said quietly. He stared down at the piece of parchment laid out before him on the wooden table.

"No!" Evan exploded. "I will see Mercer rot before—"

"She is my daughter, Vaughn, and I will do everything in my power to protect her."

"Jordan is my betrothed. But I will not give Mercer—"

"They will kill her!" James exclaimed. "Is her life worth a decrepit haunted castle and some useless lands?"

Evan ground his teeth.

"You don't give a rat's ass about those lands. Your father never did and you never have either. Give him the lands!"

Evan dropped his head and paused before a tapestry of a hunt hanging on the wall. He studied the embroidered tableau, looking at the men on horseback, the dogs giving chase to a fleeing fox. Evan gritted his teeth. "It is not that I care about the lands. It's Mercer. He's been like a festering wound that refuses to close."

James could see the anguish Evan was going through, could feel it himself. The Black Fox had given both of them plenty of headaches over the years. More times than he cared to remember. "I know, Evan," he said softly, soothingly. "I know how you feel about Fox. But we must get Jordan back. At any cost. She's the only child I have." He stood, placing his hands behind his back, and stared out the window at the half-moon shimmering faintly in the night sky. "The king has called me to court. I must leave on the morrow." He turned to Evan. "I am entrusting her safety to you. You must get her back."

Evan nodded and turned to James. "I will get her back." He strolled over to the table and stared down at the note. "I am to meet him at the Harvest Moon Inn." He picked up the paper.

"Do not mistake the Black Fox for a fool, Evan," James said. "If you risk my daughter's life for some misguided notion of vengeance against him, or to heal your wounded pride, I will wage war with you. Do you understand?'' His expression was grim as he spoke, his intent to follow through on his threat deadly serious.

Evan nodded again. ''Do not fear, Lord Ruvane. I will see Jordan safely back to your side.'' He crumpled the ransom parchment in his hand. ''This I promise.''

CHAPTER FOURTEEN

The next morning, sitting before the cold hearth of the meal room, Fox could not stop thinking about Jordan. The sight of her. The smell of her. The feel of her. *Damn,* he thought, trying to erase the lingering sensation of her body pressed to his, trying to forget the scent of fresh lavender that surrounded her, trying to wipe away the image of her magnificent eyes staring woefully up at him with such innocence. Despite his best efforts, the memory of her sweet scent overpowered him, filling his senses. He was so used to the smell of sweat and of hard work that the scent of her had been so refreshing, so womanly, so powerful.

He gritted his teeth, staring into the mug of ale he gripped in both hands. His reflection swirled around in the golden liquid. Haunted eyes stared back up at him.

Were there ghosts in the castle? he thought, echoing Jordan's question in his mind. Yes. Yes, there were. And he knew his family was one of them. A mere shadow of what it used to be. He was one of them, too. A mere shadow of what he, as a boy, had always imagined he would become. He was supposed to be lord of this castle. Now he was nothing more than an outcast on his own lands.

His hound, Doom, lifted his head, his ears pointing straight toward the door.

"Ahhh," a voice greeted from across the room, "the fox rises early."

Fox did not look up at Frenchie's warm greeting, recognizing the voice of their cook. Doom put his head back down at Fox's feet.

"Could it be for my delicious tarts?" Frenchie wondered, scratching the three white hairs on his balding head.

Fox glanced up at him in surprise. "You have tarts?"

Frenchie shrugged apologetically. "No. But you sitting there reminds me of the days I cooked for the king. Everyone rose early just to get my scrumptious tarts fresh from the ovens. Ahh, they were glorious. Flaky and golden brown, rich with fruit." Frenchie licked his lips.

"You never cooked for the king," Fox retorted, looking back at the blackened logs on the fire. "You can barely even cook for us."

"No, but if your father can say that he is lord of this castle, then I can say I cooked for the king!" Frenchie exclaimed and pulled up a chair beside Fox. "I do have bread."

"Is it moldy?" Fox wondered.

Frenchie straightened his back. "No. A bit crusty. But no mold ever grazes my bread."

Crusty. That meant hard as a rock. Fox declined with

a shake of his head. "I think I'll wait until Beau and Pick return with some berries."

"Always no. But you'll see. Someday I'll cook a meal fit for a lord . . . and I won't be offerin' you any!" Frenchie grinned a toothless grin. " 'Sides, you kind of get used to the bread."

Fox rubbed his sore arm, gingerly. The physical battle with Jordan last night had done nothing to help it heal. He was beginning to wonder if it would ever be fully healed again.

"There was no one there," Beau's voice echoed from the corridor outside the room, interrupting Fox's thoughts.

"I say someone was there," Fox heard Pick retort.

Fox stood as they entered the room. He crossed the room, concern etching his features. "You saw someone?"

"Yes," Pick answered quickly.

"No," Beau replied just as quickly.

Fox's gaze burned into Pick. "Which is it?" he demanded.

"I swear I saw someone in the forest just west of the castle as we were returning," Pick said.

"Soldier or villager?" Fox asked.

"It was too far to see."

Beau shook his head, his blond locks waving across his shoulders, denying Pick's words. "When we got there, there was no sign of anyone. No branches broken, no footprints. Nothing," Beau added.

"Hallucinating again," Frenchie chuckled at Pick. "Why can't you hallucinate about my bread being soft?"

"No one can hallucinate that well, old man," Pick retorted to Frenchie.

Beau chuckled. "I keep telling him to stay away from those green berries."

"I want a wider perimeter set up around the castle today. If anyone's out there, we'll find them," Fox ordered. "Beau, you take the north end. Scout will take the south."

Beau grabbed a handful of berries from his sack before handing the rest to Fox. "You and your hallucinations," he mumbled to Pick.

Pick halted Beau with a wave of his hand. "We also heard a new rumor in town today."

Beau nodded and laughed low in his throat. "Apparently, someone saw the castle crying tears of fire last night."

"Tears of fire?" Fox asked.

Pick nodded. "We overheard the miller and the baker talking about it in the village this morning."

"Imagine!" Beau hooted as he walked toward the door. "Tears of fire!"

Fox's gaze involuntarily rose to the northern ceiling, toward the north tower. It appeared Jordan's plea for help had helped them more than her. He grinned at the thought, imagining her expression when he told her the news.

Jordan turned toward the door of her prison room as she heard the lock being undone. The door swung open and the woman she had seen earlier entered, holding a bowl in her hands. What was her name? Scout, she thought, remembering one of the men calling her that earlier. Wordlessly, Scout placed the bowl down on the bed.

The smell of sweet porridge reached Jordan's nose and her mouth watered at the thought of tasting a decent meal. Jordan turned her gaze to the bowl to see that the wooden container was indeed filled with porridge, on top of which was a piece of bread.

Jordan lifted her gaze to the woman standing darkly

silent before her. Scout was slender, clothed in well-worn breeches and a nearly sheer tunic. The tunic hung open halfway down her chest to her navel, almost revealing the entire rounded globe of one of her breasts. Her hair was long and wild, falling down her back in thick tangles of curls. Jordan frowned at her wanton, almost primitive appearance.

Scout glared at Jordan, then turned sharply away from her and slammed into a small girl. The child tumbled to the floor. Scout stared down at her for only a moment, then stepped out the door.

Aghast at Scout's chilling behavior, Jordan raced to the girl's rescue. She picked her up and set her on her feet. "There you go," she said softly and brushed off the girl's dress. Jordan looked at the girl's face to see large tears glimmering in her large brown eyes, her lip puffed out.

Jordan's heart twisted at the girl's pain. She lifted a hand to the girl's knotted brown hair, wanting to soothe her, but the child pulled back from her touch.

"It's all right," Jordan whispered. "I won't hurt you."

But the small girl stepped away from her, her face a picture of horror.

Jordan immediately released her, letting her go. She didn't want to, but she knew if she tried to restrain her, the girl would resist her help even more. She studied the girl in the second that she hesitated. Her hair was a mass of tangled strands, her face streaked with dirt. Jordan met her gaze. Large brown eyes stared at Jordan in confusion and uncertainty.

"I won't hurt you," Jordan repeated in a soft tone.

The girl dashed for the door, disappearing into the corridor beyond. Scout appeared for just a brief moment in the doorway to glare at Jordan before slamming the door shut hard, again sealing her in her prison.

Jordan stared at the heavy door, the young girl's mask of fear burning in her mind. She thought of her children—little Kara with that brown curl that remained forever in the middle of her forehead; willful Jason with an unending supply of energy; Ana, who was growing into a beautiful, if shy, little woman; John, the smartest of the lot, quick with a solution, and baby Emily, her pudgy little cheeks begging to be kissed, her bright brown eyes shining with joy. Was she crying now? Who was watching to make sure she stayed away from the spring?

She could only imagine what they were thinking about her, the fear they were feeling. They would all be afraid of being alone, of being abandoned by her.

Jordan collapsed onto her bed, her grief coming hard and fast. But through her hot tears a determined voice made a vow: *You will pay for this, Fox. You will pay.*

CHAPTER FIFTEEN

Just as Fox finished breaking his fast with a few handfuls of berries, his father entered the room. Frederick sat beside his son at the table.

Fox studied his father, his old eyes, the wrinkles of worry permanently crinkling the corners of those eyes. His once full head of brown hair was now gray, thinning everywhere. He had been through a lot. Too much. And still he harbored the secret of who had murdered the baron. All this time, even under Fox's insistence that he tell him, his father had not once talked about it. His eternal silence about the matter had driven father and son apart, causing Fox to draw his own conclusions. And he had.

Fox looked away from his father. Now, even if he revealed to him the identity of the murderer, Fox would never believe him. His father lived in his own world now, a world where nobles still walked the halls of Castle Mercer, servants still scurried about urgently seeing to the needs of a bustling castle, and beloved friends and guests still filled the air with tales of wonder, local gossip, and news of the kingdom. It was true that ghosts haunted Castle Mercer—ghosts of his own father's forever fevered mind.

"Where is our guest?" his father asked.

"Guest?" Fox echoed blankly, still thinking of the invisible nobles that roamed only in his father's disturbed imagination.

"Lady Jordan," Frederick said, his tone thick with the obvious.

Fox's gaze shot to him, startled.

"Don't tell me she has already left!"

"No," Fox admitted. "She dined earlier," Fox lied, hoping his father would drop the subject.

Frederick nodded, accepting Fox's answer. He took a now cold bowl of porridge and stared into it for a long moment. "It's been a long time since we've last seen her."

"Longer than you think," Fox grumbled.

"She certainly has changed," Frederick said.

Fox nodded in agreement, thinking of her large luminous eyes, the way her girlish figure had matured into curvy womanhood. The way her hair seemed so . . . soft and vibrant. And her lips . . .

"She would make a good wife, don't you think?"

Fox bridled. So that was where his father was going! "For someone," Fox admitted.

"Why not you, my boy? You've always been fond of her. She's quite a lovely creature. I'm certain Lord Harding agrees, don't you, Edward?"

Fox looked over to see his father staring at an empty space opposite them. His father always amazed him, no matter how many times he sat to speak with him. He would be carrying on a normal conversation for a while, then suddenly address his ghostly companions. Only then would Fox realize that to his father these ghosts had always been in the room with them, listening and watching. Sometimes it was just downright eerie to be around him.

His father continued, looking back at Fox. "We could petition Lord Ruvane and—"

Fox stood suddenly. His jaw tightened and his eyes burned with rage and fierce anger. That was the past! He would not petition Lord Ruvane for a piece of bread, let alone his daughter! As Fox stared at his father, at his earnest expression, his look softened and he turned his gaze to the floor, shaking his head. "I don't think that the Lady Jordan would want to marry me."

"Why Fox? Why do you say that?"

"She's in love with Evan Vaughn."

In love with Evan Vaughn. Saying the words aloud had left a bitter taste in Fox's mouth. He wasn't sure why, because what did it matter to him who she loved? Whether it was a man marked for death or not.

Fox had taken his turn scouring the north side of the castle for intruders, but he had found evidence of none. He wasn't surprised he hadn't seen anyone. His thoughts were not on his duty. Not on his duty at all.

When he returned for the evening meal, the sun was setting and the wind had picked up. He entered the castle and noticed Mary Kate sitting in the inner ward near the stables. Fox smiled to himself. A wild dog had made her home in the stables and was expecting puppies any day. Mary Kate was anxiously awaiting them, checking every day for their arrival. Fox moved over to the girl and sat beside her. "No puppies yet?" he wondered.

Mary Kate shook her head and turned her large brown eyes to him.

Fox tousled the girl's straight locks. "It will be any day now," he told her. "Have you eaten?"

She shook her head.

"Come on, let's go." Fox stood and lifted the girl up, setting her onto his shoulders. He entered the keep, being extra careful to duck into the opening so as not to bump Mary Kate's head on the door frame. He moved down the hallway and into the room.

He stopped dead in his tracks when he saw Jordan eating at a table beside his father. What was she doing out of her room? Rage filled him, and he shot an accusing glare at Beau, who sat beside the door.

Beau shrugged helplessly. "Lord Mercer ordered me to," he said around a mouthful of bread.

Fox lifted Mary Kate from his shoulders and set her on the floor. "Get yourself one of the trenchers," he said and patted her bottom lightly before moving over to the table. He stood, meeting Jordan's gaze for a long moment before his father looked up.

"Join us, my son!" Frederick exclaimed.

Fox clenched his jaw tightly. His father was treating her as some damned guest rather than a prisoner! It was ludicrous. But it was no use arguing with him. Fox sat in the chair beside his father.

He looked past his father at Jordan. Rings of exhaustion darkened her skin beneath her clear blue eyes. Yet there was something bright and innocent and pure in those depths, something that instinctively called to Fox. He grimaced and looked away, taking a trencher of vegetables, bread, and roast duck. He smiled at the sight of the duck. Scout must have had a successful hunt today.

"Where have you been? Seeing to the peasants?" Frederick asked. He directed his next words to Jordan. "Fox is very dedicated to seeing his people get what is needed to survive. He is always making sure the woods are secure and the stores are plentiful for the winter."

Fox didn't look up. He didn't need to reply to his father's questions. He learned long ago his father would make up his own answers. Fox took a bite of the bread.

The uneasy silence stretched.

Fox chewed quietly, not even aware of the bread's hardness. He chanced a glance over at Jordan, unable to avoid the temptation. She was finishing up with her portion of duck, her vegetables already gone. The rock-hard bread had one bite out of it, but then had been subtly pushed aside.

He watched her place the last piece of duck into her mouth. The way her lips closed over the piece of meat, the way the slight hint of the bird's moistness glimmered on her lips, immediately enflamed desire throughout his body. Fox ground his teeth and tore his gaze from her. He lifted his ale to his lips, draining the cup.

Someone bumped his arm, and he looked over to see Mary Kate pushing her trencher next to his. She tried to pull herself onto the bench, struggling to climb into the seat beside Fox.

Fox reached down and grabbed her arm, pulling her onto the bench. Mary Kate placed her bottom on the bench and looked up at Fox, smiling.

Fox couldn't help but grin at the proud smile on the girl's face. She immediately turned to devouring the duck.

"Who is she?" Jordan asked, drawing Fox's attention.

Fox looked at Jordan for a moment, for some reason

surprised she had even spoken to him. Her right hand was hidden from view in her lap, but she quickly placed it back onto the table as he gazed at her. There was an odd look on her face for a brief second, but then it quickly vanished. "Her name is Mary Kate," Fox finally responded, looking down at the child.

"Lady Jordan tells me she is staying in the north tower," Frederick said, holding his ale cup and gazing into it.

Fox groaned to himself. His father would think that the room was not good enough for her. And it wouldn't have been if she were truly a guest. But it was fine for an enemy. "That's right," Fox replied.

"Don't you think it inappropriate for a woman of Lady Jordan's stature?"

"It fits Jordan just fine," Fox replied shortly. "As a matter of fact, I think it's time Lady Jordan be returning to her room." Fox shot a meaningful look at Beau as he finished.

Jordan shot Fox a withering stare that he easily ignored.

Beau climbed to his feet, setting his trencher on the floor. Doom immediately lumbered over to the food and ate it.

"But Lady Jordan hasn't seen the entertainment! The minstrel has a fine rendition of the King Arthur—"

Fox rose. "I think Lady Jordan is looking weary. She begs for pardon, Father."

Jordan looked hard at Fox, but then nodded at Frederick and stood. "Yes. Your minstrel will have to wait for another day. Good eve, Lord Frederick."

"Good eve, my child," Frederick replied and smiled at her.

Fox took a step forward, but halted immediately when his father cleared his throat loudly. Fox groaned inwardly.

He knew his father was expecting him to personally escort Jordan back to her room. He looked back at Jordan, staring at her for a long moment. She was beautiful. Damned beautiful. If it had been another time, another life . . .

Fox reluctantly offered her his arm, steeling himself. But even his guarded preparation couldn't lessen the effect of her touch. When she placed her hand on his arm, bolts of lightning pierced his body, sending tingles from his fingertips to the tips of his toes. He lifted his gaze to hers. Had she felt it as well? The blue of the bluest sapphire didn't do justice to the color of her eyes. Like precious gems, they glinted innocently, unaware of the raw beauty emanating from them. His gaze dropped to her lips as if summoned to them. God's blood, how he wanted to taste her!

He moved forward, jerking her into motion.

When they exited the room, he waited for her to break contact with him. But she didn't. And he couldn't bring himself to do it, despite knowing that every moment they remained together, touching, he dropped another inch of his defenses.

They moved up the spiral stairway toward the tower. He wondered what she would do if he pressed her against the wall and kissed her.

As if sensing his intent, she dropped her hand from his arm and picked up her skirt to continue up the stairs.

Disappointment settled over Fox. Disappointment and frustration—and a great sense of relief. He felt somehow he had just escaped a deadly trap.

The door to the north tower room rose before them. Fox opened it, allowing her entrance. He stepped deeper into the room to light the candle.

And turned back to find Jordan holding a dagger out before her, pointed right at him!

CHAPTER SIXTEEN

Jordan held the small dagger before her, clutching it tightly. She had taken it from the dining table when no one had been looking and had managed to keep it hidden in the folds of her skirt.

Fox's dark eyes glowed with grim amusement in the candlelight. "What do you plan to do with that?" he asked mockingly.

Insult speared through Jordan at the obvious ridicule in his tone. He perceived her as no threat to him, and his blatant scorn made her blood simmer in her veins. "I plan to escape," she said, and stepped toward him, brandishing the dagger before her. If he still doubted she knew how to wield a blade, then so be it. He would become a fast believer.

But Fox did not move away from her threatening step. His gaze remained locked on hers, not even bothering to look at the deadly weapon in her hand. "I will not let you go," he said softly.

Jordan held the dagger firmly before her, adjusting her grip with her suddenly moist fingers. "Are your damned lands and title so important to you?"

He tilted his head quizzically, as if the answer was painfully, obviously staring her right in the face. "Yes, they are," he replied. "Much more important than inconveniencing you."

"I have more important reasons to leave than my inconvenience," Jordan retorted. "And I will not let you stop me."

He lifted his eyes to hers.

Jordan was shocked to see the fierce, deep anger that whirled in their depths.

"Then you will have to plunge that dagger into my heart, Jordan. Only then can you be reunited with your lover. Take my heart and you can go to him. Go on. Take it. Take it, damn you! You tossed it aside once before. Surely you can do it again."

Jordan stared at him, unable to move, unable to take action.

"Take it!"

The thought suddenly seemed horrific. She looked away from his intense glare, turning away from his harsh tone to stare at the weapon she held in her hand. A swirl of orange and red and yellow candlelight played along the metal, the colors flickering and flaming as they danced on the reflection of her eyes. Her eyes looked tired, haunted, almost as if she, too, might become nothing more than a specter in this eerie, decaying castle. Then she noticed a slight tremor in her fingers and willed them to be still. She looked away from the blade, back to Fox.

She could kill him, she realized, to get back to her

children. She knew just where to put the blade, knew just where to throw it to stop him dead in his tracks. But then quick images, quick memories flashed through her thoughts. She pictured him again with the little girl, Mary Kate, seated on his shoulders as he entered the room. Mary Kate had been beaming with joy as he carried her. She obviously had great affection and love for Fox.

And then Jordan pictured Fox's lips so close to hers the other night. The smell of his closeness flooded her senses, her memory taking on a ghostly life inside her mind.

Then she pictured Fox bleeding at her feet on the cold stones of the north tower floor, her dagger lodged deep in his heart. The thought was so sudden and so horrible that she almost dropped the dagger. She couldn't hurt him, not even after he had stolen the herbs that would have saved Maggie's life. She could never bring herself to hurt the friend she remembered from long ago.

Fox acted immediately, taking advantage of the obvious doubt and confusion playing out across her features. "Little girls shouldn't play with daggers," he scorned, then slapped the dagger from her fingers with a quick snake-like strike.

She snatched her hand back and rubbed her smarting fingers. Outrage and anger shot through her.

Fox bent to retrieve the dagger. He inspected it in the light of the candle. "I'll have to tell Frenchie to keep the daggers out of the meal room when you're eating. You can gnaw on his bread with your teeth like the rats do."

Hurt, Jordan whirled and raced from the room, moving down the steps of the north tower. Humiliation flared in her cheeks as she ran away from Fox and his mocking tone, from his teasing and degradation. How could she hope to escape him when she knew she could never even hurt him, let alone contemplate killing him? How could she hope to be free of him when she knew that her only defense against him was one she could never use?

Jordan hadn't made it down two steps before Fox caught her from behind. He grabbed her wrist and spun her around, pressing her hard against the stone corridor wall.

"I told you before you could not escape," he whispered hotly.

He held her firmly against the wall, his body pressed against hers.

Jordan knew he spoke the truth, but not the truth as he believed it. It was the truth as she knew it. How could she escape from Fox? And how could her children ever depend on her again if she couldn't fight to get to them? She couldn't hold even a trembling dagger to Fox. Uselessness, frustration, and helplessness all welled up inside her, spinning and churning until Jordan couldn't keep her feelings inside. Warm tears slipped from her eyes and dripped onto her cheeks, and her body trembled with a sob.

Fox placed a finger under her chin and lifted her face to his, studying it for an eternal moment in which Jordan fought hard to bury her feelings. She lifted her chin slightly, waiting for his scorn, waiting for his berating words.

But when the silence stretched on, she lifted her gaze to his. She was unprepared for the tenderness she saw in those blue depths. He lifted a finger to trace the path of one of her tears. Then he pulled his hand away from her, slowly rubbing the tear in his fingers, staring at the glistening drop for a moment.

His blue eyes seemed confused, and a slight scowl marred his brow as he continued to inspect the tear on his fingertip. Then he looked at her again and his gaze swept every inch of her face. A warmth spread throughout her body that suddenly brought her senses to life, sharpening them. The muscles in his strong chest pressed against her breasts. The power in his thighs crushed against her. And something dangerous stirred inside her—something powerful that threatened to engulf her.

Her vision dropped to his lips, lips that were so sensual, so entrancing. Lips that were slowly moving closer and closer.

Jordan didn't fight him; she wanted to feel his kiss. She wanted the intoxicating feeling rushing through her body to grow. His kiss would only make the dangerously delicious sensation run wild inside of her.

And then his lips closed over hers, a startlingly gentle caress, a warm, wet brush of his lips. But with that simple touch, exhilaration filled Jordan's body. It was unlike anything she had ever felt, tender and warm, but filled with a fiery spice all the same.

Then his tongue touched her lips, gently sliding along the length of her mouth, caressing, coaxing. She felt a jolt igniting its way through her entire body from the tips of her hair to the edges of her toes. She gasped against his lips and he dropped his hands to the small of her back, pulling her closer to him as he delved into the recesses of her mouth.

Jordan felt herself being swept away by the emotions raging through her. Her world was spinning on its axis, and she had to cling to Fox as if he were the only thing keeping her from falling. But the tighter she clung, the greater the waters seemed to swirl about her.

"I won't let you go, Jordan," he whispered against her lips. "Not this time."

It took a long moment for the words to sink in. *Won't let you go.* She pulled back suddenly, fighting against the emotional current that was now threatening to drown her.

She almost hit her head on the stone wall as she tore away from him so abruptly. Was this another way to keep her trapped, to hold her prisoner? To play with her emotions? To leave her dizzy and confused? Her fists clenched, her body shook, but not with passion this time. How had he known she would react as she had? Willing, wanton? Her cheeks flushed a deep red and she had to look away to hide her humiliation. *Damn her traitorous body!*

She shoved against his chest, but for a long moment he was unmovable. Jordan pushed harder. Finally, he stepped back. Wordlessly, she turned away from him and headed back toward the tower.

Fox took hold of her, but Jordan yanked her arm free and continued to marched up the steps toward her prison of a room. She had failed. And she would continue to fail unless she could battle her own emotions and defeat them. She had to fight against the control Fox somehow had over her. She had to fight it and win.

But she had no idea where to begin, or even what kind of weapon would be useful in such a battle.

Jordan slammed the door hard, sealing herself alone in the darkness.

Fox stared at the door for a moment before reaching out to lock it. Jordan's kiss was still fresh on his lips, the feel of her soft body a tantalizing memory, one he would not soon forget. The painful hardness in his groin was not a feeling he could easily banish from his thoughts.

His admission that he would not let her go echoed in his mind, for it was more of a confession of his soul than a statement of fact. *God's blood! How has the little vixen bewitched me? What was I thinking?*

But he knew exactly what he had been thinking, because her tears had tugged on more than his thoughts. They had called to his heart.

I have to let her go, he thought. *When Vaughn gives me my lands and title back, I must relinquish Jordan.*

Fox turned and walked away down the stairs. He found himself hoping Vaughn would refuse.

Silence surrounded the room as Jordan slept. Suddenly, a loud click sounded, jarring her awake. She lay absolutely still for a long moment, clutching her blanket to her neck, staring at the door. Was it Fox coming to see her? Was it someone bringing her a meal? Or was it a ghost? But when the door didn't open, Jordan wondered if the sound had only been in her imagination. Slowly, she lowered the blanket from her neck.

Then the door moved.

Just slightly, but it moved nonetheless. A faint sliver of light slipped into the room from the corridor beyond.

Jordan stood up, the blanket falling to pool around the ragged hem of her skirt.

Who had opened the door? And why?

She stood motionless for a moment, waiting for someone to enter. "Who's there?" she called out. But her question remained unanswered and the doorway remained vacant.

Then another thought jarred her into action. The door was open! What more did she need? What difference did it make who had freed her? She was free!

Jordan moved toward the door, reached for the handle—and stopped.

What if it was a trap? What if Fox was testing her? She stood for a long moment. She had given Fox her word that she would do everything in her power to escape. She might as well live up to it, she thought with a cold grin.

Her hand closed over the handle and she pulled the door open to peer outside.

The spiral stairway was empty, no movement, no sound coming from the dark passageway. A faint, flickering light illuminated the very bottom of her view of the stairway. "Hello?" she called.

Only her soft, hesitant echo returned.

Jordan stepped out of the room into the darkness of the stairwell. She gnawed on her lower lip as she moved forward. Her stomach felt like it was in her throat, and her heart raced in her chest. She took one step down the stairs, then another.

The light didn't grow brighter or recede. It remained still. Was someone with a torch waiting for her at the bottom of the stairs? She glanced back up toward her cell, but her room remained dark.

She continued down another step and another. Finally, the light touched her toes. It was nothing more than a torch on the wall.

Relief washed through her and she hurried the rest of the way down the stairs. She braced her hands on either side of the stairway to lean out and peer down the hallway. The narrow corridor was empty, illuminated by moonlight streaming in through a gap in the mortar. She swung her head the other way. A soft glow emanated from inside the meal room.

She hurried through the empty corridor, racing past the stray moonbeams, hoping this hallway would lead to her freedom. She hoped desperately that her memory served her correctly and she was heading in the right direction.

Suspicion gnawed at her. Someone knew she was roaming the hallways. Someone had set her free. Why?

Jordan turned a corner and froze.

A large, ghostly white figure was standing still in the hallway, floating above the stone floor, its shimmering cloak flapping in the night wind that slipped in through the castle's decaying mortar.

Jordan gasped as the ghost began to move toward her, its cloak billowing out behind it as it moved. She turned to flee, but tripped over a loose stone and fell to the ground. She fought to regain her balance, and turned just in time to see the ghost almost on her. Jordan lifted her hands to cover her eyes and flinched back, a scream of terror welling in her throat.

Something brushed over her and she instinctively pushed it away. Her hands shoved against more fabric and she jerked away, spinning to be rid of it. But the white cloak covered her completely and Jordan fought against it, gasping in fear. She kicked at the clinging cloth again and again until finally she was free. She crawled a few steps away and looked over her shoulder.

The ghost lay in a crumpled pool of white on the ground.

Jordan sat absolutely still for a moment, staring at the lifeless mass of cloth. Her heart beat madly in her chest. Had she killed it? Why wasn't it moving? Hesitantly, she moved forward. But the ghost didn't rise before her, didn't resurrect itself. It just lay inert in a mound of white fabric. Jordan reached out and tentatively kicked at it with her foot. But still it didn't move.

Slowly, curiosity overcame her fear and she crawled forward. She reached out a shaking hand and touched the ghost. It was just empty fabric! Jordan picked it up, laughing at herself for being so scared.

Then the ghostly cloth shifted in her hands. She let go

of the fabric with a cry of alarm, but immediately saw that something was pulling at the cloth, jerking it. Some sort of string was attached to it. She reached out and clenched the thin string in her hand, following its path upward, seeing that the fabric was connected to some sort of string that hung from the ceiling.

This was no ghost! But it was obviously intended for someone to believe it was. Amazed, she stared at the gadget. Someone was going through a lot of trouble to make everyone believe Castle Mercer was haunted.

Jordan stood, grudgingly admiring the work. Footsteps suddenly echoed down the hallway. She glanced toward the noise, fearful someone had heard her battles with the make-believe apparition. She dropped the ghostly fabric and pressed herself against the wall.

But no further noise came. She waited an extra moment to be certain and then started again down the hallway.

She turned a corner and breathed a sigh of relief. She was not lost! The huge double doors that led to the outside loomed ahead of her. Jordan almost raced down the hallway toward them.

Then she saw the huge hound that lay in front of the doors.

She pulled back quickly. How was she ever going to get past the hound? He would hear her if she dared to approach the doors. She was half-surprised he hadn't smelled her already. Then he would bark and wake Fox and she would never . . .

From the darkness of the hallway, through the moonlight that flooded in through the partially open doors, the shape of a man materialized and moved toward her. He was cloaked in a long, brown robe—a monk's robe, she guessed from the long piece of rope tied about the man's waist to hold the robe closed. She gasped and pulled further back into the shadows.

As the man stopped to pat the hound's head, Jordan studied him. There was something about him. Something familiar.

Suddenly, the dog's ears jerked toward her hiding spot and a low growl issued from its throat.

The man rose, staring in her direction. "Who's there?" he called.

Jordan hesitated a moment, but knew there was nowhere she could run. She stepped out of the shadows.

"Who are you?" he demanded in a sharp voice as she stepped into view. "How did you come to be at Castle Mercer?"

His eyes triggered her memory. Flecks of hazel shone in the light from the torch. Where had she seen those eyes before?

He moved toward her, scrutinizing her face as closely as she was looking at his. Then, his eyes narrowed in unpleasant recognition. "Lady Jordan?"

Confusion etched her features, her scowling brow. She nodded. "How did you—"

Fierce, brutal anger slammed down over his features. He gritted his teeth. "Michael. I'm Michael."

"Michael?" Jordan gasped. "Michael!" Fox's younger brother! That's why his eyes looked so familiar! They still held that enigmatic, pain-filled look she remembered from that fateful day so long ago.

She moved forward to embrace him.

But Michael caught her around her neck with a fierce hold and shoved her back into the wall, cutting off her breath.

This is a mistake, Jordan thought before his grip tightened. *This is all a grave mistake.* Instinctively, she fought, struggling for a breath. Her nails raked along his arm, pried at his fingers. But his hands tightened around her neck like a vise, squeezing, suffocating her.

With one last effort, she reached down to the dagger on her thigh, fighting the blackness that threatened to take over her vision, her mind. She fought for a breath, but Michael's hand only tightened around her throat, cutting off her attempt. Finally, she reached the sheath.

It was empty.

She wanted to scream in frustration and anger, but a wall of darkness closed around her, settling about her like a warm blanket.

And then she felt nothing. Nothing at all.

CHAPTER SEVENTEEN

Fox leaped out of bed, grabbed his sword, and raced toward the sound of Doom's barking. Were they being invaded? Had Vaughn found their location? Were scores of armored men already combing the ruins of his former home, hunting him down? A dozen different scenarios played out in his mind.

But even in his worst imaginings, he was unprepared for the sight that greeted him as he bounded down the stairs of the keep and raced into the main hallway.

His brother, Michael, stood in a beam of moonlight that penetrated the double doors at the far end of the hallway, his hands locked around Jordan's neck. The wan moonlight painted Michael's usually pale face an even starker shade of white. Panic and dread welled within Fox. He forced himself to go faster, forced his legs to pump harder.

But he couldn't get to her fast enough. Jordan's hand

dropped from Michael's arm, and her body went limp. The corridor seemed to stretch on forever. A horrible dread filled him. He slammed into Michael, sending the three of them flying to the floor. His sword clattered to the ground nearby.

Fox quickly lifted his head to look at Jordan. She had fallen to the stone ground, just before him. Fear froze his body. She wasn't moving.

He was at her side in an instant. "Jordan," he called.

"Get away from her, Fox. Cast the evil demon from your castle," Michael ordered.

Fox ignored his brother. His gaze stayed riveted on Jordan's pale face, her closed eyes, the ugly red welts around her neck. His heart pounded in his chest. He lifted his hands, but then held them still over her. He was terrified if he touched her she would never open her eyes.

"Jordan," he called again, and was surprised that the voice that came forth was thick and husky.

A firm hand gripped his shoulder, pulling him roughly away from her. "Don't touch her!" Michael thundered. "Remember the spell she had over you? She is nothing but evil!"

Suddenly, Jordan took a sharp intake of breath and her eyes flashed open. She looked momentarily disoriented, but then she quickly focused on Fox and on Michael behind him. She sat up abruptly and backed quickly away from them, pushing herself along the stone floor.

Fox yanked his shoulder free of Michael's hold. But Michael stepped past him, blocking his path, holding a cross before him like a shield, pointing it at Jordan. "Out, demon! I rid our lands of you!"

Jordan's back hit the wall, stopping her cold. She cringed away from Michael's tirade.

Fox strode forward and pushed Michael's arm down,

shoving him out of his way. "That's enough, Michael!" he ordered in a roar that sounded like thunder bursting forth from the emotional storm churning inside him.

Fox glimpsed movement out of the corner of his eye and saw his father and Beau race down the hallway, but he kept his eyes on Michael's hot gaze. He stood before Jordan like a wall of stone, refusing to let Michael take another step toward her.

"What is the meaning of this?" Frederick demanded as he approached. He stepped behind Fox and reached down to Jordan, helping her to her feet.

"Father!" Michael jerked forward, but Fox shoved him back.

"She is no demon," Fox said to his brother, keeping his voice calm.

Michael's gaze shifted to him. "It's too late," he murmured. "She already has you under her spell."

"I won't let you hurt her," Fox told him.

Michael's gaze swung back to Jordan. Fury churned in his eyes. "I have worked long and hard to rid Castle Mercer of evil." He looked back at Fox. "And now you invite the devil to our very table."

"She is a guest, Michael," his father said over Fox's shoulder. "And you will treat Lady Jordan as such."

Michael's gaze narrowed. "She will never be a guest in my home." He whirled and moved into the Great Hall.

"Michael!" Fox's father called out after him.

Fox put his hand on his father's shoulder, stopping him. "I will speak to him," Fox said. He turned to look at Jordan. She looked small beside his father, her brow furrowed with lines of concern and confusion. Fox stepped toward her. "Are you all right?"

Jordan nodded, and a lock of her hair spilled forward in a long winding curl that stretched past her throat. Fox could not take his eyes from her neck, from the ugly red marks that now marred what had once been perfect, flawless skin. Michael had done this to her. He reached out a finger and touched her chin, forcing her head up to bare her throat to his scrutiny.

Michael could have killed her—would have killed her if Fox hadn't heard Doom's wild barking. Fox clenched his teeth against the rage flooding through him. He hadn't been there to protect her.

Doom nuzzled Fox's hand and Fox patted the hound. He turned and picked up his sword, then handed the blade to Beau. He leaned close and spoke in a whisper. "Beau, see Jordan to my room."

"Your room?" Beau asked quietly.

Fox glanced back over at his father to see that he was now holding Jordan's hand tightly, apologizing profusely. "She is no longer safe in the tower," Fox explained quickly, turning toward the Great Hall. He paused and added quietly, "Don't tell my father."

Fox continued on to the Great Hall and paused in the doorway, his glare sweeping the large room. He could see very little in the dark. Cobwebs hung in long strands over the doorway, and Fox did his best to duck his head and leave the strands undisturbed. He entered the room, blindly making his way through the darkness.

A light came from behind him and he turned toward it. Mary Kate moved to him, her small hand cupped around the flame of a candle. She stopped just before him and lifted her gaze. Her lips were thin and her brow was furrowed.

"You should be sleeping, little one," Fox whispered to her.

"Doom was barking," she said simply, extending the candle to Fox.

Fox took the candle with a grateful half smile and shushed her back to bed. He watched her scurry off and then moved deeper into the room. Finally, he spotted Michael pacing before the long-dead hearth.

Michael paused when he saw Fox approaching him. "Are you mad?" Michael demanded. "To have her come to our castle? Our very home contaminated by her infidelity—by her disloyalty. Don't you remember how much she hurt you?"

"Yes," Fox answered. "I remember." He paused before his brother, facing his wrath with a calm demeanor.

"Then why in the name of the Lord did you bring her here?" Michael demanded, his hands clenched into fists.

"Because of Vaughn," Fox growled. "I will destroy him as he did us. I have taken what he treasures most in the world. For her safe return, I demand our lands and title back. A fair exchange."

"She will take your soul long before then," Michael cautioned him. "Our lands and title mean nothing if your soul is gone. Do not give yourself to this demon, Fox. She is not worth it."

"Jordan means nothing to me," Fox proclaimed.

Michael studied Fox for a long moment. Michael shook his head slowly. "I will pray for your soul, my brother. Pray that you will have the strength to withstand her temptation."

Fox hid his growing concern behind a wall of calm. *I can resist her,* Fox told himself. But even as he thought the words, images of her soft lips, memories of the way her body pressed against his taunted and beckoned him.

Fox turned away from Michael and headed for the large double doors. Would he be devastated if Vaughn didn't pay the ransom? Or would Fox be the happiest man in all of England?

CHAPTER EIGHTEEN

Alone in the darkness of Fox's room, Jordan lifted her hands to her neck and rubbed her skin softly. It was still raw and painful to the touch.

Why had Michael tried to kill her? They had been such good friends. She had been a big sister to him, a protector. They had played knights and dragons many times in the woods near Castle Ruvane, on the riverbank near Mercer Castle, on the dirt roads that connected their homes. She'd lost track of how many foul-smelling, fire-breathing beasts Michael had slain to save her.

Jordan recalled his bright hazel eyes, the way his blond hair always hung over his left eye in a soft curl. He had looked at her with happiness and a child's delight, clutching his wooden shield tightly to his chest, swishing his wooden blade through the air with the brave swings of a future champion.

But that had been so long ago. So long ago.

The images faded from Jordan's thoughts, replaced by the face of a dangerous man who wanted her dead—a man of God who reviled her so much that he would tempt the Lord's wrath to see her dead at his feet by his own hands.

She scowled darkly, thinking of the day that ruined the lives of the Mercer family forever. It had ruined her life, as well. It had taken Fox from her and changed him into someone she feared she no longer knew or understood, someone who was not interested in letting her know him.

That was the hardest part to bear. She still had strong feelings for this Black Fox, whatever name he chose for himself. In her heart and in her thoughts he would always be just Fox.

She took a step into the dark room. She had been in his room many times as a child. If she remembered correctly, and if he hadn't moved anything around, his bed would be against the left wall and there would be a window straight ahead against the opposite wall.

Jordan took two cautious steps toward the opposite wall. He could have moved his bed. He could have changed everything around. It was so dark she couldn't see anything very clearly. Maybe if she opened the window, she would be able to see more. Jordan moved forward, step by step, waiting to bang into the bed or a trunk or a stray chair. But nothing stopped her steps until finally her fingers brushed the stone wall at the other end of the room. She moved carefully to the left, skimming the wall with her fingers, searching for the window. The stone was cold and rough beneath her fingertips. Then her fingers brushed against the wood of the shuttered window. She palmed the window until she found the middle of the shutters, then grabbed the latch and pulled them open. The cool night air wafted in around her, sending shivers running up her arms. The moon was a mere slit in the night sky, casting only a weak, pale light.

"Jumping out?"

Jordan whirled to find Fox standing just inside the door, holding a candle in his hand.

"Trying to see," Jordan retorted.

Fox took a step deeper into the room, then shut the doors behind him.

Sealing her inside. Alone. With him.

He moved across the room to a table, where he set down the candle. He was so confident and powerful, even with such simple movements. Then he turned to face her. When his penetrating blue gaze rested on her, another shiver shot up Jordan's spine. This time it had nothing to do with the chill wind blowing in from outside. She looked away from him, from his deep stare.

"How did you get out of the tower?" he asked.

She glanced back up at him. "You left the door open."

Fox scowled at her. "That door was always locked."

"Then one of your ghosts must have unlocked it for me. Because it was open."

Fox stared grimly at her, but said nothing.

Jordan cleared her throat, getting up her nerve to ask the question she needed an answer for. "Why did Michael try to kill me?"

"He sees you as an enemy," Fox answered immediately, without hesitation.

"An enemy?" Jordan said, the word stinging her. "I've never done anything to him. How can he see me as an enemy?"

Fox's gaze narrowed. "You turned your back on us when we needed you the most. You turned your back on the entire Mercer family. On me. On him. That is something he can never forgive you for."

"I never turned my back on you. I—"

"You left us. You left me!" Fox hollered. "Without even so much as a farewell!"

Jordan was shocked at the vehemence in his voice.

"How can you say you never turned your back on me?" Fox continued, his tone hot.

Jordan frowned, then gestured toward Fox with an open palm. "I tried to help you. I did everything in my power to get your title and lands back. I wrote the king, I—"

"You did everything but remain my friend," Fox ground out. "That was too difficult for you, wasn't it, Jordan? You promised I wouldn't lose you, that you would always be with me. But you lied." He turned away from her, moving past her to the shuttered windows.

Hurt by the pain she heard in his voice, Jordan felt guilt weigh heavily about her shoulders. "You have no right to accuse me of that. It wasn't I that refused to see you."

"It certainly wasn't I that left the castle without a word." He slammed the shutters closed with a bang.

Jordan felt desperation burn in her heart. She approached Fox, standing before him, making him face her. "Father commanded me to denounce you," she said softly. "He wanted me to have nothing further to do with you."

"You did that all right, didn't you?"

Jordan frowned at Fox. His words were not making any sense to her. "But I went against his wishes, Fox. You know that. I wrote you letter after letter."

Fox nodded, his eyes narrowing. "Just like you wrote the king?" His lip curled in contempt. "I never received any letters from you."

Shocked by his response, Jordan could only stare in silence. He hadn't received her letters! But . . . what had happened? She had given the letters to Evan, who swore he would deliver them. Why had he told her Fox refused to take her letters?

Fox read into her silence. "Caught in your own lies!" he snapped. "I have heard enough. You and Vaughn belong together." He whirled and stormed toward the door, but then paused once more to glare at her. "And have no fear. You will not escape *this* room." He shut the door with a resounding thud.

Jordan sat heavily on the bed. Fox had never received her letters. He hadn't refused to see her. He hadn't even known she had wanted to see him all these years.

The fact that he hadn't refused to see her should have relieved her, but instead she felt a horrible churning in the pit of her stomach.

Why had Evan lied to her?

Letters, Fox scoffed as he stormed toward the meal room. His fists were clenched tight, his jaw ground. There had been no letters. No letters to him, no letters to the king on his behalf. She was an unfaithful liar. He should want nothing to do with her.

As he stormed down the hallway, he saw Beau at the door leading into the meal room.

"Is she all right?" Beau asked as Fox neared.

"Just fine," Fox retorted shortly and swept past him into the room. He paced for a moment, then sat heavily on a stone bench.

"Fox, might I suggest this might be the wrong way to go about getting your title and lands back?"

Fox lifted burning eyes to Beau.

Beau grinned. "Or it might be a perfect way to do it."

"It's the only way," Fox said. "Jordan is my only chance at getting what was stolen from my father."

"Your meeting with Vaughn is tomorrow night," Beau said, crossing his arms over his chest. "Do you really expect him just to hand over the lands?"

"No," Fox admitted.

"Then what will you do?"

Fox sighed. He rubbed at his temples, closing his eyes. "I don't know yet."

"Have you considered it might be a trap?"

"I would expect that traitorous Vaughn to do no less."

"Then why not let me and Pick accompany you?" Beau sat beside him. "At least that way you might come back without a sword in your back."

"I need you here to watch Jordan, especially now that Michael has returned."

"Scout can—"

"I need Scout out patrolling the north." When Beau opened his mouth to reply, Fox added, "And Pick needs to patrol the south."

A moment of silence passed between them.

Finally, Beau shook his head, voicing their concerns. "I don't like this, Fox. I don't like this at all."

CHAPTER NINETEEN

After a fitful night of little sleep, Jordan watched out the window as the rays of the sun stretched over the walls of the castle. Long ago, when she had first known Fox, she couldn't understand why he liked this room so much. The view was anything but spectacular. There was nothing to see, only stone walls and a glimpse of the countryside beyond. From her spot at the window, she could see the stone archway of the inner gatehouse and, beyond that, the rusted portcullis of the outer gatehouse. Then she remembered long ago Fox's telling her why he liked this room so.

"You can see who comes in," he had told her. "If I don't like any of my father's visitors, I can hide and not see them all day."

Jordan imagined Fox used the room for much the same reason now, keeping a wary eye out for unwanted guests.

The door opened and Scout entered, carrying a trencher

of food. She placed it on the bed. Jordan frowned at her. The woman was always so quiet in her presence. Eerily, uncomfortably quiet.

Jordan's gaze moved past the enigmatic woman to the doorway where Mary Kate stood forlornly, her little hands clenched before her, her large brown eyes gazing at Jordan. Her gaze swung to the trencher on the bed, then quickly back to Jordan.

Jordan lifted her gaze to Scout to say something to her about Mary Kate, but the woman was already moving toward the door.

Jordan quickly waved for Mary Kate to enter.

Mary Kate looked at Scout, then hurried into the room. Scout seemed not to notice. She closed the door behind her as she departed the room, leaving Mary Kate behind like some forgotten piece of baggage.

Jordan sat on the bed and glanced at the food. A piece of bread and some porridge. Despite the hunger gnawing at her belly, the fact that the bread from the previous night was still sitting heavy in her stomach left her more cautious about jumping right into the meal. Jordan wondered if the cook used iron to make the bread.

She lifted the trencher to her lips, but stopped short as the little girl pulled herself onto the bed and sat at the far edge of it. Her gaze was still wide and uncertain, the expression on her small face making her look as though she were ready to flee at any moment.

The nearness of food to her mouth was too much for Jordan to resist and she continued to raise the hard crust of bread to her lips, taking a sip of the porridge the trencher contained. It was cold and too thick, but it was better than nothing. She placed the trencher back on the bed and noticed the girl was still watching her with those wide brown eyes with a fearful silence.

"Would you like some?" Jordan asked.

Mary Kate looked at her and then looked at the food. She nodded.

A head full of knots and brambles. Jordan was sure of it from the looks of the child's matted hair. *Poor girl,* she thought. *She obviously has no one to take care of her.*

Jordan picked up the bread and struggled to tear a piece off. It was so hard she felt guilty giving it to Mary Kate, but the poor thing looked so hungry. She held it out to Mary Kate and the girl practically snatched it from her hand.

Jordan watched her gnaw at the hard bread. "Didn't you eat this morning?" she asked.

Mary Kate shook her head. "There wasn't enough," she answered around a mouthful of bread.

Jordan looked down at the trencher of porridge. There wasn't enough for a child? She pushed the trencher toward Mary Kate. "You can have it. I'm not that hungry."

Mary Kate lifted rounded eyes to Jordan. She inched closer on the bed and reached out a hand to take the trencher.

Jordan grinned at her, but there was no warmth in her smile. Not enough food. She saw how thin the girl was. "You should eat every day, Mary Kate," she told her softly.

"I know," she said. "Fox told me I have to or I might get sick again. But my mother needs to eat more than I."

Jordan clenched her teeth. What mother would deny her child food? But she knew no matter how cruel parents were, a child would always defend them, so she didn't press the subject. "You were sick before?"

Mary Kate nodded. "Once. I had the fever."

Jordan's heart missed a beat. "The fever?" Maggie had the fever. It had killed her.

Mary Kate nodded and put a piece of bread into her mouth. "Fox said I almost died."

Jordan stared hard at the girl, trying to mask her disbelief. How had Mary Kate not perished when Maggie had? "When?"

"A little bit ago," she said, concentrating on chewing the food.

Jordan couldn't breathe. She couldn't move. "What happened?"

Mary Kate lifted her large brown eyes to Jordan. "Fox got some herbs for me."

Jordan's chest constricted as she stared at the girl and tears welled in her eyes. Fox had stolen Maggie's herbs to save Mary Kate!

Jordan covered her mouth and turned away to hide her incredulity. Maggie's life for Mary Kate's. Fox hadn't done it to get back at her, or take vengeance on Evan. He had stolen them to save Mary Kate's life.

Damn you, Fox Mercer, she thought. *You aren't the coldhearted outlaw you pretend to be, are you? There's still some of the Fox I knew inside you somewhere.*

"Are you all right?" Mary Kate asked.

Jordan slowly looked back at Mary Kate, but found that the strange mixture of relief and sorrow left her unable to speak. All this time, Jordan had thought he stole the herbs for some selfish, vengeful reason, perhaps even to spite her. But that couldn't have been further from the truth.

With a saddened heart for Maggie, Jordan knew she would have done exactly what Fox had done to save one of her children.

Suddenly, there was a tugging at her elbow. Jordan

lowered her gaze to find Mary Kate sitting beside her. The child lifted one of her hands and held out a piece of bread to her.

Jordan smiled and laughed. She wanted to embrace the little girl, but she held back her emotions because she didn't know what would happen if she let them loose. Maggie died so this little girl sitting so innocently before her could live. Was her life more important than Maggie's? Did her life justify what Fox had done?

Jordan did not know the answers, and she would never have an answer that would put the questions to rest. Instead, she took the bread from Mary Kate and gently stroked her knotted hair.

She had misjudged Fox. As he had her. Perhaps there was still time . . . to make a friendship.

The fire in the hearth of the Harvest Moon Inn was slowly dying, the final flames nothing more than weak sputters. Outside, visible through a small window in the wall near the hearth, the moon had long since risen in the sky and was well overhead.

"Where is the varlet?" Evan whispered to a man sitting at a table behind his. "It is almost midnight." His gaze swept the room imperiously.

The innkeeper was leaning against the door frame of a rear room, almost falling asleep. Another one of Evan's men sat alone at a far table, clutching a mug of ale in his hand. Behind him sat a group of hooded monks—monks who wore chain mail beneath their robes. They were his men as well, all waiting to spring the trap. They had arrived well before dusk, the scheduled meeting time.

But the Black Fox had yet to arrive.

One of the monks threw back the last drops of ale in

his mug and then stood, moving toward the door. Evan watched the man step outside and then thought of doing the same thing. It had been hours since he had relieved himself, and his bladder was full from all the ale he had consumed. But he quickly dismissed the thought. He would take no chance on missing the Black Fox's arrival, no matter how slim that chance might be.

The logs in the hearth sputtered again, growing ever weaker as the minutes passed, until the last flame spit out a final spark and then died completely. Gray-white smoke drifted up from the charred embers.

"He is not coming," Evan finally announced and stood up.

A small boy rushed into the inn, but Evan paid him no mind. He began to pace before the cold hearth. *The insolent cur,* Evan thought. *Coward.*

The boy stopped at his side. "Excuse me, sir, but are ya Sir Vaughn, strongest knight in all of England?"

Evan looked down at the boy as he nearly knocked him over in his pacing. "What, boy? What do you want?"

The boy repeated his question. "Are ya Sir Vaughn, the strongest knight in all of England?"

A bemused grin came to Evan's face. "Yes, lad. That would be me."

The boy held out a piece of parchment.

Evan's brow furrowed. He took the parchment and unfolded it. His eyes darkened as he read.

Vaughn—

Your troops cannot fool me, even hidden beneath monks' garb. By your own actions, you force Jordan to remain with me. Mercer lands and the restoration of my father's title in exchange for your future wife.

That is the one and only offer I make you. Thanks for the ale, old friend.

Friar Fox

Jordan is quite beautiful, isn't she?

Evan shook with anger and fear. The monk! Fox had been sitting amongst his men. He was the monk who had left. And now that Evan pondered it for a moment, he suddenly recalled the monk had never returned to the inn. Fox sitting right under his nose for hours!

With a snarl, he crumbled the parchment and hurled it into the hearth. But the note did not burn. It sat atop the cold remains of the fire, taunting him.

The thought of Jordan even standing in the same room with Fox enflamed his senses. And the image of Fox looking at her with lust-filled eyes drove him mad with rage. Evan clenched his teeth so hard he heard his jaw crack under the angry force of it.

I will kill you with my own hands, Fox Mercer, Evan vowed. *Next time we meet, you will die.*

CHAPTER TWENTY

Jordan had discovered ink and a quill on the table in Fox's room and was using another piece of her ragged skirt hem as parchment to write a note. "Baked in the oven for too long," she mumbled to herself, concentrating on printing the letters. She leaned over the small table and struggled with the makeshift parchment. It was hard to write anything on the fabric, let alone a coherent note to the cook. "You need help with the—"

Suddenly, the door swung open.

Jordan jumped and hit the inkwell. It teetered and she shot a hand out, just missing the small jar as it fell over. The black ink spilled across the piece of cloth, smearing most of the words she had written. She grabbed the torn fragment of material and shoved it behind her back.

When she stood and looked up, Fox was standing in the doorway, his gaze locked on her. Jordan squared her shoulders and faced him.

He shut the door softly and turned back to her.

Her hand tightened convulsively around the fabric as dread shot through her. The spilled ink soaked through the cloth to her fingers.

Fox stalked toward her, grimly silent as he approached. He stopped in front of her, glanced at the spilled inkwell on the table, then slowly shifted his gaze to bore into her eyes.

She felt like a deer trapped in the path of a marksman's arrow. Her hand seemed to move of its own accord, appearing from behind her back, holding the fabric out to him in an open palm. Dark ink stained the tips of her fingers. Fox took the ragged piece of cloth from her and opened it. His scowl deepened as he read her words, and then he simply grunted in disgust as he tossed the cloth to the table. "Again you seem to prove that your word means nothing," he declared.

Jordan frowned at his remark. "My word? I was just giving your incompetent cook a piece of advice. He obviously—"

"Liar!" Fox snapped, taking a threatening step toward her.

Jordan put her hands protectively across her chest and took a step away from him, shocked by his outburst.

"Every time you open your mouth nothing but lies come out!" Fox spat. "You and your betrothed were meant for each other!"

"What are you talking about? You don't know what you're saying, Fox."

Fox grabbed the cloth she had written on and thrust it toward her. "You have the nerve to lie to my face and tell me I don't know what I'm saying?" Fox pushed the cloth even closer to her, as if daring her to take it.

Jordan took the cloth and looked at it. Two words

caught her attention immediately, the only two words not smeared beyond recognition. *Need help.* She read the words again, and then glanced up at Fox's enraged face. "It's not what you think, Fox. I was writing a note to your cook. I was—"

Fox snatched the cloth from her. "Do you think my men would help you escape? Your noble life of luxury has grown mold on your brain."

"I was not pleading for help to escape," Jordan shot back. "I was trying to give your fool cook a little advice! His bread is harder than a rock! But now I think you are the one who needs a little advice."

"And do you expect me to listen? Do you expect me to care about what you have to offer me? The only thing you offer me are lies and deceit. You and Vaughn belong together. I can see that now."

Jordan grew silent as rage flared in Fox's eyes. But there was something else behind his anger—disappointment. "Fox, believe what you like, but I am telling you the truth. I was writing a note to your cook because I felt bad for Mary Kate. The poor girl won't have any teeth left by the time she is ten years old."

Fox suddenly unclenched his fist and let the cloth fall to the floor at his feet. He kicked at the piece of fabric, pushing it away from him, then took in a deep breath and exhaled slowly.

Jordan studied Fox in the long stretch of silence that followed. Something else was wrong. She could tell by the troubled furrow on his brow. "What is it?" she finally asked. "What's happened?"

He glanced up at her. "As if you couldn't guess."

Jordan did not rise to his goading.

"Vaughn set a trap for me."

Jordan's eyes raked him with concern. But she saw

no wounds, no blood. "Which you obviously escaped unharmed."

Fox nodded, moving into the room away from her. "As I have many times before . . . including escaping from a clever trap that almost snared me in the glen near a farmer's house."

Jordan looked away from him. That had been the trap she had set for him, the trap that had captured one of his men. The trap that had started all of her misery into motion.

"It never occurred to me it wasn't Vaughn who set that trap. I know he's been after me for years. But after his pathetic attempt to capture me tonight, I know now he is not capable of coming up with such an ingenious plot."

Fox approached her again until he stood a mere foot away. Jordan refused to look at him. "Don't underestimate Evan. He is more dangerous than you can imagine."

Fox ignored her warning. "I saw you there near the farmer's house."

Jordan looked up at Fox, as if compelled by his sharp gaze. His blue eyes were locked on hers, capturing the essence of her soul and reflecting it back. "Yes, I was there." She could feel his body close to her, feel the power radiating from him. Strange, warm tingles danced across her flesh, moving all over her body.

"What would a lady of such grand nobility be doing waiting with a group of dirty, sweating soldiers to ensnare a fox?" he wondered in a soft tone, his voice a silky caress.

Jordan watched the way his lips formed each word. "Why do you care?" she asked softly.

He reached out a hand to smooth back a curl of hair from her cheek.

The touch sent a shock of pleasure through her entire body.

"Once, and only once, have my men and I been outsmarted. I would know who, exactly, is my most worthy adversary. It apparently is not the fool Vaughn."

Jordan swallowed hard. "Evan is a master in battle. Who else could have thought of such an elaborate plan?" She hoped her voice didn't sound as shaky to Fox as it did to her.

A sly grin touched Fox's lips, and Jordan almost collapsed with shock. Just the merest hint of amusement on his face, just the slightest touch of happiness on his lips made his already handsome face that much more appealing. If he ever turned a full-fledged smile on her, could she resist his charm?

"Who indeed," he murmured. His gaze swept her slowly and she felt invisible fingers behind his look, fingers touching her face, her neck, her breasts. His gaze dipped lower, and the invisible fingers followed his heated look.

Jordan quickly escaped to the window, throwing open the shutters, hoping that the cool breeze would restore her composure, help her regain some measure of her senses. She chewed her bottom lip softly.

Fox approached her again. "I see you still chew your lip when you're nervous," he said with a quiet laugh. "At least one thing I remember about you hasn't changed so drastically over the years."

Immediately, she stopped toying with her lip and turned to look at him, unnerved that he could read her so well.

"It was you, Jordan, wasn't it?" he asked.

Jordan didn't know how to respond. If she denied it, he would see through her façade. If she admitted it, would he take out his anger on her right here? She opened her mouth to respond, but Fox pressed a finger to her lips, silencing her.

"Only you can set a trap that almost captured me," he whispered.

Suddenly, guilt weighed heavily on her shoulders. She reached up and took his hand into hers, pulling his finger away from her lips. "Yes," she admitted in a breathy sigh.

"Why, Jordan?" Fox asked. "What do you want from me that you haven't taken already?"

Her body began to tremble and her eyes filled with tears. "You stole the herbs I needed so badly. I wanted to punish you for killing Maggie. Those herbs were meant for her."

Fox froze. "Killing Maggie?" he echoed weakly, his voice trailing off. "I didn't . . . I . . . Mary Kate needed those herbs. She had the fever. She would have . . . died . . ." Fox looked away from Jordan, taking his hand away from hers. He curled his fingers into a tight fist and clenched his teeth hard.

Silence stretched between them. Jordan could clearly see the pain her news had caused him. It was glaringly obvious that he hadn't known the herbs had been intended for her. The immediate agony and sorrow on his face was too genuine.

"Jordan, I . . . I didn't know." Fox closed his eyes tight and stood motionless for a long moment. "Who . . . who was she?" he finally asked.

Jordan could hear the tremor in his voice as he battled for control of his emotion. "She . . . Maggie was an orphan. She came down with the fever suddenly, and we tried everything to bring her temperature down, but we couldn't."

Fox nodded knowingly.

Her mind conjured up images of the rest of her children. She could see John as plain as day, smiling at her with joy as she handed him a wooden sword. Jason jumping up and down, barely able to stand still. Kara bending to pick the wildflowers. Ana swiping a lock of her dark hair from her eyes as she cleaned the dishes. And Emily. Little Emily. She could almost hear her laughter, could almost feel her hands around her neck. A million questions about how they were doing, what they were feeling flashed in her mind. "Fox, you have to let me go." More tears welled up in Jordan's eyes. She missed her children so much.

His hand moved to the nape of her neck and he pulled her to his chest. Jordan leaned into him, letting him soothe her, letting him embrace her.

Fox wrapped his arms around her and held her for a long time. "I cannot let you go, Jordan. Not until I finish what I have started."

Jordan felt more tears flood her eyes. She knew what his answer was going to be before he spoke it. The determination that burned in his eyes every time she looked into them never wavered. The children would have to continue on without her. She prayed Abagail would have enough strength to take care of them.

"Vaughn will not give me back my lands," Fox whispered into her hair. "But there is one way I can get lands and a title."

"How?" Hope seared through her chest.

He pushed her back to look into her eyes, and Jordan felt an unwanted chill come between them as their bodies separated. But the words he spoke next sent a rush of heat throughout her entire body.

"I can marry you," he stated.

CHAPTER TWENTY-ONE

Fox stared into Jordan's eyes. For a moment, he thought he saw a curious flash of happiness. But in an instant, it was gone. Jordan pulled away from him, her fists clenching in rage.

"You are no better than every man on that field at the tournament," Jordan snapped. "You see me as a prize, a means to an end. I could be an ugly lout for all you care, a shriveled, infertile, barren wasteland, because the only thing you care about is your land and your title." She crossed her arms over her chest. "I will be married to someone I love and someone who loves me. Not for a name, not for a piece of property."

Fox stared at her for a moment, bewildered. She stood strongly before him, that little chin lifted in defiance, her eyes dancing with fury. She was the most beautiful woman he had ever seen. Her outraged righteousness made her beauty only that much more of a marvel to behold.

"Your father held that tournament with you as the prize. From what I saw, you seemed willing to stand there and display yourself to all the men who had gathered there. I saw no chains about your wrists. I saw no rope about your neck. You could have been married to a complete stranger. Don't speak to me of marrying for love."

Jordan's eyes narrowed. "Father thought Evan would be the victor."

Fox froze, his own eyes narrowing suddenly. "So you do love Vaughn, then?"

Jordan opened her mouth and then closed it, remaining uncharacteristically silent. She looked away from him, but Fox could see her brow was still furrowed with anger. He looked at her curiously, wondering why such a simple question brought about a complicated display of emotion on her face.

Fox felt a strange emotion moving through him and then realized he was overjoyed that she could not answer him. It seemed she did not understand or even know what her true feelings for Vaughn were. But from what he could see in her eyes when Vaughn's name was mentioned, whatever feelings they were certainly did not seem like love to him.

He stepped forward until he was standing just before her. He lifted her chin with his finger until she was looking at him with those large blue eyes. Those big, beautiful blue eyes. "Do you look for him when you enter a room?" he asked softly.

She gazed into his eyes, her brow slowly smoothing.

"When he speaks, do you watch the way his lips move?"

Her gaze dropped to his lips.

"When he says your name, does your heart race a little faster?" he wondered. "Does it, Jordan?"

Fox could hear her breath catch in her throat.

"Does his kiss make you forget all the rest of the world?"

Fox drew closer to her lips, anticipating the feel of their softness, the taste of sweet honey he knew he would find on them.

"Would he give his life to make you happy?"

"Fox," Jordan whispered. "We can't do this."

His breath caught in his chest. Her warm breath touched his lips and he looked down at her mouth, entranced by the glistening wetness he saw there. Suddenly, Fox realized that everything he said was how Jordan was making him feel. He pulled away as if she had suddenly grown horns and quickly stepped back.

Jordan stumbled, but caught herself.

Shocked, angry, and confused, Fox moved to the door. He hesitated for a moment before commanding, "You will marry me. In love or not."

Fox moved out into the hallway, slamming the door behind him. Beau looked up at him from his seated position across the hall. Then he looked back to sharpening his sword, moving the rock across the sharp part of the blade.

Fox's jaw tightened. He was not in love with her! He would never let himself fall in love with a woman who deserted him. Not her. God's blood! Did she always have to affect him like that? Fox turned to move down the hallway.

"Every moment she is in the castle, she makes you more and more angry," Beau said.

Fox grunted, but did not turn to him.

"Get rid of her, Fox," Beau suggested. "Before you lose your sanity."

"That will be hard to do," Fox said, moving off down the hallway. "Since I'm going to marry her."

Shock settled on Beau's face. Then a grin. "I see my suggestion has come too late."

The sun seeped into the castle through cracks in the walls and broken mortar. Fox moved past several rusting suits of armor as he walked down the hallway. Skeletal faces peered out from behind the tarnished metal head-gear. Dead sentries—in case anyone ventured too close to some of the castle windows.

Fox entered the meal room, but stopped cold as he saw his father seated at the table. He hesitated for a moment, then turned to leave. He was in no mood for his father's ramblings today.

"Fox!"

Fox grimaced, then slowly turned back to face his father.

"I can't find Lady Jordan," Frederick said.

Fox looked into his father's eyes. He had his suspicions about who had released Jordan from the tower the night before. It could have been his father in one of his delusions. He didn't know if he should tell him where she was. "I've taken your advice, Father," Fox said, hoping to change the subject. "Jordan and I are to be wed."

"Well done, boy!" his father exclaimed, placing both his hands on Fox's shoulders. "I knew she couldn't have truly loved Evan. The two of you were meant to be together. I've always known that. Some things are just fated to be."

Fox nodded, but with far less enthusiasm than his father's words.

"You've petitioned Lord Ruvane for her hand?"

Fox clenched his teeth. He didn't like to lie to his father. He opened his mouth to answer, but then thought of something. "I won the tournament," he said. "Jordan was the prize."

"Excellent! My training has taken you far! I knew you'd make a great warrior someday!" Frederick exclaimed. "I will begin the necessary announcements immediately. I'll invite all the wealthiest lords, all my old friends." He began to walk down the hallway. "There is much work to do." Suddenly, Frederick paused and turned to Fox. "Well done, my boy. I'm very proud of you." He turned and called out to the empty air, "Duke Harrington! My son is to be wed to the Lady Jordan of Ruvane!"

With sad eyes, Fox watched him walk away down the hall, in his own world, surrounded by imaginary friends and imaginary people whom he believed held great love for him. Fox wished his father would wake up from his eternal daydream and look around. He was already surrounded by real friends and real people who loved him; he did not need his make-believe world for that.

Fox turned to head out of the room, but stopped immediately.

Michael stood two horse's paces away from him, his eyes red with fury, his jaw clenched tight. "It isn't enough that you invite her into our home. Now you take her as your wife?"

"It is for land and title only," Fox said, approaching the raging storm cloud that was Michael.

"I warned you about giving her your soul," Michael said grimly. "It seems I have arrived too late."

"She is no devil, Michael. She is just a woman."

"A woman who as a child took your trust and betrayed you. What will she take as a woman? Your heart?"

"I know Jordan for what she is."

"You know nothing of her. She is one of the nobles who deceived you and abandoned you. She will betray you again, Fox. Mark my word."

Fox clenched his teeth and moved past Michael.

Michael's hand shot out, capturing Fox's arm. "You are a fool to think to marry such a devil. Your children will be demons, connected to Satan."

Fox yanked his arm free of Michael's hold, tired of his brother's ridiculous speeches. "Have you ever considered that you were the one who almost committed a grievous sin?" Fox retorted. "You would think that for a man of the cloth, a follower of God, killing a woman would be a serious sin, punishable by an eternity in hell."

Michael's jaw clenched tightly and Fox could see the turmoil in his brother's eyes. "It would be a sin I would gladly commit for you, brother," Michael declared.

"Don't do me any favors," Fox retorted and brushed past him.

Evan paced back and forth before the warm hearth in the Great Hall within Castle Vaughn. Firelight danced over his features and made his hair seem to glow with an unearthly sheen. His fists were clenched behind his back, his strides fueled with frustration and anger.

Three mercenaries stood in the room, watching him. A thin man with a patch over one eye scratched his stubbled chin. "What are you offering for this?"

The rest of the men grumbled as they waited for his response.

Evan stopped pacing to stare at the one-eyed man. "Two horses and a suit of armor."

Astonishment spread through the group assembled in the large room.

Evan scanned the motley men. His eyes narrowed. "Plus a new sword and a bag of gold for the one who brings me the location of the Black Fox's lair. But you are not to approach him. I will deal with him myself. I simply want him found. And I will pay dearly for it."

CHAPTER TWENTY-TWO

Jordan ducked behind the dusty tapestry that lined one wall of the room. It had been several days since she had last seen Fox, and she had no idea what he was planning next. His threat of marriage weighed heavily upon her. Would he simply bring a monk, perhaps even Michael, to perform the ceremony? If they *were* married, would he expect an act of consummation on their wedding night?

In her mind's eye she saw Fox standing before the bed, slowly pulling his shirt off, revealing his strong chest to her, showing her the flesh that would soon cover her own. His muscles would be warm beneath her fingers, warm and hard and . . .

A sneeze tickled her nose. She rubbed her nose and pinched it so the sneeze wouldn't escape.

"Ready or not, here I come!" Mary Kate called out.

The young girl's voice brought Jordan out of her reverie. She had spent most of the last few days with Mary Kate, playing with her, talking to her—or at least trying to talk to her. The young girl wasn't very communicative. Hide and seek seemed to be Mary Kate's favorite game, and they played it over and over again.

There weren't many places to hide in Fox's room. Jordan had found only two. So this was about the tenth time she'd hidden behind the tapestry. But it didn't really matter. She was having fun, and Mary Kate would find her quickly. She was probably checking next to the bed now. Jordan had lain down beside it many of the other times they had played.

Sure enough, the tapestry moved as Mary Kate poked at it and Jordan couldn't help but let out a small giggle. Then the heavy tapestry shifted and Mary Kate's little head poked in.

"I found you!" she squealed.

Jordan hurried out from behind the tapestry. No sooner had she done so than she sneezed. She looked at Mary Kate, who was smiling, and then started to laugh herself. Every time she hid behind the tapestry, she sneezed.

Mary Kate laughed with her, the sound a delightful, joyous giggle that Jordan worshipped.

But it also made her sad. It made her think of her own children. Who was holding Emily if she wept? Was John hungry? How were they eating? Who was supplying them with food? Jordan's laughter faded and she looked at the window. She wanted to go to them, knew somehow she had to get to them.

And yet she didn't want to leave Fox. She was afraid if she did she would never see him again.

Mary Kate touched her hand softly, as if sensing her troubles. "Do you want to play again?"

"I would like to speak with Lady Jordan, Mary Kate," a voice boomed from the doorway.

Breathlessness shot through Jordan as the darkly serious voice penetrated to the core of her being. She lifted her gaze to Fox. He filled the entire doorway, radiating power and authority. Jordan's breath caught in her throat.

Mary Kate nodded to Fox and moved to the doorway. She paused beside Fox to glance back at Jordan.

Jordan's eyes dropped to the girl. Mary Kate gave a little wave to Jordan. Jordan smiled and waved back. Mary Kate lifted her gaze to Fox.

Fox smiled down at Mary Kate, his dark gaze softening. Jordan almost reeled under the vibrancy of his smile. Fox reached down and gently tousled Mary Kate's hair before giving her a gentle nudge out the door.

Mary Kate smiled back and scampered from the room.

Fox closed the door.

Jordan felt a strange sense of pride fill her. "She worships you, you know."

He stood near the door, his gaze intense and unrelenting.

"Where are Mary Kate's mother and father?" Jordan wondered.

"Her mother lives in the castle. Her father is not here."

Jordan had seen only one woman in the castle the entire time she had been here. Could he be talking about the woman they called Scout? Her eyes widened. That woman had dismissed Mary Kate with nary a word. Surely she couldn't be Mary Kate's mother. The woman didn't seem fit to be anyone's mother. But there were no other women in the castle; she was sure of it. "Scout?" she finally asked aloud in disbelief.

"Why do you need to know?" Fox demanded.

"I'm concerned about Mary Kate," Jordan replied, meeting his stare evenly. "She always seems to be so alone. She needs love."

"She has that here," Fox said defensively.

Jordan saw his shoulders square and his eyes harden and knew the offense he had taken at her statement. "She needs to be a child," Jordan corrected quickly. "She needs someone to play with."

"And you know this so well?" Fox demanded, still hurting from her insult.

"Yes," Jordan whispered in a desperate sigh.

Fox stared at her for a long moment. Just when Jordan thought he was not going to say anything more, he added, "Mary Kate is the result of a rape."

Rape? Jordan felt her skin crawl at the mere mention of the word. It was a horrible, brutal act.

"Her mother wants nothing to do with her," Fox added in a softer voice.

The poor child! The rape wasn't her fault. Jordan sat heavily on the bed. No one to love her. No one to hold her. No one to see to her needs at all. "Who looks after her?"

"Mary Kate has learned to find food herself, to steer clear of trouble, to survive. Just as all of us have had to do over the years," Fox informed her. "Our lives are not easy, Lady Ruvane." He did not bother to disguise the spite in his voice.

Jordan overlooked his bitter tone, concentrating on the child. "The poor girl is all of maybe three!"

"Four," Fox corrected her.

"Four?" She was so small.

"Is Mary Kate the reason you asked to see me?" he wondered suddenly.

Jordan had momentarily forgotten she had asked to see him. She had come up with a compromise. Well, she was sure Fox wouldn't see it as such, but it was a desperate move on her part. She had decided she would marry him.

She would risk her father and the king's wrath. If only . . .

"No," she answered and stood, turning her back to him. Jordan chewed her lower lip, wringing her hands. She had no right to put demands on a forced marriage. But it was Fox, and somewhere beneath the Black Fox was *her* Fox. Desperation and hopelessness bloomed within her heart.

Finally, she turned to him. She lifted her chin and straightened her back, meeting his gaze. Her heart beat quickly in her chest and she forced her nerves to stay under control. "I'll marry you," she told him quietly.

Fox chuckled. "It wasn't a request. I will marry you with or without your consent. By rights of my victory in the tournament, you are mine to do with as I please."

Jordan scowled at his callous response and his brutish attitude, but continued undaunted. "I'll marry you willingly . . . if you take me back to Ruvane village."

Fox stared at her in disbelief. Slowly, his jaw clenched, and then true anger began to bubble hotly in his veins. "Do you take me for a fool?" Fox finally thundered.

Jordan's face remained calm. "I'm asking a simple request."

"If I take you there, your people will protect you and take you—and my chance for lands and title—away from me. I don't think so."

Jordan took a step toward him. "No! That won't happen. I give you my word."

Fox growled, rage churning inside him. "Is that the same word you gave me ten years ago? You said you would always be with me. I can't trust you any more now than I could then."

"Fox, listen to me. I'm not trying to trick you."

"I've listened enough to you. I will marry you without any compromises." He turned to leave.

Jordan raced forward, seizing his arm. "They're my children. I have to reach them!"

Jordan's children? Fox's gaze dropped in shock to her flat stomach. Then his eyes narrowed and slammed back to hers. "Another lie. You have had no children." He yanked his arm free and stormed for the door.

"Fox! Listen to me! I'll marry you! All you have to do is take me to Ruvane village!"

Fox slammed the door on her pleas. Cursing, he moved through the hallway. She was not to be trusted. Not now, not ever. Children. She had no children.

But the image of her playing hide and seek with Mary Kate played again in his mind. The easy interaction between the child and her. Their laughter. She obviously had great experience with them. Did she have children?

And if she did have children, who sired them? Vaughn? The mere thought that Vaughn had touched her made Fox mad with rage.

"Fox!" his father called.

Fox faltered and clenched and unclenched his fists, trying to get his anger under control.

Frederick joined him in the hallway. "Are you quite sure Lady Jordan is all right?"

Fox ground his teeth. "Fine," he answered shortly, wishing his father would find something else to concern himself with.

Frederick rubbed his chin. "Very strange," he said thoughtfully. "I found this on my strolls through the wards." He held a piece of parchment out to Fox.

Fox took it from his father. His eyes scanned the writing and his teeth ground even more. The piece of parchment read: *Help. I am a prisoner in Castle Mercer. Lady Jordan of Ruvane.*

Fox let out a fierce howl of frustration.

Jordan sat at the window, gazing forlornly toward Ruvane village. Deep in her heart, she had been sure Fox would agree to her compromise. After all, she was promising to marry him. But she should have known he would see lies in her truth. He wouldn't even let her explain. He wouldn't let her tell him why she wanted to go back.

Suddenly, the door slammed open and Jordan jumped. Fox stood in the doorway, looking more like a demon than a man.

Jordan's fingers tightened on the window ledge. She had never seen such explosive anger in Fox before.

He stalked toward her, his fists clenched tight. "I warned you about trying to escape again."

Jordan backed away from him, racing around to the other side of the bed. "I don't know what you're talking about."

Fox came up short opposite her, the bed acting as a barrier between them.

"No?" he held up the piece of parchment his father had found. "Then what's this? Enough of your lies." He raced toward her, moving around the bed, but Jordan skittered away, keeping the bed between them.

"How would you have me act?" Jordan demanded.

"Like a lady."

"A desperate lady! Fox, let me explain."

Fox held the note up in a clenched fist. "This is all the explanation I need from you." Fox bolted around the bed, and Jordan raced away from him.

"I have to escape! The children—"

"You have endangered my friends and my entire home! For that you will be punished." Fox leaped over the bed.

Jordan turned to flee, but he caught her from behind, wrapping his strong arms around her. As she struggled in his hold, he twisted, wrestling her to the bed, falling on top of her to pin her flailing arms above her.

When he had her pinned, he growled, "Do you realize what you've done?"

"The children need me!" she hollered back, struggling. "I will do whatever it takes to return to them."

"You have given away the only place where I feel secure. My friends are now in danger because of you." He shook her hard. When she stopped her fight, he added, "That I will not tolerate. There is only one place where you will not be a threat to us." He hauled her to her feet, holding her wrist tightly, pulling her through his room and out into the hallway. "A place where I should have put you from the beginning."

His steps were large and quick and she almost had to run to keep up with him.

Until she realized where he was heading—the dungeon. There could be no other place to put her. Jordan dug in her heels and began to pull against his hold.

"No," Jordan pleaded. "Fox, no." She tried to twist her arm free, tried to pull her hand out of his hold, but his grip was unrelenting.

"No!" she hollered as they neared the stairs that led down to the depths of darkness. "No! Fox!" Jordan tried to grab onto a suit of rusted plate armor that decorated the hallway, but it tumbled to the ground, the crash echoing hauntingly through the crumbling stone corridors.

Drawn by the clamor, Beau rushed down the hallway,

followed by Scout and Frenchie. But no one moved to stop Fox.

"Fox!" Jordan screamed, tears rolling down her cheeks as Fox pulled her roughly forward. "No!"

"Noooo!"

Fox effectively silenced her pleas in his mind, steeling his heart and soul against her cries. If she dared to endanger his friends, then the dungeon was the only place to keep her.

He moved down the hallway toward the dark door at the far end. He refused to think of the condition the dungeons would be in, as they hadn't been used for over ten years. But if Jordan acted like an enemy, Fox had no choice but to treat her as one.

As he moved, Fox noticed a dark figure standing in an open doorway. At first Fox thought the figure an apparition to be paid no mind, but as he neared he recognized the ghostly figure. Michael nodded at him in smug satisfaction.

Fox froze, faltering in his determination. He turned to look over his shoulder. Beau and Pick and Scout and Frenchie and Smithy were all standing in the dark hallway. They were all watching him silently, confusion and grim acceptance on their faces.

But it wasn't his friends that caught his attention. It was Mary Kate. She stood just slightly to Scout's right, holding a candle. Tears glistened in her young eyes and smeared down her cheeks. He hadn't seen Mary Kate cry for a long time. The little girl turned toward Scout, lifting up her face, looking for some kind of comfort. Scout rudely pushed past her and marched off down the hall, leaving Mary Kate standing alone in the dark hallway.

What am I doing? Fox thought, appalled at what he was about to do to Mary Kate's one true friend. Fox felt the bruising grip he had on Jordan's wrist and turned his gaze to her. He could feel her trembling. Her face was tragic and scared. Tears glinted off of her cheeks.

God's blood! I am destroying her. Horrified, repentant, he took a step toward her. "Jordan . . ." he began softly. But in the face of her agony, there was nothing he could say.

Ashamed, he released her arm. How could he hurt her like this? How could he treat her like this?

Fox took a step away from her, turning his gaze from her. He didn't even deserve to look at her. "Beau, watch her," he commanded and turned, moving down the hallway. He kept his back straight, trying to muster some form of dignity. But slowly his walk turned into a run.

CHAPTER TWENTY-THREE

Fox hung his head. Around him, the branches of the willow trees housed him while a downpour of rain pelted the lands outside his rudimentary sanctuary. Wind lashed the branches, and the river churned with fury.

What is wrong with me? he thought. *I almost threw Jordan into the dungeon.* He ground his teeth. *She is working strange magic over me, making me think emotionally instead of rationally. But she endangered my friends. How can I marry her without trusting her? How can I force her to do something she doesn't want to?*

Fox shook his head. The image of Jordan's tearful face rose in his mind again, and her cries of desperation haunted his memory. *How can I force her into marriage?*

And then he thought of something he hadn't before. What if he had taken Jordan just to be with her again?

The reality of the thought jarred him. He had wanted to see her for years after that fateful day, had yearned for her. They had been kindred spirits. There was nothing he could not talk to her about. But he had forced her from his thoughts, forced the memory of her from his mind, concentrating instead on taking care of his father and his brother and the welfare of his friends.

But when he'd seen her at the tournament, so regal, so statuesque, looking like a goddess, he knew her memory still burned brightly just below his conscious thoughts. It had taken the mere sight of her to rekindle it into a roaring inferno.

When he came across her in the hallway of Castle Ruvane, he acted impetuously, not thinking or caring about the consequences of his actions. He could have escaped the castle without her. That would have been simple. But when he saw her standing there with her beautiful eyes wide, he grabbed for her, clinging to her.

He had been compelled to grab her. He knew that now. There was no denying the powerful force that still bound them together. Only now it was stronger. The attraction she had for him was unequaled. Part of her was permanently seared into his heart from their childhood. And now part of her was permanently scorched onto his memory as desire.

Thunder rumbled, and a sudden gust of wind parted some of the willow branches, whipping a blast of rain into the shelter. The cold water stung his face. He wiped at his eyes, clearing his vision of the chilling rain.

The icy gust sent his thoughts tumbling to his father, his brother. Men without lands, without titles, without honor. And then his thoughts grew darker, moving to the man who was the cause of their misery.

Evan Vaughn.

Vaughn had killed the baron. Vaughn took his father's title and lands away. *His* title and lands. If he was not willing to give the lands back, then there was only one thing left to do.

Painful images flashed through his mind. He remembered his father standing tall as the heavy hammers slammed at his spurs, remembered him dropping to his knees as the sword split in two over his skull, remembered the sickening sight of blood trailing down his forehead into his eyes. Fox's jaw clenched hard and tight.

Someone had to pay for those memories that haunted his dreams. He'd lost his father that day. And now Vaughn would lose something just as precious. His wife.

Yes. Fox stood up. He would take Vaughn's wife from him and make her his own. It was unfortunate that Jordan had to be mixed up in their battle, but so be it. Vaughn had to pay for what he did.

Fox stormed through the field toward Castle Mercer. He would marry Jordan and make her his wife. Her lands would be his. He didn't give a damn how she felt. He couldn't let himself give a damn about how she felt. That road was far too treacherous to follow. He didn't care that she didn't want to be with him as his wife—couldn't care for his father's sake, his brother's sake, the sake of the Mercer family. He couldn't let himself care at all.

He entered the castle, moving through the downpour of rain through the outer ward, the inner ward, and finally into the keep. His decision played itself over and over in his thoughts. It was his only chance to regain what he had lost. He approached the meal room, ready to announce his intentions to Jordan.

When Fox entered the room it seemed unnaturally quiet. He noticed his hound, Doom, near the wall. The dog lifted its head to gaze at Fox but did not rise. The animal seemed to gaze at him with reproach, but Fox knew that was ridiculous.

Fox turned his gaze to the table where Beau sat. His friend stared at him with narrowed eyes, as if in disapproval, and then swung his look to Jordan. Beau bowed his head and shook it, his gestures mirroring the same condemnation Fox saw in Doom's eyes. *Now what have I done?* Fox wondered. But deep down he knew. He had treated Jordan badly. Even if she had deserved it, dragging her down a hallway intending to toss her into the dungeon had been no way to treat a lady.

Fox swung his gaze to the hearth. Jordan sat before the cold fireplace, a blanket draped over her shoulders. In her hands, she cradled a mug of ale. Her shoulders were slumped slightly and her hair drooped down to touch her lap.

Fox halted as she turned to gaze at him. She rose and came toward him. She looked weary and sad, so very sad. Fox knew she had not slept from the rings beneath her eyes, eyes that were full of sorrow and remorse.

''Fox.'' The word came from her lips softly, full of repentance. ''I shouldn't have endangered your family. I shouldn't have endangered your friends. I never should have sent those notes.''

Guilt filled Fox. Where others, even Doom, would cast blame on him for his shameless actions, for his fit of rage, Jordan took responsibility for the incident herself.

His plans immediately evaporated before him as he looked into her troubled face. One second. That's all her doe eyes needed to make him forget himself, forget anything else he thought he so fervently desired. There was so much pain in her eyes. How could he force her to marry him? How could he hurt her like that and live with himself? How could he sentence her to a life of misery with him when all he wanted to do was make her happy?

She opened her mouth as if to say something, but suddenly Pick raced into the Great Hall, skidding to a halt just before Fox. "Mary Kate is missing," the big man panted.

Fox scowled at him. Fox impatiently brushed a drop of rain from his eyes, waiting for Pick to go on.

Pick continued, "She didn't sleep with Scout last night, and Scout hasn't seen her all day."

Great. The one day Scout showed any interest in her daughter was the day the girl disappeared. Fox bolted for the door. "Find her," he ordered his men. They sprang into action, forming search teams.

Fox looked at Jordan for a moment, urgency filling his gaze. She stood forlornly before the dark hearth. It could never be between them, he knew suddenly. With that thought came a sense of great loss and great anger. He looked away from her.

"Go," he said. "You are free to go. I can't bear to look at you like that." Once the words were out of his mouth, he regretted them. But there was no time to take them back, no desire to keep her caged.

He raced out of the meal room without a glance backward. He had to concentrate on Mary Kate, had to find her. An even bigger storm was threatening.

Then why did he feel as if his heart was being wrenched out of his chest?

Jordan stood at the hearth, gazing after Fox with her jaw agape. *Go?* she silently wondered. *Go?* He was releasing her! *Go!* She could go to her children! She ran toward the door, but then halted at the threshold. She would never see Fox again. Such a great sense of loss filled her that she didn't take a step for a long moment.

But I have to go. I have to make sure my children are all right.

She ran to the door of the keep. The sun was setting, the darkness coming. The rain had lessened, but the clouds were still very dark above. In the distance, an even darker mass of clouds appeared to be heading their way. She would be crazy to leave the safety of Castle Mercer now, risking robbers and highway men and the approaching storm. But did she really have a choice? What if Fox returned and changed his mind? What if he didn't let her go? Would that really be such a bad thing? *Yes,* she quickly answered herself. *Yes, it would. I have to get back home.*

Jordan squeezed through the opening of the keep just in time to see Fox thunder past on his great black stallion, racing toward the outer gatehouse. Jordan watched him go, feeling forlorn and lost and so very alone.

She wanted desperately to be here when Fox returned. After all, he did want to marry her. *No,* a voice inside her said. *He doesn't want to marry you. He wants your lands, your title. He even said he couldn't look at you anymore. He doesn't want you. He doesn't need you. And you don't need him.*

She had to leave now—before she lost something far more important than her lands and title . . . her heart.

With that, Jordan set out from the castle, moving into the forest beyond.

CHAPTER TWENTY-FOUR

Fox's horse pranced anxiously beneath him. He had to force the animal to move slowly with firm yanks on the reins as his gaze swept the empty hilltop, searching for the child. Lifting a hand to his mouth, he yelled, "Mary Kate!" But his own echo was the only response.

He had searched narrow trails in the forest, across muddy paths, but found nothing. No broken branches to mark her direction, not even a single footprint. It was as if she had vanished.

He heard the echoes of Pick calling out to Mary Kate, but there was no response from the child. He cursed Scout for the hundredth time. She should have told him immediately about Mary Kate's disappearance. She could be hurt.

It wasn't like the little girl to venture out of the castle. Fox couldn't remember the last time she had taken more than a dozen steps beyond the castle walls. She usually only came out with her big branch to help cover their tracks when they returned from an outing, and that was about the extent of her ventures into the world.

She was only a child, for the love of God. How far could she have gone? She had to be around here somewhere.

Frustrated, Fox reined in his horse and headed back toward Castle Mercer, wanting to try a different direction. Why would she have gone out alone? he wondered again. They had actually searched the castle again quickly before heading outside in case she had been hiding. But she wasn't in there.

Lightning flashed, and Fox cursed again. The damned rain that had plagued the land the night before in torrential downpours was threatening again. That was all he needed. He decided to move closer to the village. Maybe someone there had seen something.

His thoughts tried to drift to another female out alone in the dark beneath the threatening sky, but he refused to let them linger longer than a moment on Jordan Ruvane.

Jordan moved quickly through the field outside of Castle Mercer. Thunder rumbled overhead, and she glanced up. The sky was dark, and blackened clouds churned above her head. The grass was still wet from the previous night's rains, and the dampness clung to her dress, slowing her down, as if the forces of nature were trying to hold her back.

She glanced back at Castle Mercer. She wished she could have made Fox believe all she wanted was to make sure her children were all right, but he wouldn't have listened to her. All he wanted was the lands and his title.

She certainly shouldn't care about him. After all, he had said he couldn't stand to see her. Then why did she feel this empty ache in her chest? Why couldn't she erase the sadness that encompassed her? Why couldn't she forget him?

She hung her head. Fox thought she had turned her back on him, abandoned him. He despised her. Yet he hadn't locked her in the dungeon when he could have done so. What had made him stop? Maybe he did care for her. Maybe he did have feelings for her that were not full of anger and hate and hurt.

Why? Because she wanted him to? Because she had feelings for him? Because she wanted those warm feelings she had for him to be given to her in return?

Jordan entered the forest. Her feet were soaking wet, her slippers heavy with mud and leaves. She pushed on, knowing the farther she got from Castle Mercer, the closer she would be to her children.

She wanted to help find Mary Kate, but this might be the only chance she got to see her own children. And they needed her. Fox would find Mary Kate. She would be fine.

Jordan shoved her way through the thick tangles of branches, moving toward the path she knew was near the river. Could she find it before it became too dark to see?

Thunder boomed above and a jagged tail of lightning lit up the trees around her.

Jordan increased her pace, trying to run. She slipped on the wet earth and went down on one knee. When she rose, her hand was slick with mud and her knee was caked with the wet dirt. She wiped her hand on a nearby tree.

Another spear of lightning lit the forest and cast odd shadows all around her. For a brief, mad moment she feared the woods might be as haunted as local gossip said the castle was. Thunder followed the hot light almost immediately.

Jordan pushed on. Ahead the river rumbled. She was almost at the path. She pushed urgently through the trees, and some of the gnarled branches snatched at her, catching in her long hair, as if nature herself was trying to hold her back.

But Jordan pulled through them, tearing them away from her, desperate to reach the path before she could no longer see it in the deepening darkness. It would lead her back to her children. Surely she could get a ride from a passing merchant, maybe even get to the children before morning.

Lightning lit the sky again, forming a bright halo of light on the ground. This time, Jordan didn't look up. She kept her attention riveted on the forest, memorizing the way ahead in the momentary burst of light.

The rush of the river sounded close by, much stronger and more ferocious than she remembered. It had rained fiercely the night before. The water was probably much higher than normal.

Thunder boomed, rocking the ground beneath her feet. She slipped again in her hurry.

And fell flat on her stomach right onto the path. A sense of profound relief filled her. She glanced down the sodden, muddy trail and broke into a tired smile. Jordan rose to her feet.

But she froze as she heard a faint cry over the rush of the river. She paused, glancing around, wondering for a moment if she had heard anything at all. She took a step down the path.

The cry came again, distant but unmistakable. A cry

filled with fear. A child's cry. It had come from near the river.

Mary Kate.

Jordan glanced down the path that would lead her to her children, and then toward the child's cry. With a muttered curse, she made her decision.

CHAPTER TWENTY-FIVE

The child's cry came again, this time much closer.

Jordan pushed past the bushes near the river's edge. Lightning speared the sky, illuminating the rushing river. A strong current churned down the river. Then the light faded and the night fell once again.

"Mary Kate!" Jordan shouted above the rushing waters.

The scream came again from Jordan's right. Jordan looked for the girl, but the darkness was thick and consuming. "Where are you?" she shouted.

"Help!"

Jordan rushed forward, following the voice, almost tripping over a splintered tree in her frantic haste to get to the child.

"Help!"

Jordan followed the fallen tree toward the river. Its end was well in the rushing water. But what caught Jordan's attention was a small head barely visible above the water's surface. Mary Kate lifted a hand toward Jordan, but then slipped. Her face went under the rapidly moving river.

Jordan's heart leaped into her throat, but the little girl reemerged seconds later, gasping and sobbing, her small hand still clinging desperately to a tree limb.

Jordan raced to Mary Kate, sloshing through knee-high water, then thigh-high water, to reach her. She grabbed the child as she got close. Mary Kate's small hands went around her immediately, clinging to her soaked dress.

"I've got you." Jordan attempted to pull Mary Kate up and out of the churning water, but Mary Kate caught on something and screamed in agony. Jordan quickly lowered her back down.

"I'm stuck," Mary Kate said, desperately. "My leg is under the tree. It knocked me into the water when it fell over."

Jordan held Mary Kate firmly to her with one hand and followed her leg with her other hand to where the girl was trapped beneath the fallen tree. The tree was far too massive and heavy for her to budge, let alone move it off the girl's leg.

Suddenly, large drops of water began to hit the river around them. Jordan looked at the sky with growing alarm as the downpour began. The river was going to rise again, probably very quickly. "I have to get you out of here," Jordan told her. "Can you hold yourself above the water while I move the tree?"

Mary Kate nodded. "I'll try."

Jordan released her, and the girl was just barely able to hold her head above the raging waters, clinging to a branch just above her head. Jordan hurriedly moved over to the tree next to Mary Kate. "When I lift it, move your leg out, all right?"

Mary Kate nodded.

Jordan positioned her hands on the bark, doing her best to wrap her arms around the thick trunk. Heavy rainfall continued to pelt them both. She tried to lift the tree, but it would not budge. Jordan wrapped her arms around the large tree again, fighting for a better grip, and tried to pick it up. It would not move.

She sat in the churning waters and placed her feet against the tree, trying to get more power into her shove by bracing herself against the ground. She pushed with all her strength, but it was not moving even an inch. Her hands sank into the soft river bottom, the mud not letting her get a good position.

Mary Kate slipped and went under the water again.

Jordan scrambled to her and grabbed her, pulling her up. Mary Kate was sobbing now, her tears mixing with the chilling rain. Jordan held her tightly. "Don't cry. Don't cry. It will be all right. Everything will be fine."

"I'm scared," Mary Kate whispered, her tiny voice barely audible amidst the noise of the river and the rain.

"I know," Jordan answered. "Here. I'll dig your foot out. Hold yourself up." Jordan touched Mary Kate's leg and again followed it down to her foot. She began to pull the mud out from beneath her foot and away from her leg. But the more she struggled with the mud, the more the heavy tree just pushed Mary Kate's leg deeper into the muddy bank.

Mary Kate went under the water again and Jordan had to reach over and grab her. "Hold yourself up," she ordered.

"I can't," Mary Kate wept. "I can't."

Jordan went to her and sat in the river, holding her. The girl wept in her arms. Jordan wanted to cry with the futility of it all, but she refused to give up. She held the girl to her, letting her rest for the moment. The water felt as if it were getting colder and higher by the second. Jordan looked desperately around the area, searching for something, anything that might help her. She spotted a group of large rocks near a tree on the shore.

"Mary Kate," Jordan said. "I have to go for help. I'm going to move one of those rocks over here. You can hold yourself out of the water on it."

"No, no. Don't leave me."

"I'll be back, Mary Kate. You have to be brave. I'm going to get Fox."

"Don't leave." Mary Kate's little fingers dug into her arm.

"Please, Mary Kate. I promise I'll be back." She almost choked on the words as tears rose in her eyes. "Do you believe me?"

Mary Kate struggled to answer, but her sobbing prevented any words from coming out. All she could do was nod.

"I won't let anything happen to you," Jordan whispered, kissing the top of her head. "But I have to go now."

Mary Kate screamed as Jordan released her. Jordan had to steal herself against the child's fearful wails as she moved to the rocks. She looked over them quickly, finding the largest one. Jordan bent to it and tried to pull it toward her. For a moment, the big stone refused to relinquish its hold in the ground, but then it jerked free of the mud with a loud sucking noise, almost sending Jordan to her bottom.

Lightning ripped through the sky and thunder rumbled almost immediately after it, drowning out Mary Kate's fear-filled cries.

Jordan pushed the rock through the mud, tumbling it end over end. She slipped and fell to one knee, but quickly recovered and pushed the rock toward Mary Kate. The girl was floundering in the water, trying her best to keep her head above the river, but Jordan saw the weariness in the girl's slouched shoulders.

She pushed with all her might, through the thick mud that threatened to stop her progress, refusing to let the mud and rain win. When she reached the water, the rock moved easier and she pushed it to Mary Kate's side.

When the girl grabbed it and was able to lift her head out of the water, her cries lessened. She moved up as much as she could on the rock, resting her body against the stone.

Jordan straightened when Mary Kate was situated. "I'll get Fox," she told the girl, wiping a strand of brown hair from the child's cheek. "I'll be right back."

Mary Kate bravely nodded her head, looking at Jordan with the trusting eyes of a small child. The rain splattered against her cheeks, washing away the last of her tears.

Jordan smiled bravely back at her, admiring the little girl's courage. She squeezed her hand once quickly, then turned and headed off to find help.

Jordan dashed into the dark forest, the mud, much worse than before, sucking at her slippered shoes. Her dress was heavy with the river and rainwater. Disgusted with her slow movement, Jordan peeled off her shoes and tossed them aside. Then she pulled up her skirt and held it in one hand, fending off the branches with the other as she raced through the trees.

Thunder rumbled around her, but she paid it no attention. A flash of lightning lit up the forest, and Jordan knew she was heading in the right direction. She waited until she could no longer hear the rush of the river behind her before she began to scream, "Fox!"

She had to move faster. Mary Kate didn't have a lot

of time. The river was still rising. The rain was coming down in heavy sheets, and Jordan had to swipe the rain from her eyes every few seconds just so that she could see. "Fox!"

What if she couldn't find Fox? The thought came unbidden. She had to have another plan. She would keep going until she reached the castle. Surely someone there could help. "Fox!" she shouted at the top of her lungs. With any luck at all, she would run into Fox or Beau or Pick first. "Fox!"

She burst from the forest into the meadow. She was soaked through to the skin and her dress felt as if it weighed a hundred extra pounds. Desperation seeped into every pore of her body, along with the chill the rain brought with it. "Fox!" she screamed, looking out across the meadow.

But a flash of lightning revealed only an empty field, the high stalks of grass bent over in the wind and thick rain. Jordan dashed into the field, running as hard as she could toward the castle. Her lungs felt like they were going to explode, and her legs ached from the exertion. But she pushed on. She swiped the rain and hair from her eyes and dashed toward the castle. Mary Kate needed her. Damn it, she wouldn't let the girl die.

Jordan stifled the tears that threatened to overwhelm her.

"Fox!"

Jordan raced toward the castle, but for a long frustrating moment, it seemed no matter how fast she ran, she wasn't getting closer to the crumbling walls. Where was Fox? She needed him. Mary Kate needed him.

Then Jordan was at the drawbridge. Her heart was hammering so hard inside her chest she found it difficult to catch her breath. She paused for only a moment before hurrying inside the castle, rushing through the outer ward and then the inner ward to the keep. Relief filled her as she entered the keep. There would be help here.

She burst inside and raced toward the meal room, screaming, "Fox!"

But it wasn't Fox that emerged from the meal room. It was Scout. She was casually eating a piece of rabbit, seemingly without a care in the world.

"Oh, thank God!" Jordan gasped. "I . . . I found Mary Kate. She's trapped."

Scout's gaze swept her impassively.

"She's trapped," Jordan repeated.

But Scout didn't move, didn't blink. She bit off another piece of rabbit and slowly chewed it.

"Did you hear me? I need your help to free her. She'll die!"

Something darkened in Scout's eyes and she turned her back on Jordan, beginning to move back into the meal room.

Jordan seized her arm. "She's your daughter. Don't you care?"

Scout ripped her arm free of Jordan's hold. "I want nothing to do with her."

Jordan's jaw dropped. Outrage and horror seared through her. "What kind of woman are you? She's your daughter!"

Scout pushed her face close to Jordan's. "Who are you to judge me? You don't know what it's like to have your legs held open while a man pushes his cock into you! Do you?" Scout snarled. "You don't know what it's like to find out you're pregnant with a rapist's baby! Don't you dare judge me!"

Shock and repulsion warred with Jordan's sense of

urgency and desperation. "Mary Kate had nothing to do with that. She's just a child."

"She's *his* child. I can't stand to look at her. Every time I do, I'm reminded of what happened, of what he did to me. I hope she dies. Then I can be done with both of them." Scout whirled away from Jordan and moved back into the meal room.

No, Jordan thought helplessly. *No.* There was no one to help her. She ran back out into the rain, racing out of the castle. She had to keep moving. *Keep looking. Keep thinking. Think of another plan.*

But suddenly another image rose before her eyes, the memory of Maggie's still form as she lay on the bed. Dead. Then the image transformed. Maggie's face became Mary Kate's. She, too, was lifeless and still, dead. Tears rushed into Jordan's eyes. She tried to swipe them away, tried to erase the memory from her thoughts, but they lingered to torment her. *God, help me,* she begged silently. She couldn't lose Mary Kate, too.

An immense tidal wave of helplessness threatened to overtake her. She wanted to just collapse and sob, but she couldn't. It would paralyze her completely. She had to do something.

She paused at the drawbridge, trying to collect her thoughts, trying to come up with a plan. But she couldn't. The rain only made the night that much bleaker and that much blacker. She needed help. Mary Kate was depending on her.

Maggie had depended on her, too.

Her throat closed tight. She had to get help. The river was rising! She couldn't free Mary Kate by herself.

She wiped at her eyes and a sob escaped. What if the little girl died?

Jordan began to run back toward Mary Kate. She would

at least try to free her again, even though she knew it would be useless.

"Fox!" she screamed again and again, racing toward the forest. She could hardly see, she was sobbing so hard. It was hopeless, and her time was running out.

"Fox!"

CHAPTER TWENTY-SIX

Jordan raced through the field, sobbing. She could feel her hope diminishing, but she refused to give up. Fear threatened to well up inside her, clawing for her soul, waiting to drag her down into despair and defeat.

Fox, she silently begged. Where was he? Her vision blurred as she scanned the forest ahead and prayed that Fox would find her. She opened her mouth to scream for him again, but only a sob came forth.

Lightning flashed over the field. Jordan tripped on a rock and fell onto her hands and knees in the mud. A sob raked her body, and it took all her willpower to push herself to her feet.

The rumble of thunder boomed over her head. More lightning lit the sky, followed by a piercing boom that shook the ground. Jordan jumped and looked left, where the crack had originated.

For a moment, Jordan thought it was a hallucination.

On the hill to her left, silhouetted by the lightning, was a rider. Hope surged inside her. She waved her arms, desperate to get his attention.

"Help!" she cried as thunder boomed overhead, rocking the land. "Help!"

For a long moment, the rider didn't move.

He can't hear me over the storm, Jordan thought. Frantic, desperate, Jordan raced toward the rider. "Please!" she called.

The rider slowly rode toward her. In the darkness he was barely visible, but as they moved closer to each other, she saw his long black hair, his strong shoulders. "Fox," she gasped, almost crying out her joy.

He came to a halt just before her, staring down at her in confusion.

"Fox," she cried. "Mary Kate. She's trapped by the river."

Fox looked toward the river, then reached down and grabbed Jordan around the waist, pulling her up into the saddle before him. He spurred his horse toward the river, moving around the forest. "Where?" he demanded.

"Just off the path," Jordan instructed. "South of the willows."

Fox urged his horse faster with a slight kick, holding Jordan close to him as the horse charged forward.

Jordan turned her head slightly so he could hear her. "A tree fell, trapping her leg. When I left, she was just able to hold her head up out of the water. The river is rising." As if in reply, lightning streaked across the sky.

The horse reared slightly and Jordan grabbed the pommel.

Fox steadied the horse with a firm hand and urged it on, moving across the path and into the forest.

Jordan tried to see beyond the dark shapes of the forest

trees. But suddenly, tears blurred her sight. "I couldn't move the tree, Fox. I couldn't help her." Her voice cracked as she thought of her helplessness, her weakness.

"You did enough," Fox said softly, kindly.

He nuzzled her wet skin, and Jordan thought she felt his lips against her temple. She was afraid to look at him, afraid it had been nothing more than the brush of a wet leaf.

The roar of the river sounded as they moved toward it. Jordan listened for Mary Kate's cries, more fearful of the silence.

"Where?" Fox demanded.

Jordan was silent, listening for the girl. What if she was too late? Jordan shook her head. "She was close to here."

Fox reined his horse into a walk. "Mary Kate!" he hollered.

Jordan's heart pounded in her chest. Dread consumed her. Why wasn't she answering? Fear closed around her body so completely that she couldn't even get her lips to call out her name.

"Mary Kate!" Fox called.

Desperately, Jordan slid from the horse and moved to the river. They had to be close. Jordan scanned the dark river bank, but couldn't see. She prayed for lightning so she could find the tree.

"Mary Kate!" Fox called again, just behind Jordan.

Jordan moved closer to the water, searching. Despair was settling over her shoulders, moving through her veins, freezing her blood.

"Fox!"

Jordan whirled at the cry, running up the river bank toward the shout. Relief speared her heart. Fox raced ahead of her, splashing into the water.

Mary Kate was just holding her head out of the rushing water, clinging to the rock Jordan had moved. Jordan collapsed by her side, grabbing the girl and holding her, rocking her slightly. She stroked Mary Kate's hair, relief filling her. A sob escaped her lips as she held Mary Kate tightly. They had made it. She would be all right!

Fox bent and attempted to lift the tree. "When I lift, Jordan . . ."

Jordan nodded.

Fox groaned and attempted to lift the tree. But it remained on Mary Kate's leg.

Jordan released Mary Kate, making sure the child was positioned on the rock so her head was above the water, and moved to Fox's side. She put her hands beneath the tree.

Lightning lit the sky and the rain pelted them.

"Ready? Go," Fox said.

They pulled together. Jordan lifted with everything she could. She strained at the tree as hard as she could, pulling it up. The tree budged and then they lifted it.

"Move your foot, Mary Kate," Jordan said.

The girl slid her foot out and slipped, going under the water. Jordan released the tree and seized Mary Kate's arm, hauling her away from the tree. Fox held the tree as long as he could and then released it when they were clear, stepping away from the falling log.

Jordan pulled Mary Kate from the water, holding the shivering child to her. The girl was crying, her small arms wrapped around Jordan's shoulders.

Jordan was sobbing into Mary Kate's hair.

Fox put his hand on Mary Kate's head. "Are you all right?"

Mary Kate nodded her head.

Jordan leaned into Fox to find herself trembling with

relief. His arm swept around her, holding her close for a long moment. "It's all right," he murmured, his voice strangely soothing.

From the bushes, a one-eyed man watched with interest and joy. *I can use a new horse and a good set of armor,* he thought, grinning.

Jordan's eyes were still red with worry and tears long after they had reached the meal room. A fire had been lit in the hearth, and Mary Kate was sleeping curled up in a ball, exhausted.

But it wasn't Mary Kate who held Fox's gaze. It was Jordan. She was soaking wet, a blanket wrapped around her slumped shoulders. Her hair hung in long waves until it disappeared beneath the blanket. She was looking at her hands, which had finally stopped trembling.

Fox moved from his place near the hearth and sat at her side on the bench. "I'm sorry, Jordan," Fox whispered. "If it hadn't been for me, Mary Kate never would have left. I shouldn't have treated you like that."

Jordan placed her hand comfortingly atop his.

For a long moment, they said nothing.

"I couldn't move the tree," Jordan said. There were tears in her voice and her chin quivered.

"It's all right, Jordan," Fox said quietly. "Mary Kate is safe."

She sniffed. "You don't understand. There was nothing I could do. Just like Maggie. I thought . . ." She shook her head. "If I couldn't find you . . ."

She looked at him and Fox's heart broke. Her blue eyes glistened like diamonds. Jordan leaned her head against his shoulder, exhausted. She smelled of clean rain and forest. He rested his cheek against her hair for a long moment. His arm went around her of its own accord, rubbing her arm to warm her, holding her.

Jordan lifted her head to him and opened her mouth as if to say something. But no words came out. Fox found his gaze sweeping her face, every precious inch of it, flawless in its perfection. Her eyebrows arched slightly over her large blue eyes. Her pert nose almost touched his, her soft breath fanning across his lips. Her lips, so red and perfectly bowed, so luscious and ripe . . .

Fox leaned closer until her blue eyes took up his entire view, a sea of vibrant, caring life. So generous in her giving, so caring in her unselfishness. Just to touch her perfection would be like touching heaven. Fox's lips touched hers, a gentle stroke, an innocent mating. He pulled back slightly to study her face, looking for disgust or any sign of pity. But he found neither, only curiosity and trust.

Something so strong and forceful that Fox was unable to control his action took over. He pulled her to him, crushing her against him, holding her as he had longed to for ten years.

He kissed her lips urgently, tasting her innocence. He touched her soul with his need. And Jordan answered as she had always answered, unselfish in her giving. Her arms wrapped around him, the blanket falling to the bench behind her. Her wet clothing had molded completely to her skin, and her body molded completely to his.

Fox's hand moved to the nape of her neck, pulling her close to him. He could not get enough of her. Her kiss warmed him where he had never been warm.

He could feel the beating of her heart as if it were his own. *God's blood!* Fox thought. *I want her so fiercely, like nothing I have ever felt before.* He pulled back suddenly, fearful of losing himself to her.

Her eyes were full of dazed confusion. Fox could have kissed her again and again, perhaps even taken her right there. But he couldn't. He moved away from her.

Jordan straightened, drawing herself farther away from Fox.

Fox ignored the need that raged inside his body. He couldn't do that to her, couldn't force her to live the way he had to live . . . in disgrace, like a common thief. She was a lady and deserved better, no matter how much he wanted her. He could never even fantasize that she could be his. It would be far too painful.

He looked away from her, staring at Mary Kate on the floor. Jordan had saved the child's life, risking her own freedom, to save her. Jordan deserved far better than the way Fox had treated her.

"Fox, did I—"

Fox interrupted her. "I will take you back to Ruvane Village," he said quietly. "As you requested."

CHAPTER TWENTY-SEVEN

Fox was going to take her back to Ruvane village. Jordan should have been happy. After all, this was what she had been asking for, to see the children.

But Fox was distancing himself from her, releasing her to let her go back to her life—back to Evan.

The thought of Evan was like being doused with cold water, especially after she had tasted Fox's passion.

Jordan sat for a long time, trying to comprehend her feelings. She was anything but happy. She touched her lips, staring into the dying fire. How could Fox kiss her like that and have it mean nothing? How could he just let her go? She was not happy, not elated, just very confused by the emotions stirring inside her.

He was forsaking his title and his lands by letting her go. Why would he do that, especially after making it clear that they meant everything to him? She was his means to gaining at least the land.

Jordan stood and marched out of the meal room. She had to know. She moved down the hallway toward the spiral stairway. The corridors were dark except for the light of the moon that shone in through the second floor windows. Jordan marched up the stairway, having to feel her way up the stone tower. She emerged onto the second floor and walked toward Fox's door.

He wouldn't get away with it. He couldn't throw away his chance at getting back what was his.

A figure emerged into a patch of moonlight before her, startling her.

The figure wore the long brown robe of a monk. Jordan quickly halted. Michael. She swallowed and looked at Fox's door just down the hallway. If she called out, Fox would come. But something made her stay silent.

"Stay away from him, witch," Michael commanded.

His tone of voice, the degradation in his words, wounded her. "What have I done to you, Michael?"

"Don't dare to be innocent with me! I see through your façade, demon. I see through it where Fox cannot."

"What have I done that you treat me as an enemy?" she demanded.

"You are the devil's own work." Michael touched his forehead, his stomach, and each shoulder, making the sign of the cross before her. "I vow to protect my brother against you."

"I love him, Michael."

The look in Michael's eyes seemed to grow darker, more dangerous. "Love?" Michael spat. "What do you know of love?"

"I loved you, Michael," Jordan said softly. "Like a brother. I protected you and—"

"Abandoned Fox!" Michael shouted. "Is that love?

Was it love that made you remain silent while our life was stripped away?''

Jordan felt the guilt rise within her once again. ''I gave my word,'' she whispered.

''You could have at least come to our defense! Instead you turned your back on us.''

''Turned my back?'' Jordan gasped. ''How can you say that? You were there! It was because of you that I . . .'' Jordan stopped, shutting her mouth quickly. ''It was all to save you, Michael,'' she whispered.

Michael scowled in confusion. ''Me?'' His anger seemed to dissipate. He looked away, his face filling with tortured agony.

''Don't you remember?''

He rubbed his brow. ''I . . . I . . .'' He shook his head fiercely. ''It was a long time ago. I was just a boy. I remember that the baron was in my room. But . . .'' He shook his head again. ''Evan . . .''

''Evan?'' Jordan echoed. What had Evan to do with it? ''Michael—'' She stepped toward him.

He backed away quickly and his anger suddenly resurfaced. ''Your words cannot sway me! Begone, witch!''

''I'm leaving tomorrow, Michael.'' Even to her own ears, her voice sounded heavy.

''Good.'' There was no emphasis or conviction behind the word. He rubbed his forehead again. ''You will stay far away from Fox until then.''

She looked at him quietly for a moment, then turned and retraced her steps, leaving Michael alone in the hallway.

Later, Jordan sat in the meal room, her head bowed. Suddenly, something white moved past the door. Jordan lifted her gaze, but the doorway was empty.

Then a ghost appeared there.

Jordan stood quickly, taking a few involuntary steps backward and putting her hand protectively over her heart. But when the ghost moved deeper into the room, she saw it was only Beau dressed in a white robe.

"Are you all right, m'lady?" Beau asked.

"Why are you dressed all in white?" she wondered.

Beau smiled sheepishly and indicated the robe. "I'm the ghost of Castle Mercer," he said. "We take turns wearing it and walking the battlements so the villagers think the castle is haunted."

Jordan smiled. Everything was making sense. The traps set in the hallway for inquisitive intruders, the ghost of Castle Mercer. It was all part of an elaborate plan to keep visitors away. She retook her seat.

"If you don't mind my saying, you look as miserable as Fox." Beau sat beside Jordan.

Jordan remained silent, studying a piece of lint on her wrinkled dress.

"That's what Fox says, too. The two of you must have long, involved conversations."

"I'm going back tomorrow," Jordan whispered.

Jordan could feel Beau's quizzical gaze on her.

"I thought that was what you wanted," Beau said.

Jordan wanted to see the children, yes. But something more powerful, something she couldn't fight, wanted to stay with Fox. Her shoulders slumped. She couldn't do both. What would she do if she had to choose? Jordan dropped her head to her hands. The choice was simple, really. She couldn't live with herself if she didn't return to the children, but her heart would ache for the rest of her life without Fox.

"I know this seems like a terrible way to live," Beau commented. "Barely any light, no fires. Having to scrounge for food. But Fox would do anything for us." Beau looked at the stone ceiling, putting his hands behind his head. "When Vaughn captured me, I knew Fox would get me out. I had no doubts." He looked at her. "And he did."

Jordan slowly lifted her head to look at him. "It's not a bad way to live," Jordan said. "Surrounded by people you trust."

"It's just not the way you're used to living."

"That's not it," Jordan said softly. "I have people to look after, people who depend on me. My children."

"You have to do what you feel you must," Beau said. "No matter how hard the decision."

Jordan looked at him. She wanted to cry. She wanted to die. She could not stay with Fox. And she knew she couldn't.

Beau stood and moved to the doorway. "Michael has gone to bed," he told her softly.

Jordan lifted shocked eyes to him.

His grin was lopsided. "The ghost of Castle Mercer knows everything." And with that he disappeared down the hallway.

Jordan rose immediately and moved down the hallway to the spiral stairway. She had to tell Fox why she couldn't stay. He had to understand. She would give anything to stay with him . . . anything except for her children.

Jordan moved up the stairway to the dark hall. She half expected Michael to be there, waiting for her, but no form materialized from the darkness. No one moved to stop her as she made her way to Fox's door.

She opened the door and entered the room, closing the door behind her.

As she turned back into the room, a shadowed demon rose before her and a flash of light glinted in her eyes.

The darkness concealed his features, cloaking him in blackness. He stepped from the bed, holding a weapon before him.

Jordan stood her ground as the blade neared her throat. Death was nothing compared to the agony consuming her.

A shaft of moonlight shone through the partially open shutters and Fox stepped into it, shedding the darkness like a cloak.

He tossed his sword to the floor and seized her shoulders. "I could have killed you." Half hidden by the night, he was so dark, so mysterious, so strong.

"I know," she whispered.

"Why have you come?" he demanded, drawing closer to her.

"You're going to let me go."

"It's what you want, isn't it?"

Jordan couldn't answer. Her mouth was dry and the words would not come. She felt tears of sorrow and loss burn behind her eyes.

"To be lady of a castle?" Fox continued.

Jordan studied him, searching for the answer. But his face was starkly empty of emotions.

"To be with other nobles?"

She winced as his fingers squeezed her arms.

"To wed Vaughn?"

"No, Fox. Don't do this."

"What should I do, Jordan?" he asked softly.

She knew what she wanted, but she didn't know how to get it. It wasn't fair to put those demands on herself when it was impossible for her to stay with Fox. She had to return to the children. And in returning, she had to wed Evan.

Even though she wanted Fox.

She looked up into his eyes again. "Would you kiss me if I asked you to?" she wondered, her throat closing around the pain and the horrible decision she knew she was going to make.

Fox was silent for a long moment, studying her face. "I would bring you the moon if you asked it," he whispered and bent his head to hers. His lips touched hers with the gentlest of touches, as if a light wind had whispered across her mouth. But not even a tornado could produce the onslaught of emotions his kiss did. She pulled him against her, claiming him with a kiss and a touch that sent waves of fire flaring through her veins.

Suddenly, Jordan broke the kiss and flung her arms around his neck. "I'm your only hope of ever getting your lands and title back." She held him tightly, never wanting to let go, never wanting to release him. "Why are you letting me go?"

"Don't you know, Jordan?" he asked softly.

The only thing that Jordan knew was that she loved Fox. With all her heart. She shook her head against his chest. She didn't want to leave him, didn't want to feel the pain her abandonment would cause both of them.

Yet she could not forsake the children. "I don't know what to do," she whispered as a savage sob tore through her body. "I don't know what to do, Fox."

Fox held her close, his breath hot against her neck. "There really is only one thing you can do."

She pulled back to look into his eyes. He was right, but she didn't want to let him go. She didn't want to leave him. It wasn't fair! She pressed her lips to his, tears rolling over her cheeks. "I was forced to leave you before," she whispered between kisses. "I shouldn't have to leave now."

Fox pulled away, cupping her tear-streaked face in his

hands. "You shouldn't have to live like this. You're a lady. I was wrong to take you away from your life. I never should have brought you back into mine."

She pressed her fingers to his lips. "Don't say that. I love you, Fox." She pressed a kiss to his lips, to his cheeks. "I've always loved you. I just didn't realize how much until these last few days."

"Jordan," he groaned. "Don't. You'll only make this harder."

But Jordan didn't stop kissing him. She couldn't. Finally, he responded with as much regret and need as she had, their kiss full of longing and remorse. Jordan felt his strong body against the length of hers as she pressed against him. She ran her hands over his naked chest, wanting to touch him, to remember him. His skin was warm to her touch. His powerful arms locked around her, exploring her waist, her back.

His hand moved to the nape of her neck, pulling her tight to him, closer to his tongue's insistent need. She opened her mouth to his exploration and their kiss grew hotter as their tongues danced. His hand moved down from her neck and his feathery touch sent ripples of desire through her body. Finally, his hand eased down inside her dress and moved across her naked breast, cupping it, caressing it with a light, teasing touch.

Jordan gasped, thrusting her breast into his hand. He stroked it, caressing and rubbing until spirals of ecstasy whirled inside her. Then his hands were behind her back, unhooking her dress. Gently, expertly, he eased it down over her shoulders, guiding the chemise down with it. His mouth did not leave her, his hands coaxing, his fingers urging until her dress and chemise hung from her waist.

Fox pulled her close, pressing her naked breasts to his chest.

Desire, hot and urgent, shot through Jordan. She moved her hips against his, unknowing, but knowing that was the spot where she needed him the most.

Fox pulled away from her and she instinctively went after him, reaching for him. But he caught her arms in his hands and held them out to the sides, studying her. "Lord, you're beautiful," he whispered. "More beautiful than any woman has the right to be." He lowered his head to her breasts, running his tongue around one nipple, then sliding his tongue across the sweet valley between them to kiss the other. Both of them grew hard beneath the wet warmth of his mouth.

Fire exploded inside Jordan and she wrapped her arms around Fox's head, pulling him closer to her. Pressing him to her flesh.

His hands slowly lifted her skirts and moved slowly up her legs in spiraling circles, closer and closer to the spot that burned for him. A hot, urgent desire speared through her body. She had never wanted anything more than she did this.

Suddenly, Fox scooped Jordan up into his arms, sweeping her from her feet, and took two steps to the bed. He gently placed her into it and immediately fell on top of her, raining kisses down upon her face and chin, over each eye and finally claiming her lips with his own.

Jordan's world spun. One of his hands slid down her taut stomach to the curve of her hips. He eased her dress and chemise down further, inch by torturous inch. She burned for him, burned for more. For all of him.

Jordan opened her eyes to see Fox staring at her body in rapt adoration. Then he turned his heated gaze to her. For a moment, their eyes met and held.

Slowly, Fox eased her dress from her hips, revealing her womanly hair. He watched her face as he inched his fingers over her hips, around her hair, teasing, stroking, caressing.

Excitement built inside Jordan until she thought she could stand no more. Fox moved closer, ever so deliciously closer.

''Please,'' she whispered, begging for completion.

Fox touched the spot where he knew she needed him, and her instant intake of breath was enough indication that she was ready.

He eased himself from his breeches and slowly guided his manhood toward her wet, slick core.

And then he entered her.

Jordan stiffened at the unexpected agony. But Fox covered her lips with gentle, tender kisses, easing the agony and hurt with a building passion. She lifted her hips to settle him better inside her, to try to ease the growing restlessness.

Fox groaned at her movement and began to move against her. He thrust slowly at first, but gradually his tempo, his movement increased, drawing Jordan into his frenzy of passion.

She matched his movements, until they found a tempo that had them moving as one. Jordan's passion built as her excitement rose with each thrust, with each cadence. Tremors of arousal danced along her skin and whirled in her mind.

His hands skimmed her sides, moving up until he reached her breasts. His hands encircled the mounds, and Jordan's world ignited into a flaming tornado, whirling and spinning as ecstasy tore through her. She rode the spiral of pleasure until she was sure her mind had touched the heavens and exploded into a thousand bright stars.

When she opened her eyes, awed at the feelings that lingered inside her body, she saw Fox smiling softly down at her. Then he moved again, rocking back and forth until suddenly his entire body stiffened and he gritted his teeth. She felt an explosion of warmth deep inside her.

Fox was still for a long moment. But when he opened his eyes, there was such peace and tranquillity shining there that Jordan thought she had never seen a more wonderful sight.

She smiled at him. He smiled back.

Fox took Jordan into his arms and rolled over onto his back, refusing to relinquish his grip on her. He kissed the top of her head, holding her tightly against him.

CHAPTER TWENTY-EIGHT

A shaft of moonlight shone through the window, lighting their entwined hands with a soft pale glow. Fox studied her small hand, wrapping his tighter around hers, wishing she could remain with him. But that was impossible, even after the passion they had just shared. For him, there awaited only certain death. For Jordan, there was life. And maybe his life growing inside her now. She had a bright future ahead of her. He did not—not a future a woman of her stature should be subjected to. A future of misery and thievery and scraps of food and hunting. And being hunted.

The thought of the future and what was not to be was painful, and he pushed it aside. He wanted to say something, to explain to her. But there was nothing to say, nothing to explain. After he killed Vaughn, men would come for him—the king's men, no doubt—and he could either run or fight. But he knew in his soul that he would not run when the time came. He would fight. A dozen men, two dozen if that's what they sent after him. No, there was no future for him.

"Fox," Jordan whispered. "You know I cannot stay with you."

His thumb stopped caressing hers. He opened his mouth to argue the point, but snapped it shut. "I know," he finally agreed, nodding his head.

An awkward, heavy silence engulfed them.

"But you don't understand why," she said quietly.

"I understand my life is not for you, Jordan." He kissed the top of her head where it lay against his chest.

She lifted her head and stared at him with those luminescent eyes, eyes that glowed in the moonbeams with their own inner light. "I would stay with you if you were a dung farmer."

He smiled. "Smelly but still handsome."

Jordan didn't share his smile. "My children need me."

Fox ground his teeth and slid out from beneath her. He had thought at one point during their lovemaking that she had to be a virgin. But here she was speaking of her children again. He sat at the edge of the bed. He didn't want to hear that Vaughn had had her. He didn't want to hear that his hands had been on her body . . . inside her body. The very thought made him clench his teeth. "I've already said I would take you back to Ruvane village."

"I want you to understand I am not abandoning you," she said from behind him, placing her hands on his rigid shoulders.

Fox bowed his head. "I know," he whispered. He turned again to her, taking her face in his hands. "I know." He bent his head to hers, pressing a kiss to her lips. It was a sad kiss, a kiss of farewell.

* * *

As they rode toward Ruvane village, Fox held Jordan close to him, knowing this would be the last time he could touch her, the last time he could hold her.

He brushed his cheek against her hair. She belonged with other nobles. He could never subject her to the life he led. Yet to allow her to marry Vaughn was unthinkable. He couldn't imagine her in his arms. He didn't want to. And someday, somehow, he would kill Vaughn.

"This way," Jordan said, jarring Fox from his thoughts.

Fox looked down the road she pointed to. It led to the outer reaches of the Ruvane lands. He glanced back down the main road that led into Ruvane village and then steered his horse down the less traveled road.

He could feel her excitement as they rode down the barren road, the stiffening of her body, the anxiety that bubbled within her, making it almost impossible for her to sit still. Something was going to happen. He was sure of it. His body reacted to her excitement, tensing and releasing in anticipation.

As they moved over a slight hill, a house rose before them. It was a rather large house, if not a bit decrepit. A trap? The thought flared in Fox's mind. His gaze scanned the surroundings. There were no horses, no sign of soldiers in wait.

Jordan would never do that to him. Not again. Or would she? She had been writing notes and trying to get out of the castle. Fox immediately dismissed the idea.

As they neared the house, a small girl emerged from the building, struggling with a bucket that was obviously too big for her.

Jordan slid from the horse, racing toward the girl. "Kara!" she shouted.

Kara lifted her gaze to Jordan and instantly her face transformed from a scowl into a beaming smile filled with pure joy. "Lady Jordan!" she screamed. "Lady Jordan!" The girl dropped the bucket, spilling the contents, and raced toward Jordan.

The door to the house opened and a small squadron of children emerged. When they saw Jordan, they all squealed just as excitedly and ran after Kara.

Kara launched herself at Jordan and Jordan caught the girl in midflight, swinging her around once before pulling her to herself and holding Kara tightly.

Fox watched with curious eyes as the group of children greeted Jordan with huge smiles and warm hugs. *Are these her children?* he wondered. *There is a boy who must be at least nine!* She would have had to have been pregnant when he had last seen her ten years ago. It wasn't possible.

"Where have you been?" one older girl asked.

"We've missed you," a young boy complained.

"I cried for you," Kara said.

"I know," Jordan replied. "I know. I'm sorry I was away so long."

Fox stared in awe at all of the children. These children couldn't all be Jordan's! It was impossible. Two of them were less than a year apart in age!

The young boy approached him. "Who's he?" he asked Jordan, keeping his distrustful gaze on Fox.

Jordan rose with a small girl on her hip. Her eyes were shining, and the smile on her full lips was warm and genuine. "That's my good friend, Fox," Jordan answered.

Good friend. Fox hadn't heard those words for years. But the sheer simplicity of those two words, and the honesty with which she spoke them, transformed his cold soul, melting it into something warm and comfortable.

"The Black Fox?" the older boy gasped.

"No," Jordan answered. "Just Fox."

"These are your children?" Fox finally asked Jordan.

Jordan nodded, proudly. The children formed a circle around her. "I built this place for them—with father's help, of course. They have no parents. I love them as I would my own."

Shock and unabashed pride and awe welled inside Fox. He grinned sheepishly. *And I had thought she had children of her own flesh and blood! I should have known.* Then a realization struck Fox. No other man had ever touched her. He had been her first, her only. The thought was thoroughly and dangerously arousing.

There was a tug at his boot and Fox looked down. The young girl who had been carrying the bucket stared up at him. Dark curls fell across her face. "Will you eat with us?" she asked.

Fox hesitated at the idea. He looked back down the road they had just come from. He had to return to Castle Mercer.

"Please," Jordan said.

Fox turned back to look into the blue eyes of heaven. He had never been able to resist her. And now was no different. He swung his leg over his horse and dismounted.

They dined with the children that evening and Fox met the older woman who helped Jordan with the children. Abagail had been taking good care of them in Jordan's absence, but Fox could see the large rings under her eyes, the slumping of her shoulders. The children were obviously a lot of work for her.

Fox turned his gaze from Abagail to Jordan. The children sat around her, one small girl in her lap, two seated beside her, and the older two standing behind her.

" . . . and Jason fell into the muddy patch in the garden," the older girl was saying. "We told him not to go there but . . ."

The children adored her. They had fought over who would sit beside her, who would bring her ale and her trencher. Jordan was their protector, a mother to all of them.

Jordan looked up and her gaze locked with Fox's. She set the small girl onto the bench at her side and stood. "I need to speak with Fox," she said quietly.

Five sets of suspicious, angry eyes swung to him. He bridled under the impact, but followed her out the door as she promised to return to the children. When she shut the door on the strange, untrusting silence that followed them, Fox found himself grateful for the moment alone. He had felt like fighting to sit beside her, too. For just an instant as they walked quietly together, Fox knew contentment as he imagined what their life could have been together. He looked down at her and smiled. She was beautiful. She was everything he could have ever wanted—and so much more.

"I'm sorry," he said. "I didn't understand."

Jordan grinned at him. "Fox, I was thinking. Mary Kate should be here. She should be with my children. She can play with them and be with them all the time. She can be the child she is supposed to be."

Fox stiffened for an instant.

Jordan touched his arm. "It's not safe for her at Castle Mercer. Here she can get the proper food and love that she needs."

Fox ground his teeth. She was right. There was no sense in trying to make up reasons why Mary Kate should stay at the castle. But did he have to give up the girl as well as Jordan? Fox nodded. "You're right, of course," he said softly. "I'll bring her back here to see what it is like and then let her decide."

Jordan pressed a kiss to his lips.

Fox lifted his head to gaze at her. Those accursedly blue eyes would haunt him forever. He groaned softly and looked away. If only things had been different for them. But he was a criminal, a commoner.

"I don't care what you are, Fox," Jordan said quietly, as if reading his mind. Her voice was thick and husky. "You'll always be my friend."

Fox pulled her to him and kissed her, hard, desperately. He felt wetness on her cheeks and pulled back to see her eyes full of tears.

"I love you, Fox." She turned and raced for the house.

Fox couldn't move for a long moment as he watched her leave. Was he doing the right thing? If he was, then why did his chest hurt so damned much?

CHAPTER TWENTY-NINE

I love you, Fox.

Fox rode slowly back toward Castle Mercer, Jordan's simple phrase repeating itself over and over again in his mind. Jordan was lovely, more lovely and charming than any woman had a right to be. He still found it hard to believe she had actually said those words to him. Again. How could he possibly let her go so easily?

A bleak, depressing emptiness had already crept into his heart though he had been away from her for only a few hours. They had made love, and it had been the most magical, wonderful experience in his life. He already ached to hold her in his arms again, to touch her face, to run his fingers through her hair, to kiss her sweet lips.

But it could never happen again. It would only make it harder on the both of them. He had to say farewell . . . and leave her.

Fox approached Castle Mercer. The silence settled

around him, deepening, leaving only his thoughts to plague him with images of Jordan in Vaughn's arms. Her betrothed's arms. Fox gritted his teeth. They had all been friends once, the absolute best of friends. But who would have thought Vaughn would have betrayed him?

And now I have betrayed him, Fox realized. *I have taken his woman. I have taken the virginity that was to be his and stolen it for my own pleasure.* It was a treasure that could never be replaced or restored. The thought brought some sort of placating vindictiveness to Fox. Vaughn would never be able to experience that mysterious and enchanting moment.

As he approached the drawbridge, his horse suddenly pranced nervously beneath him, taking shying steps away from the castle. Alarms immediately rang in Fox's head. Not a word, not a sound greeted his arrival. Usually the birds cawed or a dog barked, but there was nothing.

And where was Mary Kate? She usually rushed out to cover his tracks with her big leaf. Fox glanced down at the ground, thinking of the girl. To add to his unease, he noticed a wide, chaotic mass of what appeared to be hoofprints in the dirt. He couldn't tell for certain.

Something was wrong here. Very wrong.

Fox had learned long ago not to doubt his instincts. He quickly dismounted and swatted his horse. The animal galloped away over the field.

Fox entered the outer ward, keeping to the shadows of the castle wall, his hand firmly gripping the hilt of his sheathed blade. He didn't see anything obviously wrong within the courtyard, but the unpleasant feeling he had in the pit of his stomach wouldn't go away. It remained, traveling through his body, tickling the hair on the nape of his neck as he continued to move through the shadows.

Fox slipped beneath the inner gatehouse, moving into

the inner ward. The inner courtyard was empty as well, the keep silent. Fox moved toward the decrepit building. Maybe he was imagining things.

Maybe.

And then he spotted something in the middle of the courtyard. In the dirt and dust, a set of tracks caught his attention. Horses' hooves. He moved to the middle of the courtyard. In the rising sun that stretched through the courtyard, Fox stared at the ground, turning round and round. All about him, the tracks of horses were pressed into the dirt. This time he was certain.

Someone had invaded Castle Mercer.

Fox's eyes slowly rose from the horse tracks to the keep. Father and Michael! His friends! He started to charge forward, ripping his sword free of its sheath, but then quickly brought himself to a sudden halt.

What if they were still inside?

Fox quickly merged into the shadows. He sneaked into the keep, pressing himself into any pool of darkness he could find, the dark shadows welcoming him like an old friend. The hallway was empty, silent. Where was his father? And Michael? What had they done to Beau or Pick and the others?

Fox's jaw clenched tight and his fingers gripped the leather handle of his weapon firmly as he thought of who would dare to enter Castle Mercer.

Evan Vaughn and his soldiers. It could be no other.

Fox continued into the keep, moving deeper and deeper into its crumbling interior. He apprehensively glanced down at the stone floor as he moved, dreading the sight of spilled blood, but he saw no sign of bloodshed anywhere in the hallway. Were they gone or were they hiding, waiting for him?

As he cautiously moved down the dark, empty hallway,

Fox's ears became more and more attuned to any noise, any sound. Where was his hound? Where was Doom? He strained to hear something, anything, any sign of life or activity, but there was no sound in the castle at all. None.

He came upon one of the traps they had rigged up in the hallway and saw that the ghost had been released and torn to shreds by an angry blade.

Fox moved more quickly down the hallway as the dread inside him grew stronger. What had happened here? Where was Mary Kate? She knew of a dozen places to hide in the castle. Surely she had escaped the invaders.

As he approached the meal room, Fox slowed his progress. He moved cautiously up to the door, listening for any sound of the intruders in the large room beyond. But the silence was deafening. He could hear his own heart beating in his chest, his own blood rushing in his ears. His own careful footsteps sounded like the heavy pounding of falling rocks.

He pressed his back against the wall beside the door. The shadows that hid him loomed up around him, suddenly becoming more like eerie patches of dangerous mystery than friendly cover. Could they be hiding his enemies as well as they hid him? He peeked around the doorway, into the meal room, scanning every dark shadow, every dark crevice.

To his surprise, the hearth was lit, which set his nerves on end, and a man sat in a chair before the fire. He was bent over, his face in his hands.

A trap? Fox wondered. His gaze again scanned the room. But he couldn't see any trace of others. Not soldiers, not his friends.

Fox took a silent step into the room toward the man. Suddenly, he heard a whimper and whirled, lifting his sword. Near the wall, he spied Doom, bloodied and lying on his side. The dog whimpered again and moved to lift his head, but it dropped back to the floor.

Fox moved to his hound, a well of grief opening up inside him. He kept one eye on the man near the hearth and stroked the wounded dog with his other hand. His palm came away from the dog's fur thick with blood. Fox's body shook with anger. What kind of barbarian curs would hurt an animal? What kind of barbarian had Vaughn turned into?

He marched across the room toward the man near the hearth. If it was Vaughn and this was some kind of trap, Fox would still kill him before his men could be upon him.

But as Fox approached, the man lifted his head.

Fox faltered and lowered his sword. His father gazed at him, torment painfully evident in his old eyes.

"I couldn't stop them," Frederick said softly. "I couldn't stop them, Son."

Fox sheathed his sword. "Where are the others, Father?" he demanded, his jaw tight.

"They took them. They took all of them," Frederick answered. "I ordered them to stop. I called my men. But they never came."

"Your men are gone, Father," Fox said. "Who took them?"

"Gone? Good heavens, where could they all have gone? Were they defeated? He did bring an army of men. Perhaps . . ."

"No, Father," Fox said firmly. "They left a long time ago. When we couldn't pay them anymore."

"Couldn't pay them? We have coffers full of gold! Of course we could pay them!"

Fox's jaw tightened. "Where is Beau, Father? And Pick? And Michael? Where are the others?"

"They left because we couldn't pay them?" Frederick seemed confused for a moment as he turned toward the fire.

Fox grabbed him and pulled him to his feet. "Your castle is crumbling around you! Your armies are gone! There are no nobles who come to visit!"

"What about Lady Jordan?" Frederick asked him, seemingly unaffected by Fox's outburst.

Fox released him with an aggravated sigh and his father fell back into his chair. "I kidnapped her. I wanted to get a title, our lands . . . your life back for you."

"My life back," his father echoed dully.

But Fox knew that was what he himself wanted. He wanted his life back. He wanted his title back. He wanted Jordan back. And now he had lost all of that and more. "What happened, Father?" Fox asked, a sudden feeling of defeat draining him and making him feel exhausted.

"They surprised us, boy," his father said softly. "They came in and . . . demanded to know where you were."

Fox groaned softly. "Who was it?"

"Evan," Frederick said. "It was Evan."

Fox shook his head, grinding his teeth. He clenched his fists, forcing his anger under control. Then he looked at his father. "What does he want?"

"He wants you," Frederick answered. "He left me here to relay the message that if you didn't bring Jordan to Castle Vaughn by sunset five days from now, he would start killing them."

Fox cursed silently and ran his hands through his hair. "Did they hurt anyone?"

Frederick shook his head. "I don't think so. Our men couldn't do much when Evan's men had a sword to Scout's throat."

Fox looked at the fire for a moment, collecting his

thoughts. But that didn't take long. He already knew what he had to do. He turned back to his father. "Will you be all right, Father?" Fox asked.

Frederick nodded.

"Take care of Doom. He needs you to clean his wound and feed him. Can you do that?"

Again, Frederick nodded. He glanced at the dog, then back to his son. "You're going after him, aren't you?"

"Yes," Fox said.

Frederick nodded. "Be careful, Son."

Fox exited the keep, moving quickly. He had to get to Castle Vaughn and free his men. He prayed his horse hadn't strayed too far. He was certain that the animal was lingering near the castle somewhere. He hoped it might have even moved into the outer courtyard of its own volition. He had to . . .

Suddenly, he stopped as he heard a soft sound. He lifted his gaze, scanning the inner ward. It sounded like . . . crying. Soft crying. Fox crossed the inner ward, listening. It sounded as though it were coming from the stables.

That was where Mary Kate had been told to hide if the castle was ever invaded.

His brisk walk turned into a run as he bolted for the door of the stables. It had long since fallen from its hinges, and was now just a piece of rotting wood dangling askew in the doorway. He brushed past the door and moved inside.

He saw her immediately. She was kneeling on the ground with her back to him, her small shoulders shaking as she sobbed. "Mary Kate?"

But Mary Kate didn't move.

Fox walked up to her and peered over her shoulder,

seeing that she was kneeling beside the pregnant dog. It was lying on its side, not moving. It wasn't until he bent down further toward her that Fox saw why Mary Kate was crying. The dog had been gutted, from her throat to her tail. The puppies were dead. All of them.

Fox grabbed Mary Kate and pulled her away from the sight. She threw her arms around Fox and hugged him desperately. "Why, Fox? Why did they do it? Why did they kill those babies?"

Fox picked her up and carried her outside into the inner ward, wordlessly soothing her with gentle strokes on her hair. He held her tightly as she sobbed. *Jordan is right,* he thought. *Mary Kate doesn't belong here. She doesn't deserve this. She's suffered enough for five lifetimes, let alone for a child of only four years.*

You will pay for this, Evan Vaughn, Fox vowed as he carried Mary Kate from the castle. *You will pay.*

CHAPTER THIRTY

Jordan scooped some water from the stream with a bucket. Some of the cold water spilled over her fingers, chilling her skin. She took a moment to study her reflection in the slow moving current. The bright moon in the sky above illuminated the water with a soft shimmering light. She looked tired. Tired with the weight of three worlds on her shoulders.

She had the children she needed to look after. She had a future husband she should have contacted the moment Fox had freed her, but had not. And then there was Fox himself. Her childhood friend. Her kidnapper. Her . . . her lover.

She quickly looked away from her reflection, part of her feeling ambivalent for what she had done. She was betrothed! Women had been hanged or burned for less. But another part of her felt no shame at all. It was the part of her that felt breathless at the mere thought of Fox taking her in his arms and holding her and kissing her.

She turned from the stream and marched through the high stalks of grass toward the house. Her eyes again swung to the road. Fox was over a day late, and she was worried about him. She had decided to remain at the house and await Mary Kate's arrival before moving on to Castle Ruvane. She wanted to make sure the child was safely situated at the house and felt comfortable with Abagail and all of the other children.

Jordan scowled, turning to stare down the road again. Where was Fox? Why was he taking so long? Maybe Mary Kate hadn't wanted to come live with her. Or had something else happened, something far worse? Jordan shook her head, refusing to imagine the worst.

Instead, she turned her thoughts to how heavy the bucket was. She had filled it to the top, and the cold water sloshed over the sides onto her dress. Her dirty white dress. The hem was ripped and the frayed edges were black. It was way past time to get to Castle Ruvane and get some fresh clothes. She brushed a lock of her dark hair away from her eyes as she neared the house.

She was almost to the door when a hand clamped down firmly over her mouth and she was being pulled roughly back.

She struggled, dropping the bucket, the water splashing along the dirt, and quickly reached for the dagger at her thigh.

But a firm hand grabbed her before she could reach the dagger and pressed her fingers tightly into her thigh, forcing her hand to be still. "It's me, Jordan."

Fox. She'd recognize his strong voice anywhere.

Relief sagged Jordan's shoulders and she ceased her struggles. She allowed Fox to pull her into the darkness beside the house, into the shadowy part even the moon's bright light didn't reach.

Fox released her, but held her close. "Vaughn took my men."

"What?" Jordan gasped.

Fox nodded, his dark hair fanning his shoulders. "He attacked the castle while you and I were here."

Jordan opened her mouth to reply, but just then a small hand slipped into hers. She looked down to see Mary Kate standing beside her. Jordan smiled down at her and picked the girl up. "Have you come to stay with us?"

Mary Kate looked at Fox, and Fox nodded. The girl turned back to Jordan. "Yes. I think so."

Fox ruffled the knotted curls in the little girl's hair. "Mary Kate stayed hidden while Vaughn was in the castle."

"Good girl," Jordan whispered, hugging her tightly.

"They killed the puppies," Mary Kate told Jordan. "The bad men killed the mommy dog."

Jordan glanced at Fox over her shoulder.

He nodded glumly.

"Let me take her inside," Jordan whispered. "Will you wait?"

Fox nodded, his gaze scanning the surrounding trees with urgency. "Hurry."

"Who's there?"

Jordan turned to see Abagail stepping outside, her eyes scrunched tight as she scanned the darkness. "It's me, Abagail. Mary Kate is here."

Abagail smiled brightly at them as she approached. Behind Abagail, five sets of small eyes stared from a gap in the doorway. Jordan could hear a few giggles.

"Hello, Mary Kate. We have your bed all ready for you. You must be very tired."

Again, Mary Kate looked to Fox for reassurance and he nodded for her to go with Abagail. Mary Kate took Abagail's offered hand and the two of them moved into the house, leaving Jordan and Fox alone in the night.

Jordan watched the door close and then turned to Fox, squeezing his hands. "What will you do?" she asked.

"I have to free them," he said softly.

"But how?" Jordan gasped, appalled that he could and would endanger his life. "Evan will kill you."

Fox nodded. "I'm sure he would like to." Fox again glanced over his shoulder. "He had some men watching the castle. They came after me as I was leaving to head here. They're looking for you."

Again guilt surged in Jordan's breast. "I was waiting for Mary Kate," she told him. "I should have—"

Fox pressed a finger to her lips. "You don't have to explain." He ran his finger along her lips.

She lifted her eyes to his. In the darkness, she could barely see them. She could only feel his breathing, the press of his chest against hers, the way his breath caressed her lips before vanishing. It was as if they were one.

"I need time to think. I can't go back to Castle Mercer, and I don't think I should stay here much longer. Vaughn is bound to come looking for me here."

She lifted her hands to touch his face. His cheeks were rough with stubble. She wanted to tell him to stay, but she knew he had to go. Loyalty was one of his best attributes. "Let me help you."

"No." The word came quickly.

She tried to pull away, but he held her tight against him. "You cannot be involved in this. If it goes wrong . . . you can still live your life."

Jordan panicked. "No, Fox. You can't ask that of me. I won't sit by while you risk your life to . . ."

His lips pressed hotly against hers, silencing the cry of despair on them. A sob escaped the heated embrace as his mouth pressed to hers. When he pulled back slightly, he pressed his cheek to her temple. "You mean more to me than all of the world. I won't risk your life."

Fox tried to pull back even more but Jordan held him closely. "Please, Fox," she whispered tearfully. "I don't want to lose you again."

"No one captures the Black Fox," Fox whispered against her ear, his cheek pressed against hers. "No one except you."

Jordan pulled back, startled. She could feel his touch on her lower back, his body pressed intimately to hers. She wanted another kiss. She licked her lips, running her tongue along the path his lips had taken. Then she tentatively lifted her lips to his, pressing a chaste kiss there.

Fox's response was immediate, his passion igniting into a blazing brand. He pulled her tight against him, holding the nape of her neck so she could not escape his kiss. Trapped, Jordan could do nothing but let Fox kiss her thoroughly, tantalizing her lips with hot caresses, until she had to gasp from want and need. Then he plundered her mouth, sweeping his tongue into the recesses of her sweetness, tasting her.

He stepped toward her, pushing her back, pinning her against the house, trapping her body between him and the wall. His hot kisses trailed down her neck until fire flamed in her veins. The hardness of him pressed against her belly, and the memory of their lovemaking sent hot desire searing through her, the heat radiating throughout her entire body, coming to a blazing peak between her legs.

His hand cupped the round part of her breast, his fingers kneading her already hardened nipple through the fabric.

The thrill of his touch resounded throughout her body, the tingles of desire roaring within her. Aching to feel his warmth, to feel his body, she lifted his tunic and touched his naked skin, marveling at the muscles in his shoulders, across his chest.

His foot parted her legs and he pressed himself tightly against her, his thigh rubbing against the most intimate part of her. Sensations of pure pleasure pulsated through her body, making her entire body tremble and throb with wanting. As if sensing this, Fox eased her to the ground, laying her on a soft patch of leaves and grass. He lifted her skirt, touching her skin, tracing a trail of tantalizing swirls across her calf and up over her knee to her thigh. Jordan sighed and instinctively reacted to his touch, thrusting her hips toward his hand.

He touched the moist bud of her womanhood and her world shattered instantly, exploding into tiny lights of glowing warmth and love.

Fox moved over her, kissing her all the while, his hot mouth seeking a haven of safety and love. She gave him that safety, if only for the moment, a place where no one would try to capture him, where no one would try to hurt him. She opened her legs wider for him, inviting him to become one with her. Fox thrust into her, groaning softly, closing his eyes, enjoying the warmth that sheathed him.

Jordan shifted her hips, guiding him deeper inside her, and saw the flare of desire sweep across his features. "Don't move," he whispered. "Not yet. Not yet. I want to feel this . . . I want to feel you . . . forever . . ."

Jordan's arms wrapped around him, holding him close. She kissed his cheeks, his eyes, his mouth, touching him all over as if she couldn't get enough of him. And she knew she couldn't. Tonight, this fleeting moment between them, would not be enough. It felt too good, too right, to last such a short time.

"Jordan," Fox whispered. "Jordan."

And then he began to move. Jordan matched his thrusts, lifting her hips to meet the deep strokes of his manhood, until suddenly he stiffened as his passion's fluid filled her. And then Jordan felt the inevitable explosion building inside her, growing stronger with each thrust, sending wave after wave of pleasure washing over her. She gasped and gripped his strong arms as she climaxed along with him. This time she kept her eyes open, watching his final wave of pleasure relax his face, enjoying the calm and peace that filled him. He slid to her side and held her against him. Jordan felt safe in his arms and let the rest of the world fade away as he cradled her against him.

Fox gazed down at Jordan as she lay nestled in his arms. She meant everything to him, as she had all those years ago. Yet he had to let her go. He was a fool for making love to her. He had claimed her as his, only to have to let her go. Unconsciously, his hand clenched tightly around her wrist.

Jordan pulled her arm from his hold. "What is it, Fox?" she asked, rubbing her wrist.

Fox sat up, running his hands through his hair. "I'm sorry it has to be like this," he admitted. He reached for his breeches. "You deserve better."

Jordan touched his hand, stilling his movements. He couldn't look at her. He had taken her like an animal, unable to control his lusting, in a wooded forest, beneath the starry sky.

"I deserve you," Jordan said softly.

Her words drew Fox's attention. When he looked at

her, with the moonlight shimmering on her white skin, he realized she could have been a woodland nymph, a creature of magic and beauty. Her hair was wild about her shoulders, her large blue eyes full of trust and mischief. Fox looked away again. "You are supposed to be another man's wife."

She released her grip on his forearm. "I don't want to marry Evan," she said softly.

Fox bridled. "I should hope not. He will be dead long before he can lay a hand on you."

"You would kill him simply because King Edward granted your lands to his father?"

Fox looked at her with such darkness and anger that she pulled slightly away. "I would kill him because he ruined my family. It was his fault. All of it. He killed the baron."

Jordan sat back on her heels.

She should be shocked, Fox thought, *but she does not appear to be.* He frowned and leaned forward to snatch his breeches up. He slid them over his legs and reached forward for his tunic. "I found this in the baron's tunic. I carry it with me every day to remind me of what I need to do." He rummaged inside his tunic for a moment before grabbing something and displaying it to her. It was a pouch. After all these years, the fabric had frayed and the colors had faded, but the crest on the pouch was still vivid. The Vaughn crest. He handed it to her. She took it, but didn't seem to see the pouch.

"Fox," Jordan whispered.

He didn't acknowledge her, lost in his own thoughts.

"Fox," Jordan said. This time he heard her, noticing there was a strange catch to her voice.

"Evan was the only one who could have done it," Fox explained. "The pouch had been filled with gold coin.

The baron's coin. My father must have known Evan had done it. I don't know why, but my father felt he had to protect him, had to take the blame for him, maybe because Evan was my friend. I don't know. I still can't figure it out. All I know is that I've waited far too long to do what's needed to be done."

"Fox, Evan didn't kill the baron," Jordan said, staring at the pouch she held limply in her hand.

"Of course he did. He robbed him, killed him, and stole his gold. My father tried to protect him and the Vaughns betrayed him, betrayed his trust."

"Evan didn't kill the baron," Jordan said more forcefully.

Fox turned to stare grimly at her. "Are you defending him?"

Jordan shook her head.

"If it wasn't him, then who was it?"

Jordan was silent. She looked away from him, her head down.

Fox noticed for the first time how pale her face seemed. The rosy glow was gone from her cheeks and there was suddenly a haunted look in her eyes. Fox scowled. "You know. You know who the murderer is."

Jordan dropped her eyes to the cloth in her hands.

"Tell me, Jordan," Fox said.

"You have to understand. Michael—"

He seized her shoulders. "Tell me who killed the baron so I can avenge my family!"

"Fox," the word came from her lips as more of a sob than a plea.

"Tell me."

She lifted tearful eyes to him, eyes full of agony, full of guilt. "*I* killed the baron."

For a long moment, Fox could not move. He felt like the

air was being squeezed from his lungs. Betrayal speared through his body like lightning. He dropped his hands and jerked back as if he had touched poison. *It can't be!* he thought.

"I promised your father I wouldn't say anything," Jordan said, desperately. "Not even to you."

Fox stood up quickly, backing away from her.

She moved forward on her knees, as if seeking forgiveness. "Fox, the baron . . . he was sick. He liked little boys. He had Michael—"

"Don't!" Fox exploded.

A broken sound came from Jordan's throat.

"You said *nothing!* You let them take everything from us. From me!" Fox took an angry step toward her, then faltered. Complete agony washed over his features. "We lost everything because of you!"

Jordan lifted a hand to him, reaching out to him. "I'm sorry, Fox."

Fox stood stoically for a moment, then swatted her hand aside and turned, racing through the forest.

"Fox!" Jordan cried.

CHAPTER THIRTY-ONE

Jordan dressed as the sun rose to meet a dreary gray sky. She still felt drained and exhausted from the events of yesterday. She had barely slept during the night. Her thoughts were a scattered mix of conflicting feelings. She warmly remembered Fox laying atop her, kissing her, touching her, loving her. But she also remembered the ugly hatred in his eyes when she confessed her crime to him.

She trembled fiercely as the image of his darkly enraged glare filled her mind. Her fingers were shaking so hard she couldn't get the buttons on the back of her dress buttoned completely. Frustrated, she gave up on the last button, leaving it undone.

She picked up the pouch and stared at it.

It was Evan's crest, all right. There was no mistaking the red background and the black dragon. What was a pouch filled with gold doing with the baron? Had Evan worked for him? Was the gold meant for him? Or for his father? Had they done the baron some service?

Jordan squeezed it in her hand. It didn't matter. She looked up toward the path Fox had taken, remembering the hate, the anger when only moments before there had been love.

Jordan moved toward the house, a numbness dulling her senses. It was as though Fox had never been in her life, as though these past wonderful days had not ever happened. He hated her now more than he had before.

Jordan entered the house to find Abagail sitting at the table.

Abagail lifted her head to Jordan. "She's sleeping," Abagail whispered.

Jordan nodded, trying to be strong. But she couldn't stop the tears from entering her eyes. She looked away from Abagail.

"She'll be fine now that she's with us," Abagail told her softly.

Jordan nodded. She hurriedly picked up a dagger and began to cut the bread for the morning's meal. But that didn't stop the tears from rolling from her eyes to drop onto the table top.

Abagail put a comforting hand on her shoulder. "You needn't worry any longer. Everything is fine."

Again, Jordan nodded silently. For the first time in her life, she wasn't worried about the children. She knew they would be fine.

But she wouldn't be so lucky.

With red-rimmed eyes, Jordan returned to Castle Ruvane in the morning only to find her father had gone to court, summoned by the king. She moved through

Castle Ruvane like a ghost, doing her duties and her chores. Servants raced up to greet her, soldiers welcomed her home and questioned her about the horrible ordeal her kidnapping must have been. But she had very little, if anything, to say to them.

Her thoughts were consumed with Fox. Her mind replayed the hate and loathing she had seen burning in Fox's eyes. He would never forgive her.

Two days later, Evan came to Castle Ruvane with a garrison of troops. He found Jordan in the Great Hall speaking to two serving women about packing up food to bring to the children at the house.

"Lady Jordan!" Evan called out excitedly as he raced across the room. He threw his arms about her, holding her, warmly embracing her.

Jordan felt strangely aloof from him, absently returning his embrace. He was obviously glad to see her, but there was no feeling of warmth for Evan inside her as there had been for Fox. There was no breathless anticipation of his touch or nervous excitement about what he might say to her, no stirring of desire. Not even a slight twinge of need or tingle at his touch.

He was not Fox.

Evan pulled away from her, a scowl on his brow. He studied her face. "Tell me, m'lady," he said in a strangely quiet voice, "how did you escape from the Black Fox?"

"He let me go," she said, quietly.

Evan's eyes narrowed. "He just let you go?"

Jordan looked away from him. "Yes."

"It was a horrible experience for you, wasn't it?" he asked. "He's a ruthless bastard. Did he hurt you?"

Only in ways you could never imagine, she thought,

but remained mute to his question. Jordan's brow slowly furrowed as she remembered the letters. "You never delivered my letters."

"Letters?" he asked, genuinely confused.

"The letters I entrusted you to take to Fox," Jordan said, her voice growing sterner with each moment.

Evan lifted his gaze to the serving women, who were glancing at each other dubiously. He gently took Jordan's arm and led her away from them toward the hearth. "What in heaven's name are you speaking of?" Evan demanded.

"The letters to Fox," Jordan explained in clipped tones. "Ten years ago. When his father was first stripped of his lands and title. You never gave my letters to him."

"Of course I did," Evan said quickly. "I tried everything to get him to take them!"

"He knew nothing of them!" she hissed.

"Is that what he told you?" Evan snarled. "Of course he would say that to turn you against me. And you believed him? I'm disappointed, Jordan."

Jordan scowled. "Fox had no reason to lie to me."

Evan straightened. "And neither do I."

Jordan studied Evan's face. But she couldn't tell if he was lying or not, couldn't read anything in his empty stare. What reason would he have to lie to her?

"I have been entrusted with your safety while your father is away. I have been doing everything in my power to get you safely home. And this is how you greet me? This is how you greet your betrothed?"

Jordan opened her mouth to apologize, but then snapped it shut. "There are lies here, Evan. I will discover the truth."

Evan gritted his teeth. Jordan could see his jaw working as he stared at her. "We will be going to Castle Vaughn in the morning. I need to return to help guard the prisoners.

The Black Fox will go there to try to rescue his men. I will be there when he does. He will not get away with taking you from me.'' He stared hard at Jordan. ''And then you will learn the truth.''

Jordan was tired and soaked as she entered her room at Castle Vaughn. It had been a long trek to Evan's home. The road to Castle Vaughn had been horrible, not only because of the rain that had slowed their progress, doubling the time it normally took, but also because it had left her with hours where she had spoken to no one. Hours to think of Fox. To agonize over her loss of him, to try to think of some way to mend his hate. But how could she change the past?

And then she had thought of that one horrible day that had changed all their lives. She looked down at her hands. She could still see the blood there. How many times had she prayed for forgiveness? Too many to even attempt to keep track of.

She tossed her wet cloak on the bed and lit two candles. The sky, barely visible through a thin slit in the window's curtains, was gray, casting murky shadows in her room. The light from the candles helped to ease the gloom around her, but did nothing to lift her spirits.

The long velvet curtains near the alcove to the window fluttered and Jordan glanced over at them, drawn back to the window by the sound. The window was open? It had been raining all day!

Jordan moved toward the window. Her foot stepped into a puddle of water. She looked down.

A hand locked over her wrist. She opened her mouth to scream, but when Fox stepped out from behind the curtains she bit back her startled cry, muffling it to nothing more than a whimper. Jordan's heart blossomed with joy and relief and a smile touched her lips.

But there was no joy in the face that greeted her, no smile on the lips that sneered at her. Fox's blue eyes were cold with rage, despite the reflection from the two burning candles dancing in their depths.

Confusion washed over Jordan. Fox's arm twitched and Jordan looked down at his hand. A deadly dagger glimmered in the candlelight.

"It will do you no good to scream," Fox warned.

Her eyes snapped up to his. He had come to kill her. The thought should have sent terror rushing through her, should have sent her running, screaming into the hallway. Instead, a calm resignation washed over her. She straightened her back slightly and stood before him.

A slight scowl furrowed his brow. For a long moment they stood that way, with him holding her arm, the dagger separating them.

If it would give him peace, then Jordan would gladly give her life for the atrocity she had committed all those years ago. Jordan faced Fox as she faced death, stoically waiting for him to deliver the final blow.

And waiting.

Suddenly, a knock came at the door, jarring her from her focus. She turned to glance at the door, then looked back at Fox.

If he was going to do it, he would have to do it now.

Fox dropped her hand and stepped back into the curtains.

Another knock sounded at the door.

Jordan's heart beat wildly in her chest. He had released her. But why? Why? To let her live her life knowing a love she could not have, would not ever have? Why hadn't he killed her?

Another knock sounded, this time accompanied by a call. "M'lady?"

Jordan stepped back from Fox and turned to the door. She moved to the bed, steadying her back on one of the four posts. "Come," she called.

The door opened. Two soldiers entered the room, holding a prisoner between them. Michael lifted his stare.

Jordan locked gazes with Michael for a long moment. He had a purplish-black bruise on his right cheek. She frowned and took a step toward him, studying the dirty brown cloak that shrouded his body. She turned to one of the guards. "You may leave us," she instructed.

The two guards exchanged glances. "But, m'lady!" one protested.

"I said leave us," she ordered.

They bowed slightly and left the room, closing the door behind them. Jordan knew she was taking a chance the soldiers would report her request to Evan. She was certain he wouldn't take too kindly to one of his precious prisoners being let out of his cell, but she didn't care. She was determined to get some answers.

Michael's jaw clenched as he stared at her. "What do you want? Why did you have them bring me here? Have you tired of living? I will gladly end your suffering so mine can end as well."

Jordan felt his hatred seething from him, felt the ghostly hands around her throat. She had called for Michael to be brought to her before she knew Fox was in her room. She wanted to talk to him, to try to understand his rage. Now Jordan could reunite the brothers. But she had to know first. "Why do you hate me so?" she asked, truly confused.

Michael's face twisted in a grimace of distaste. "This is the reason you had the guards bring me to you? I'd rather rot in that dungeon than stand here and satisfy your befuddled curiosity."

"We were such good friends. I don't understand what happened."

"If you were such a good friend, then why did you leave my brother, my family, like that?" Michael spat, stepping closer to her, his fists clenched.

Jordan shook her head. "I protected you," she said, her voice growing softer.

"Protected me?" Michael demanded. "You destroyed me."

"I saved your life," Jordan retorted bitterly.

"Saved me? You ruined me."

Jordan shook her head. "I murdered the baron for you."

Michael froze instantly, his gaze scanning her face. "You are mad." He turned away from her. "I don't know what you're talking about."

"How can you say that?" Jordan asked. "Don't you remember what was happening? What he was doing to you?"

Michael turned back to her. "What is there for me to remember?" he said, his anger churning, but his mind clearly racing at Jordan's questions. "That you are a murderer and a betrayer. I can remember that very easily."

Jordan looked at him for a long moment. "Michael, yes, I did kill the baron. But I killed him to stop him. I didn't mean to kill him . . . but when I saw him . . . when I saw him . . . over you . . ." Jordan paused to collect herself. She could almost see the beginnings of the memories returning in his eyes.

Michael shook his head again, fighting the memories. "It was your fault," he said, but the conviction had left his voice.

"Yes," Jordan agreed, anguish gripping her heart. "Yes, it was my fault. But not because I killed the baron. Because I was supposed to watch you. I left you alone to find a different hiding spot, an easier spot so that Fox could find me first. I thought you would be all right. I didn't know . . . when I found you, I was so afraid I was too late."

Then Jordan witnessed a strange change come over Michael. He stood very still for a very long time, frozen in place, frozen in his thoughts. Jordan saw the transformation in his eyes, saw the anger dissolve, saw the horrific memories returning with anguish. For the briefest of moments she saw the face of the young boy return to Michael's features, the sheer terror, the pain all resurfacing with a vengeance.

She stepped toward him, lifting a hand to his cheek. "It's all right, Michael," she whispered.

Suddenly, the door banged open and Evan rushed in with two guards. They ripped Michael away from Jordan, restraining him as he struggled in their hold.

"No!" Jordan cried. "Leave him alone."

Evan grabbed hold of her shoulders, spinning her around to face him. "Did he hurt you, Jordan?"

Jordan ignored his question, keeping her gaze on Michael. Michael twisted in his captors' arms, his face blank, his eyes seeing something else. "Stop it!" Jordan struggled in Evan's hold. "Let me go! Michael!"

Michael screamed out, but it wasn't the cry of a man. It was the same cry she'd heard echoing in her head for all these years, a little boy's cry.

His eyes flashed open, pinning Evan where he stood. "It was you!" Michael sobbed. "It was you."

"Get him out of here!" Evan ordered.

"You were the one!" Michael said as he was pulled toward the door. "It was you!"

Jordan turned a startled gaze to Evan.

"You were the one who brought me to the baron!" Michael shouted as he was pulled from the room.

CHAPTER THIRTY-TWO

Jordan turned wide eyes to Evan. Michael's accusation echoed in her ears as she stared in growing disbelief at the man she was supposed to marry. Could it be true? Was it even possible? Why would Michael say such a thing? A strong sense of unease churned in her stomach. The look in Michael's eyes had been filled with honest pain. Remembered suffering.

Evan sputtered. "The man is obviously a lunatic." He looked away from Jordan's hard stare.

Jordan yanked free of Evan's hold. His words did not sound convincing to her ears. "You brought him to the baron?" she gasped.

"Darling . . ." Evan shook his head in denial as he reached out for her.

Jordan pulled away from his touch. "Why? Why would you do that to Michael?" Jordan asked, trying to make sense of the insanity of it all. "Why would you do that to anyone?"

"I'm sure I have no idea what he was talking about."

Jordan scowled at Evan. Just the thought of Evan's doing what Michael had accused him of made her ill to her stomach with even the barest possibility of its being true disgusted her beyond words. She felt a warm rush in her throat and had to swallow back the nausea swirling through her.

Evan straightened. "He's done it again, hasn't he?"

Jordan lifted confused eyes to Evan.

"He's come between us," Evan continued.

"Michael?"

"No, Fox!" Evan exploded.

Jordan stepped away from him, away from his fierce anger as her own disgusted outrage grew. "This has nothing to do with Fox, Evan! This has to do with you."

"With me?" Evan gritted his teeth. "Michael is mad, Jordan! He parades around in his monk's robes and mutters to himself all day. He's as much of a lunatic as his father! Why are you even listening to him? Why do you even care what he says? He's full of lies!" Evan stepped closer to her. "All of the Mercers are full of lies! Don't you see that?"

Jordan shook her head, harshly denying his defamatory slurs. "No, you are wrong, Evan. They are not. Frederick Mercer lost everything because of me! And now I am hearing that all of their misery, all of *my* misery, is because of something you did!"

Evan glared at her, fuming in silence. Jordan could see the tension in his stiff shoulders, in the clenching of his jaw. "You disappoint me, Jordan." With that, he turned on his heel and left the room.

Jordan stared at the closed door for a moment. She

forced herself to stay calm. Disappoint him? She couldn't believe he felt disappointed in her when all she wanted was the truth. Then she suddenly remembered. Fox! She ran to the curtain and yanked it open, nearly pulling the fabric down in her hurry.

Fox was gone.

Jordan leaned out the alcove window and saw a rope hanging down the wall.

She pulled back into the room and sat in the seat near the window with a heavy sigh. Fox wanted to kill her, when just days before he wanted to hold her and love her. How had this happened? And how could she ever convince him that she never intended to kill the baron? How could he ever believe her? Yet, as she thought back on that day, she knew there could have been no other outcome, no other way to stop the baron.

She played absently with her necklace and her thoughts drifted back to Evan. If Michael's words were true, why would Evan bring Michael to the baron? And why did the baron die with a pouch with Evan's crest on it, full of gold? Was it some kind of payment?

No. No. Evan wasn't that kind of person. She had known him all her life. He would never do something so . . . so horrible. Was the baron a thief? Had he stolen it from Evan?

Jordan shook her head. The baron was wealthy. No, beyond wealthy. He had no need to steal. Perhaps Evan was under payment to the baron for some service. Yes, that must have been it. She wouldn't let herself believe that Evan had been paid to bring Michael to the baron. The thought was just too horrible.

And yet Michael's accusing words still echoed in her ears. They had the power of truth in them. And so did his eyes.

Jordan shook her head. *No, I can't believe it. I can't.*

She looked again at the rope that was hanging out the window. Her heart broke. And what of Fox? What could she do to convince him she had never meant to hurt him or his family, that she had killed the baron to defend Michael?

Then a thought struck her. Her letters, the ones she had asked Evan to deliver all those years ago. Evan had given them back to her, along with Fox's supposed words of refusal. The letters told everything.

Suddenly, Jordan knew exactly what she had to do. Fox had to see those letters from long ago. He had to read them. Only then would he realize she was telling the truth. He would know exactly what happened.

Unfortunately, the letters were at Castle Ruvane, tucked neatly in the bottom of the trunk at the foot of her bed. Somehow, some way, she had to get those letters to Fox. But how? Evan would never allow her to leave Castle Vaughn, much less travel to Castle Mercer.

Jordan sat back on the bench, her shoulders slumping. She could never get those letters to Fox. They had just gotten to Castle Vaughn and she wanted to leave again! Evan would never allow it. It would take a miracle to get away from Evan.

And then a thought struck her. Maybe not a miracle, just a lie.

Jordan had left the castle just before sunrise. Weary, excited, and desperate, she rode hard down the roads. She'd had the stable boy saddle a horse while she waited, and the castle guards had not stopped her as she rode beneath the outer gatehouse. She was not a prisoner . . . yet.

By midday, she had just turned down the road and could see the children's house. It took Jordan half the day to ride to the children. When she dismounted, she heard the gleeful shouts of the children playing down by the stream, perhaps getting water for the garden or taking a break from their chores.

Jordan dismounted and headed for the house. It was not the children she had come to see. She flung the door open to see Abagail following a naked Emily around the table. "Come here, child," she called.

But the toddler paid her no mind, dashing beneath the table and laughing.

Jordan watched as Abagail bent slowly to retrieve the girl, but Emily scooted away from Abagail, a huge smile lighting her face. Abagail finally sat on a chair, exhausted. Her usually tight bun was a mass of frantic strands, and her face was red from exertion.

Jordan's hopes sank. How could she ask Abagail to ride to Castle Ruvane and get the letters and then take them to Castle Mercer? The ride alone would wear her out.

Jordan stepped forward. She bent forward and ducked her head, smiling at Emily. The little girl cried out with joy and rushed into Jordan's outstretched arms. Jordan straightened.

Abagail was on her feet. "M'lady! I didn't see you come in."

"They're a handful today, aren't they?" Jordan asked kindly, if a bit sadly.

Abagail's shoulders slumped slightly and she nodded.

"I'll dress Emily," she said. "Why don't you rest?" Jordan took the clothes from the table and addressed Emily. "And you . . ." She tickled the girl's stomach and the child churned with laughter, twisting in Jordan's arms. "Let's get some clothes on this naked bottom."

Jordan left the house and went to sit on the grass. Emily squirmed as Jordan slid the dress over her head. She finished dressing the wiggling toddler and then sat back, letting the child run after a butterfly that flitted from flower to flower.

What was she to do now? All her hopes . . . There had to be another way, another person. She shook her head. She glanced over her shoulder in the direction of Castle Ruvane. She could get the letters. But Evan would send men for her soon, and when he didn't find her at the house, what would she tell him?

That she loved Fox and she would do anything to get him to understand why she killed the baron, why she destroyed his life?

And then Evan would lock her in the dungeon as a traitor.

"John!" Emily cried.

Jordan shifted her gaze to see the older boy carrying two buckets of water toward the house. He smiled at Emily as she ran over to him, carefully lifting the bucket away from her so she wouldn't get wet.

Jordan smiled. John was certainly getting big. He took such good care of Emily and helped Abagail quite a bit.

Slowly, revelation ran through Jordan. John! The solution to her problems was standing right in front of her. She shot to her feet. "John!" she called.

John turned to her. He put the buckets down as a large grin lit his face. As Emily dived for the water-filled buckets, John scooped her up from behind. He sauntered over to Jordan. "Hello, m'lady," he greeted.

"John," Jordan said, placing a hand on his shoulder.

She studied John's face for a long moment. "Would you do me a great favor?"

"Anything," John replied.

"It requires skill with a horse."

"You know I can ride very well," John responded confidently.

"And it requires riding through dangerous country."

"Mercer lands?" John asked, his eyes going wide with excitement.

Jordan nodded. Suddenly, she dreaded asking him to do this. There could be real danger for him. Her face turned serious. "It's important to me, John. Very important. First, you must get some letters from Ruvane Castle. At the foot of my bed, there's a trunk. They are on the very bottom of the trunk, a stack of old letters wrapped by a pink ribbon."

John nodded.

"Can you do that for me, John?" Jordan asked, hopefully. "Can you get the papers for me?"

He nodded, enthusiastically. "Do I get to get out of doing my chores for the day?"

"Yes," she admitted, smiling.

John let out a whoop and raced to Jordan's horse.

She picked up her skirts and ran after him. "Be careful, John," she said, quietly. "And be back before sunset."

"I'll do my very best!" John answered, staring down at her. Then he kicked the steed and it raced off down the road.

Jordan watched John go until he was out of sight around the curve in the road. Then she lifted her gaze to the sun. It was midday. He should make it back hours before sunset.

CHAPTER THIRTY-THREE

Jordan paced nervously before the house. John had not returned, and darkness was settling across the land. A glow of red from the setting sun coated the lands and gave Jordan an uneasy feeling.

She lifted her gaze to the road again. Where was John? Had some brigands set upon him? She cursed herself for sending the boy. She should have gone herself.

Suddenly, hoofbeats echoed down the road. Anxiously, Jordan stepped forward.

A lone rider came toward the house, moving quickly. It wasn't until he was almost at the house that Jordan could see John's face. Relief filled her in a heady sigh. She moved forward to meet him.

He was brandishing a stack of papers victoriously in one hand. "I found them!" he called out to her, handing them to her.

Jordan looked down at the stack of letters, bound by

a pink ribbon. He had found them! He had succeeded. She clutched the papers to her heart. Now Fox would know the truth. Now he would understand! "Good job, John!"

Suddenly, the ground shook. Jordan looked down the road. A group of soldiers rode hard toward the house, thundering down the road. Jordan waved John behind her with a quick flick of her hand.

John dismounted and stepped behind her. Close behind her.

Who were these men? Robbers? As they drew closer, she suddenly recognized the leader, and absolute dread filled her. Evan!

Jordan quickly, desperately, hid the letters behind her back. Her hand tightened convulsively around the stack of papers.

The door opened behind her, and the children and Abagail emerged from the house.

Jordan wanted to wave them into the house for protection, but she dared not move for fear of drawing Evan's gaze to the papers.

Evan dismounted before her, rushing to her and embracing her. "Thank God you're safe."

Jordan stood stiffly in his arms, sure he had seen the papers.

Evan's gaze scanned the group who stood mere feet from her. Then his gaze dropped to her. "What in heaven's name do you mean riding out like that?"

Jordan swallowed hard.

"Without a word to anyone! I thought that rogue, the Black Fox, had captured you again!"

Jordan chewed on her lower lip, her hand tightening protectively around the papers.

"Well?" Evan demanded.

Abagail stepped up to Evan. "Emily was sick this morn. I sent word to m'lady."

Evan's gaze narrowed as it speared through Abagail.

"That's right," John agreed. "Lady Jordan is the only one who can calm Emily when she is sick."

Suddenly, Jordan felt a tug from behind her. Someone was attempting to remove the letters from her hand! For a moment, she wouldn't release them until she realized it was Abagail.

Jordan relinquished the letters and stepped forward, drawing Evan's gaze. She took his arm and led him away from the group, giving Abagail time to hide the letters. "I'm sorry, Evan. But you know how impulsive I am with the children."

"God's blood, Jordan!" Evan exclaimed. "Do you realize how worried I was about you?"

"I said I was sorry," she replied absently, looking over her shoulder to see Abagail turning away from the group of soldiers.

"This will not happen again. You will return with me to Castle Vaughn at once," Evan told her.

Jordan bridled at the way he was commanding her about.

"It's for your own safety, Jordan," Evan said.

Jordan didn't like the way he said that, but she knew better than to argue with him when he was so enraged with her. She nodded her head. At least the letters were safe.

Fox rested in a warm valley of grass for the night. He knew he needed to concentrate on a plan. His friends were under heavy guard; he was able to discover that much in his quick foray into Castle Vaughn. He needed to figure out how to get them out, how to get them weapons. He tried to recall the layout of the castle, the hidden passageways he and Jordan and Evan had played in when they were children. Maybe somehow he could use those.

But strangely, the only image he could conjure up was of Jordan standing so righteously before him, waiting for him to kill her. He had wanted to. But his hand would not move, traitorous limb that it was. Only his heart had answered her, and its response had nothing to do with death or murder.

Fox forced his mind elsewhere. *What will Vaughn do to my men now that he has Jordan back?* Fox gritted his teeth. *Let them rot in the dungeon? Trade them for my life? Kill them?*

Fox stared at the twinkling lights above him. In the sky, two stars glistened like eyes the color of a flame's heart. Eyes that still trusted him.

Fox growled and rolled over onto his side. Sleep was going to be very elusive this night. What right did she have to trust him? After all these years, she did not know him.

He thought again, as he had a hundred times already, about what Jordan had told him. He still couldn't bring himself to believe what she had said. Jordan had killed the baron? She had confessed her crime to him. Jordan. Innocent Jordan. Why would she have done that? She had been barely out of childhood. Why would she have murdered that fat old fool the baron?

Michael. She had said something about Michael. But he couldn't remember much more. What did his little brother have to do with the baron? Nothing was making sense.

Why hadn't his father told him the truth? That was the greatest question of all. But then Fox had a strong feeling he already knew the answer. His honor dictated his silence. Honor was something his father practiced with every living breath. If he had made a promise or a vow to Jordan, then Fox knew his father would take it to his grave.

It was almost midnight when they reached Castle Vaughn, but Evan had insisted on riding through the night. Exhausted, Jordan made her way up to her room, but before she had taken two steps up the spiral stairway, Evan seized her arm, halting her.

"I was very worried for you, Jordan," Evan said quietly. "It was not very responsible of you to leave without telling anyone where you were going."

"I'm sorry," Jordan repeated for the hundredth time. "It's just that I've never had to tell people I was going to see the children before. And with Emily sick . . . I just didn't think."

"You should start," Evan said.

Something in his tone made Jordan pull back slightly, startled.

"For your own safety, you will tell me where you will be from this moment on," Evan added.

Jordan's mouth fell open, and she yanked her arm away from Evan so fiercely that she almost slammed it into the wall.

"Your father has entrusted me with your safety, a task I take very seriously. I wouldn't want anything to happen to my betrothed."

Apprehension filled Jordan and she turned away from Evan, moving up the stairs quickly. Betrothed. The word suddenly sent tremors of misgivings through Jordan. She almost raced to her room and shut the door behind her as if that would block Evan from marrying her . . . seal him out of her life.

But sooner or later she would have to confront him and tell him she had no intention of marrying him.

CHAPTER THIRTY-FOUR

Jordan moved through the hallways of Castle Vaughn, her thoughts centered on how she was going to get the letters to Fox. They were safe with Abagail, true, but that was nowhere near Castle Mercer.

Castle Mercer now seemed a very long way from here. A servant had told her about Evan's raid on Castle Mercer. Evan had gone there in the hopes of finally capturing the Black Fox, but Fox had been safe with her. In her arms. However, Evan had succeeded in capturing Fox's entire band of followers, and now they were imprisoned in the Vaughn dungeon.

Jordan moved past the large doors that led into the Great Hall, lost in thought, trying to figure out some way to get word to John to take the letters to Castle Mercer. She could write John a letter, but she didn't trust any of the guards to bring it to the boy. And besides, John didn't read.

The sound of several men laughing heartily caused her to pause. She quickly recognized one of the voices as belonging to Evan. She paused for a moment, steeling her nerves. She should tell him now she would not marry him and be done with it. Or should she wait for her father's return?

Evan chortled low in his throat. Something sinister in his laughter sent chills along Jordan's spine. She hugged the corridor shadows, moving closer to the open doorway, careful to avoid being seen.

"Which one are you choosing first?" she heard another man ask.

"That blond one," Evan replied. "His neck looks like it'll snap pretty easily."

More dark laughter from the others made Jordan cringe. Beau. He was the blond one, Jordan remembered. But what did they mean about his neck snapping?

"Then who?"

"I think that woman next. She might dangle on the end of the rope for a while and give us a good show."

The cruelty in Evan's statement made Jordan's blood run cold. He had said it so calmly, so matter-of-factly. But for some reason she did not feel as shocked as she thought she ought to. Was she finally seeing Evan for what he really was?

"So we begin tonight?" a third man asked.

"Yes," Evan responded. "Tonight at midnight. The Black Fox will arrive just in time to see us throw the first corpse into the moat." Evan laughed a cold, evil laugh.

"What will you do if he gives himself up?"

"That's quite simple," Evan replied. "We will kill them all. And that will be a fitting end to the Black Fox and his band of thieves. Either way, I will be rid of Fox Mercer and his outlaws forever."

Jordan felt her blood run even colder. Evan was going to hang them all, starting tonight! Jordan quickly moved down the hallway away from the Great Hall. She had to stop him. But how?

"I'll take that," Jordan said to the servant girl.

The girl lifted surprised brown eyes to look at Jordan. "But, m'lady, it's me job to bring the guards their food."

Jordan ignored the girl's comment and took the tray of food and the flask from the young woman. "I haven't seen those fine men in quite some time. I would like to say hello."

The servant girl looked at Jordan with curious eyes for a moment.

"That will be all."

The servant girl quickly curtsied. "As you wish, m'lady."

Jordan waited a moment until the girl disappeared around the hallway corner before moving down the murky stairs toward the dungeon. She made it halfway down the cracked stone steps before pausing near a guttering torch hanging on the wall. She set the tray down and reached into the pocket of her dress, pulling out several dried herbs. She had gone to the herbalist after concocting a plan to free Fox's men from the dungeon, and had complained of sleeplessness to the old woman. The herbalist had given her some crinkled old leaves and told her to mix them with an ale, and after but one drink she would be asleep faster than the king collected taxes.

Jordan opened the flask and crumbled two leaves into it, then quickly recorked it. *That should put the guards to sleep long enough for me to get Fox's men out,* she thought. She hesitated, then uncorked the flask to shred a third leaf into the ale. *Just to be certain,* she thought. She shook the corked flask, mixing up the new ingredients.

She continued her descent down the stone stairs, balancing the tray carefully. Raucous laughter just ahead warned her that she was almost to her destination. A light from the bottom of the stairs made her pause, her hand tightening around the tray. For a brief moment, she thought of turning around and heading back up the stairs. But there was no time for that—no time to think of the consequences, no time to think of other possibilities, other plans. The time was now to attempt this craziness. She forced her grip on the tray to relax. Then she took a deep breath and stepped out into the room.

Her heart sank.

There were four guards in the room where she had thought there would be only two.

Two guards sat around a table, scavenging at what looked like the remains of their previous meal. Another guard strolled back and forth across the floor, obviously bored with his turn at watch. Still another guard sat in the corner, sharpening his sword.

When they noticed her presence, the two guards at the table straightened, one quickly wiping the back of his sleeve across his greasy mouth. The guard in the corner stopped drawing the rock across the blade and slowly craned his neck up to study her curiously. The guard's pacing halted momentarily.

"Good evening, sirs," Jordan greeted them, forcing herself to move forward into the heart of the room.

"Lady Jordan," the pacing guard said. "What brings you to the dungeon?"

"I came to see to your needs," she said. She moved to the table and set the tray of food down, then grabbed the flask of ale and raised it. "Anyone thirsty?"

One of the sitting guards rose and jumped forward to relieve her of the flask. "Thank you, m'lady." The man quickly uncorked the bottle and drank deeply. He passed the flask to his seated dining companion and he, too, took a long drink.

"Hey, give it 'ere. Bloody hell, mate," the pacing guard cursed. He took the flask from the seated guard and took a healthy swig of its contents, then lowered the flask and made a sour face. He reached into his mouth and pulled out a small flake, flicking the herb fragment to the stone floor. He spit out another, trying several times to get the tiny piece of wet leaf off his tongue.

Jordan felt her face going pale.

"Bloody heathens. Can't anyone make a decent ale anymore," the pacing guard exclaimed. He held the flask out to the guard in the corner, who had resumed sharpening his blade with the stone. " 'Ere, mate."

The guard in the corner shook his head.

He wasn't going to drink it. Jordan felt her heart rise up into her throat. Now what? Her plan would all be for naught if one of the guards was still awake! And what would he do when he saw his fellows suddenly dropping off to sleep!

The pacing guard took another drink. He lowered the flask to look at Jordan. "Is there something else, m'lady?"

Again, Jordan forced herself to remain calm. "No," she replied. "Thank you." She looked at the guards at the table who were already eating heartily from the platter of food she had brought. The eyelids of the greasy-mouthed guard already seemed to appear heavy to her. She turned back to the pacing guard. "Well, have a good watch, men."

The pacing guard nodded and moved toward the food.

Jordan turned and moved out of the room, heading for

the stairs. She heard the guards talking as she moved into the shadowed stairwell and she paused at the bottom to listen, careful to stay out of sight.

"You better not be taking that mutton leg, or I'll bash you over the head with it," she heard the pacing guard say.

"She's quite a sight, ain't she, boys?" she heard another say, but couldn't figure out whose voice it was. "I'd give a bag o' gold to give her a romp, eh?"

The men laughed.

Jordan felt an angry blush rise into her cheeks.

"Give me some o' that before you drain it dry, you dog," a gruff voice demanded.

Jordan thought for a moment it was the pacing guard speaking, but then after a moment she realized it wasn't him. She prayed it was the guard who had been sharpening the sword, but there was nothing she could do about it now. And she couldn't just stand in the stairway. She might be caught, and she would have a devil of a time explaining what she was doing. She would have to leave and come back later to see if the old woman's potion worked.

She headed back up the stairs.

Jordan moved into the Great Hall and had one of the serving women bring her an ale. She sat alone at one of the long tables, sipping her warm drink as servants bustled about her doing their nightly chores and duties.

"Hello, Jordan," a voice whispered in her ear.

Jordan jumped, startled by the sudden, close greeting, and sloshed ale all across the table in front of her. She sat stock still for a moment, collecting herself, biting back a hot retort. She glanced up to see Evan moving around the table to sit across from her.

"You'll be happy to know I am setting a trap for the Black Fox," Evan said. "You can rest easy."

Jordan felt a moment of panic, but she forced it aside. "You couldn't capture him before, Evan. Why do you think you can now?"

Evan leaned across the table closer to her. "I have something he wants," he whispered.

Jordan nodded. "His men."

"Not quite," Evan said.

Jordan looked at him, scowling.

Evan brushed her chin with a gentle, if a bit possessive, caress. "I will not give you up, Jordan," he said in a soft voice. "Not ever."

Something cold in his tone, something challenging, put all of Jordan's nerves on edge. She took another drink from her ale, avoiding his stare.

When she glanced up, he was gone.

Jordan slowly made her way back down the stairs that led to the dungeon. She already had a reason to give the guards for her return. She would say she was coming back to get the tray. She reached the bottom of the stairs and cautiously peered around the corner into the room.

This time, her heart soared.

The sleeping powder had worked! Three of the guards were slumped over the table, all of them snoring loudly. The fourth was on the floor not too far from the table, fast asleep. Jordan grabbed the candle and started searching for the keys, quickly finding them dangling from a hook on the wall near the table. She grabbed the keys and turned back to head deeper into the dungeon toward the cells.

But froze in her tracks as she saw the guard laying on the floor staring right at her.

CHAPTER THIRTY-FIVE

Jordan held her breath, her feet rooted to the stone floor, as the dungeon guard looked at her with a strangely blank stare. For the briefest of moments, he struggled to raise his head off the floor, but then his eyelids grew heavy and finally closed. Jordan watched him for a long moment, but he did not move again. She let out a soft, slow breath.

Jordan quickly moved down the hallway to the first dungeon door. She unlocked the large padlock, threw the bolt aside, and stepped into the room.

Darkness greeted her. The candle she held in her hand cast only a small circle of illumination around her. "Beau?" she called, unable to see in the dark, "Scout?"

"Jordan?" Michael's voice came to her from out of the blackness.

Jordan stepped forward, the candlelight washing over a small group of battered men and one woman. They winced and cringed from the light, holding up their hands to protect their eyes.

"I'm here to free you," Jordan said.

Jordan stared up the stairs from the bottom of the dungeon, chewing her bottom lip anxiously. Behind her, the guards all still slept soundly.

Beau stood by Pick's side near Jordan. Scout had her arm around Smithy who was limping badly. Frenchie moved up to Pick, cautiously stepping over one of the snoring guards. "What are we waitin' for?" he demanded in a harsh whisper.

"You must be careful and watch out for the changing of the gatehouse guards," Jordan said. "This is all I can do to help you."

Michael emerged from the darkness, approaching her.

Beau stepped protectively in front of Jordan.

Michael stopped before him, his stare on Jordan. "You have to come with us," he said.

Shocked, Jordan stared at him. She should go with them. There was only a life she wanted nothing to do with here. Yet how could she abandon the children? She shook her head. "I can't leave the children," Jordan answered.

"We can bring them with us," Michael said hopefully.

Grateful that he was treating her as a friend, grateful that he was trying to find an answer, Jordan grinned glumly at him. "They can't live like that. I can't force them to go back to scrounging for food."

"When they find out what happened, you'll be in danger," Beau said.

Jordan shook her head. "Evan would never hurt me."

"You don't know him as well as I do. I remember

everything now. I know what he is capable of. Come with us."

With all her heart she wanted to go with them. She wanted to be with Fox, but she would not abandon the children. Some way, somehow, she would figure out a plan of safety for them. Only then would she return to Fox.

Jordan shook her head. "No. You'd best go quickly. You have to get out of the castle before an alarm is sounded." She glanced at the guards. "You have to go before they wake up. The sleeping potion will wear off soon."

Beau squeezed her hand as he passed. Frenchie nodded his head. Jordan watched them move up the stairs, regretting with every fiber of her being that she could not join them.

Michael paused before the spiral stairs and looked back at her. "You're making a mistake about this, Jordan. Fox cares very deeply for you."

Jordan shook her head, but she felt the tears welling in her eyes. "I know," she whispered. "I'll find him as soon as I see the children to safety. I just can't leave them."

Michael returned to her. "Let us help you, Jordan. We can see the children to your father's castle. Surely there they would be safe."

Castle Ruvane. Yes. Here, she was a prisoner, but in her father's castle she and her children would be safe.

"Don't abandon us again," Michael whispered. "He wouldn't be able to stand it."

And neither would she. Jordan nodded.

Michael took her hand, a grin of satisfaction and approval lighting his face.

"The children are in a cottage on Ruvane lands just

north of the Mercer border. It shouldn't take but half a day to get to them if we can find some horses," Jordan whispered as they moved up the stairs. "We can get the children and then head for Castle Ruvane."

Michael nodded.

The others had halted at the top of the stairs, and they glanced back as Jordan joined them. She nodded and the group started out of the darkness and down the hallway. Jordan led the way toward the Great Hall and the large double doors that led to the inner courtyard. She would have the stable boy saddle horses for them. Maybe Beau and Pick could help to hurry things along.

She halted as she heard footsteps echoing down the hallway. She moved back a step and bumped into Michael. The footsteps disappeared into an open doorway.

Jordan waited until she heard the door close and then let out a sigh of relief. She continued forward until they were only steps away from the large double doors and freedom.

"Jordan!"

Jordan froze and looked up. Evan was strolling toward her down the hallway just before the Great Hall. Panic streaked through Jordan. She instinctively stepped forward to greet Evan, hoping to put enough distance between herself and Fox's friends for Evan not to notice them.

"What in heaven's name are doing up so late?" he asked.

"I couldn't sleep," she answered softly. "I . . . I was worried."

"About what?" Evan wondered.

"Emily," Jordan said. "She was sick and . . . well, I just hope she is doing better."

"I can send a man to check," Evan offered.

"No!" Jordan said a little too emphatically. "I mean, I'm sure she is all right. I think all I need is an ale."

Evan nodded. He held out his hand.

Jordan hesitated for a moment. It was almost as good as a shackle. If she took his hand, she sealed her fate, but she ensured the escape of the others. Jordan nodded and placed her hand on Evan's.

Jordan raced into her room. She had sat with Evan for what seemed like an eternity, waiting for a cry of alarm to ring out. But total silence had engulfed them. There were no shouts, no cry of alarm. She hoped Beau and the others had escaped, and something in her heart told her they had gotten away without being detected.

Jordan knew she had to leave Castle Vaughn before Evan discovered that the prisoners were gone. But first she had to get the children out of the cottage so they would be safe. Castle Ruvane was her only hope.

She donned a cloak and moved toward the doorway, planning to sneak out of the castle in the middle of the night. She should have felt horrible. She should have felt devious sneaking around like this. But she didn't. Not when confronted with someone as untrustworthy as Evan.

Jordan stepped out into the corridor, shutting the door quietly behind her. She moved down the corridor to the spiral stairway and descended toward the main hallway.

Outside, thunder rumbled. Jordan paid the weather no heed as she stepped from the stairway into the corridor. She was already formulating the trip to Castle Ruvane. They would ride in the wagon, using her horse to pull it.

For the thousandth time, she wished her father were here. He would see to it she was safe. He would protect the children. But he still might very well take Evan's side about the marriage.

Jordan moved past the Great Hall quietly, hoping Evan had retired for the night, and toward the large double doors of the castle. She opened the door, pausing to gaze out at the sheets of rain that pelted the earth. The storm had arrived so quickly!

"A very nasty night for a stroll, wouldn't you say?"

Jordan whirled to find Evan standing behind her. Fear gripped her in its taloned fist. For a moment, she couldn't say anything.

"Tell me why you find it necessary to go out in this horrible weather."

Jordan straightened slightly. "I was worried about the children."

"Always the children, isn't it?" He shook his head and took hold of her arm, pulling her back into the castle. "They are safe." He closed the door behind her.

Jordan swallowed hard, watching with growing dread as her escape route was cut off. She pulled against Evan's hold. "You can't be sure. I—"

"There is another matter I would speak with you about."

Jordan's heart hammered in her chest. She allowed him to lead her into the Great Hall, knowing there was no escape.

Evan led her to the hearth. The dancing firelight flickered over her body, but she felt none of its warmth. Evan released her and leaned his arm against the mantel, staring into the fire for a long moment. He reached in and picked up a stick that was burning on one end. "The prisoners have escaped," he said quietly.

Jordan waited for the accusations to come, waited for his rage to surface.

"They had an accomplice."

Was he mocking her? Testing her? "Evan," she said, taking a step forward. "Why have you felt the need to lie to me all these ten years?" She had to take the opportunity to go on the offensive before he did.

"Lie?" he asked, turning to her. His eyes were strangely alight.

"The letters . . ." she began.

He rolled his eyes. "We went through all that before."

"But you never gave me a real answer. Why didn't you take them to Fox? Why weren't they sent to the king? They should have known—"

"Known what?" he demanded, stepping toward her with the glowing stick clenched in his hand. "That you were a murderer?"

Jordan gasped. "You read them!"

Evan began to pace. "That you should have been stripped of your title, your lands?" He stopped suddenly. "Never." He tossed the stick back into the fire. He stared into the fire for a long moment. "Don't you see, Jordan? I was protecting you. I couldn't marry some commoner. Some peasant woman."

"How dare you make that choice for me?"

Evan looked over his shoulder at her. "You were emotional. You were incoherent. You were feeling guilty. I couldn't let you make that choice. The wrong choice."

"I asked you to deliver the letters for me. I trusted you to do that." Jordan stepped away from him. "And you lied to me. I didn't want to believe it, Evan. I didn't want to think you would do that. How can I marry you now?"

Evan turned to her, straightening. "You would deny becoming my wife because I didn't send your letters ten years ago?"

Jordan shook her head. She opened her mouth to reply, but Evan held up his hand.

"Think carefully before you answer," Evan warned.

Something in his voice was dark and scary.

"The prisoners that escaped . . . they couldn't have done it alone. We found some ale that the guards drank. It was tainted with some sort of sleeping herb." Evan lifted his eyes to her. "Do you know what the penalty for aiding criminals is?"

Jordan's hands clutched together. She swallowed.

"The dungeon," Evan whispered. "Or possibly death."

Jordan's mouth suddenly felt very dry. She had to see her children safely to Castle Ruvane. She had to. Death. She lifted her chin slightly.

"You see," Evan said softly, "even now I protect you."

"Are you threatening me?" Jordan asked.

"Do I have a reason to threaten you?" Evan wondered.

"Don't do this, Evan," Jordan retorted. "You know. You know what happened in the dungeon."

Evan nodded. "Yes. But no one else needs to know."

If I marry you, Jordan silently finished the sentence. She had abandoned Fox ten years ago. She would not make that mistake again. She shook her head. "I can't, Evan," she said. "I don't love you."

Evan's jaw clenched. He looked at the ceiling, at the hallway, at the Great Hall doors. "I've waited for you for ten years." His fist clenched and unclenched. He took a deep breath. He stared at the ceiling for a long moment before facing her. "I have no doubt that the prisoners and the Black Fox will return for vengeance."

He was acting as though he hadn't heard her. "Evan—"

Evan's voice rose to override any interruption from

her. "I knew you would be worried about the safety of the children."

Jordan froze, fear spearing through her body.

"So I took the liberty of seeing them to safety." He swept his hand toward the door of the Great Hall.

Jordan followed his movement to see all of her children standing forlornly in the doorway of the Great Hall. Two armored guards were standing behind them.

Jordan began to shake. She moved to run to them, but Evan bolted forward, his hand capturing her arm, stilling her movement.

"Again I protect your welfare."

Jordan pulled her arm free and raced across the Great Hall to her children. "Are you all right? Is everyone all right?' " She tried to embrace all of them in a protective hold, but they didn't fit. She couldn't hold them all. She couldn't protect all of them against Evan. She looked into their faces.

They weren't hurt. Maybe scared, but unharmed.

Jordan pulled Emily into her arms and stood slowly.

"What's happening, Lady Jordan?" John wondered softly. "Why are we here?"

Jordan turned to face Evan.

A smug, if not somewhat disappointed, look washed over his face as he watched the tender scene.

He had her exactly where he wanted.

CHAPTER THIRTY-SIX

Fox sat in the darkness staring at the dark silhouette of Castle Vaughn. He had managed to steal a dagger from one of the guards who had carelessly left it on one of the battlements. Fox flipped the dagger in his hand. It wasn't much aid to him in helping his friends.

He had not taken his eyes from Castle Vaughn. Jordan was there somewhere. What was she doing? Was she looking out into the darkness thinking of him?

The thought sent agony through him. Why had she done it? He couldn't in his wildest imaginings ever think that Jordan would kill anyone, let alone a baron!

He turned his gaze from the castle. All his life had been centered on Vaughn and how his life would end. Now, Fox found that his anger and vengeance had been misdirected. He felt lost. He felt confused.

Suddenly, like the smoke from a chimney, Fox noticed a plume of puffy smoke lifting skyward. Something was on fire. It seemed to be coming from Ruvane lands. Somewhere in the vicinity of . . .

His eyes widened slightly.

The cottage!

Fox rose and mounted his horse. He was going to get no sleep tonight. He might as well find out what was burning, and check up on Mary Kate.

As he rode down the road, an acrid smell suddenly stung his nostrils. It was faint, but still a very familiar smell. The biting smell of smoke. He scanned the surroundings as his horse continued on. Great plumes of black smoke rose into the sky just west of his position, forming dark clouds in the otherwise clear air.

He jerked the horse to a halt, studying the smoke as it billowed upward. The puffs of white against the black night seemed to be coming from the Ruvane lands. The outer reaches of the Ruvane lands, by the looks of it.

Dread seized Fox's heart. It could only be the children. There were no other houses out here. The children had no one to protect them.

And then another chilling thought froze his spine. What if Jordan was with the children now? Trapped in the blaze with them?

Fox spurred his horse on. When he rounded the road before the house, his worst fears were realized. The house was smoldering, still smoking, a burnt-out skeleton of what he had seen before. He reined his horse in and stared in shock. What had happened?

His gaze dropped to the dirt path before the house. He could make out several sets of tracks. Riders. It looked like a half dozen or so from the hoofprints. He lifted his gaze to the surrounding woods, but the trees were still and the bushes seemed empty. He scanned the area around the house for any sign of a trap.

And saw someone lying near the side of the house.

Jordan! Fox quickly dismounted and raced over to the prone figure, fighting back the queasiness churning in his stomach. As he neared the figure, he saw it was a woman lying in a large puddle of blood. Fox moved to her side, carefully turning her over.

It wasn't Jordan. It was the old woman who had run the place. Abagail. She groaned softly and opened her eyes.

"Rest easy," Fox told her.

"The children," she moaned, clutching her side.

Fox looked down to see that her cotton dress was ripped and an ugly, gaping sword wound spurted blood. Fox instantly knew it was a fatal wound; she had lost far too much blood already. He was surprised she was still alive at all. Fox knew all he could do was try to make her comfortable in her last moments.

She grabbed at his shirt with what must have been the last ounce of strength she had left. "He's taken the children."

"Who? Who's taken the children? Who did this?"

"Lady Jordan is in danger," she gasped, clenching her teeth against the pain.

Fox scowled as her fingers tightened around his tunic.

"You have to get to her."

"Where is she?" Fox asked. "Is she here?"

"Lord Vaughn . . ." The old woman paused as she sucked in a deep breath. "He has her."

"Did he do this?" Fox asked.

Abagail nodded her head, wincing. "You're the only one who can . . ." Her voice faded and she jerked her hand from the ground, reaching into the front part of her dress.

Fox watched her for a moment, thinking her heart was hurting her. When she removed her hand from her dress, she held a bundle of papers tied with a neat pink ribbon.

Abagail held the parchment out to Fox. "She loves you so," she whispered.

Fox took the bundle from her hand, studying it.

Suddenly, Abagail's eyes rolled back into her head and her last breath released from her body in a soft gush of air.

Fox looked at her for a final moment. Then he set her head down on the ground carefully. He stared at her for another long, sorrowful moment. She had been a good friend of Jordan's and had done her best to help with the children when she could, and all she had gotten for her troubles was a pointless death at the hands of Evan Vaughn. He lifted his gaze to the burned-out shell of a house, his jaw clenching tight.

Where had Vaughn taken the children? *Why* had he taken them? Dark and unsettling thoughts filled Evan's mind. He had an impending sense of doom shrouding his future. Jordan, his men, the children—all of their lives were in peril. All were the prisoners of a wretchedly devious man.

He clenched his fist and crumbled the bundle of parchment. He looked down at it.

A thin ribbon tied the papers together, a simple pink bow holding the package together. There must have been thirty rolled parchments all bound together. What the devil could they be? Fox wondered. And from whom?

Fox pulled the pink ribbon, opening the stack of parchments, and the documents spilled onto the ground. He picked one up and gazed at the crest stamped in the wax that sealed the letter closed.

The Ruvane crest.

Fox stared at the crest for a long time. He glanced at the other letters. All of them were sealed, all unopened. The edges of all of the parchments were crinkling, shriveled and old. They had obviously been sitting somewhere for a long time. Fox grabbed one of the letters and ripped open the seal, gently unfurling the old parchment. There was a spider web inside, smeared across the leathery paper, and he dusted it away before reading the letter.

Fox,

I know you will never forgive me for what I have done, for the terrible misfortune I have brought to your family. But I want you to know what happened. Your father has told me not to tell this to anyone, but I must tell you. Please don't tell him I wrote you this letter.

As you know, your father took most of the visiting lords out hunting that day. He charged me with watching Michael. I love Michael like a brother, you know that, so I gladly agreed. But when you came back from the hunting party early, how could I resist playing hide and seek with you? It is my favorite game! I would have played even if it had not been my favorite.

Michael wanted to play, too. I found the best hiding spot for him—behind the flour bags in the storage room. You counted and I hid in your horse's stall. Remember? You found me almost immediately because I couldn't stop giggling. Then you went looking for Michael. I went to find him behind the flour bags, but he wasn't there. I thought he had found a new hiding place. You know how he loves to hide inside the wardrobe cabinet in his room. So I went to his room to look for him.

I found him, Fox. I found him.

Fox paused for a moment, brushing away another spider web from the parchment, then continued to read.

It is hard for me to tell you what happened next. Because it was my fault. . . .

The baron was standing over him, over Michael, holding his head, pushing his face down into the straw mattress. Michael was strangely still. His breeches were pulled down to his knees. It was awful, Fox.

The baron heard me enter the room and quickly turned to me. I didn't know what to do. I called Michael's name, but Michael didn't move. Then the baron let him go. He shoved Michael aside and struggled with his pants. Then he came right at me. His eyes were filled with hate, Fox, an ugly, ugly hate. He reached into his tunic and pulled out a dagger. He told me he was going to kill me. And after he finished with Michael, he was going to do the same to me.

I screamed and raced for the door, but the baron caught my hair. I turned and clawed his face in my panic. He raised the dagger and tried to strike at me, but I caught his hand and twisted his wrist as much as I could. He was still coming toward me and . . . he tripped. He fell toward me, the dagger coming down. Somehow, something happened.

We landed on the floor, he on top of me. Something warm spread across my stomach. Something sticky. I tried to push him away, but he was so big that all

I could do was squirm out from beneath him. I was ready to run. But he didn't move.

Then I saw the blood start to seep out from beneath him, moving toward me. I backed up a step and as I looked down at the floor, I saw my dress was stained with red. I lifted my hands to touch it. But they were covered with red, too. It took a moment for me to realize that it was blood on my hands, on my clothing. I started to cry and scream.

Your father came in and hugged me and helped calm me. Michael was fine, thank the Lord. Your father made us both leave the room immediately. He brought me to your mother's room. He cleaned me up himself and bid me change into one of the dresses I kept at your castle for when we visited.

Fox, he made me promise not to say anything to anyone. He didn't want anyone to know Michael or I was involved. I was so scared that I gave my word. I didn't know then that the baron was dead. I didn't know until the day they took your title and lands away. I didn't know. But I had given my word. Your father made me promise again. He said I had saved Michael's life and now he was saving mine. He told me that if the king knew I had killed the baron then I, too, would be killed. I would be hanged or burned at the stake. The baron was like a brother to the king. I was scared, Fox. I was so scared.

Fox looked up from the parchment, realizing for the first time how much Jordan had needed him all this time. He glanced down at the pile of parchments. Jordan had been just as alone as he all these years. Alone with her shame and guilt. She must have felt that he had abandoned her as much as he thought she had abandoned him. Fox realized with a burning pain in his heart that all of this happened because she had saved Michael from a monster.

His hand ached and he looked down at it to find it curled tightly around the parchment as another memory struck him hard. He remembered that just as he was leaving Jordan's room, just as he was climbing down the rope, he thought he heard Michael accuse Evan of bringing him to the baron. It had made no sense then. But now—now it all made sense.

All of his misery, all of Jordan's misery. Everything! It was all because of Evan Vaughn!

A crackle of bushes and Fox whirled, his sword out, his lips curled with rage.

He half expected Vaughn to be standing there, half hoped he would be.

But what he saw made him lower his sword.

CHAPTER THIRTY-SEVEN

Beau held up his hands. "We surrender."

Fox moved forward quickly. "What the devil are you doing out?"

"Disappointed that you won't be able to rescue us?" Beau wondered.

"Lady Jordan freed us," Pick told him.

"Fox," Michael added, "she gave the guards a sleeping potion. When Evan finds out, she'll be in great danger."

Fox's jaw clenched and he looked back at the smoldering cottage. "I think he already knows." Fox stalked back to his horse and swung himself up.

"Where are you going?" Beau asked.

Fox looked into the dark forest toward Castle Vaughn. "I'm going to free Jordan."

"Is he afraid to show his face?!" Fox demanded.

Fox sat atop his horse before the castle, riding back

and forth before the moat. The drawbridge was raised, the castle not yet open. Fox whirled his horse, charging across the field before the castle. "Where is your lord?" he demanded of the battlement guards staring down at him. The rising sun splashed over the guards, and the shifting patterns of light and dark shadows slithered across their faces, making them all appear grotesque.

"Enough! I am here, you black dog! Have you come to surrender?"

Fox spun his horse around to see Evan staring down at him from the battlements. But what caught Fox's eye was Jordan at his side. Mixed feelings warred within him. Was she there as a prisoner or by choice? At least Vaughn had not harmed her.

"You hide behind Jordan like a coward!" Fox called. "Come and face me."

"You must be mad!" Evan called down from the walkways of the castle.

Jordan jerked forward, but was pulled back.

"I have come to claim what is rightfully mine."

"I will never give up your lands!" Vaughn hollered down.

"I have come for my betrothed. Give Jordan to me and I will leave you in peace."

There was a long moment of silence. Fox locked eyes with Jordan. She turned to Evan and must have said something harsh to him because Evan shoved her roughly away from him. Fox gritted his death.

"She isn't yours! She will never be yours! Surrender to me now or I will have my archers shoot you down," Evan commanded.

"Come and face me, Vaughn. Come fight me," Fox called. "I have already beaten you once. And I would thoroughly enjoy doing so again. They still say you are the best fighter in these lands. I say they are wrong, and I stand here before you to prove it.''

''Why would I accept your challenge?'' Evan demanded.

''Because if you don't, your villagers and guards will know what a coward you truly are.'' Fox reined in his horse and circled again, staring at the walkways, wondering if at this very moment they were preparing an archer to shoot him down.

Jordan reappeared at Evan's side and he again shoved her abruptly away after a brief exchange with her. ''I accept your challenge!'' Evan hollered. ''To the death! I will meet you at midday in the Vaughn field!''

Fox ran the stone across his sword, sharpening the blade. He had been impulsive. One might even call him foolish. But Fox refused to think of that. He had no armor, only a sword and a steed. Still, he felt undaunted. Righteous. He had to win the battle for Jordan.

He sat at the far end of Vaughn field, awaiting Vaughn. He had arrived hours early, honing his skills, practicing, preparing his weapons. But his mind could not erase the concern and worry he had seen on Jordan's face.

Always worry for others. Never a concern over her own fate.

He lifted his head toward the road. He hoped his friends were all right, although he knew they were. They always were. They were probably on their way back to Castle Mercer—Pick and Beau arguing, no doubt.

Fox grinned and ran the stone across the blade again.

Mary Kate. Where had Vaughn taken the children? Did Jordan know? He hoped so. He hoped she was there to watch over them.

Because after the battle they would either be free . . . or Fox wouldn't be around to worry about them.

Jordan watched Fox across the field, preparing his weapons. He inspected the length of his sword and then sheathed it. Anxiety filled her. She had goaded Evan enough on the battlements to get him to accept Fox's challenge. She had been trying to buy some time, hoping Fox would flee. But now, as the battle was about to begin, she wondered if she had done the right thing.

Fox lifted his head and their eyes met for a moment. Anguish filled Jordan. Why was he doing this? He had said he had come to claim his betrothed. Her. Had he really meant those words? Or was this just his way of getting back at Evan? Was he using her to take revenge?

Her gaze swung angrily to Evan, who stood nearby watching Fox. He turned his gaze to her. His mouth grimaced and he strolled to a soldier who stood a mere two feet from her. "I will take no chances," Evan told him. "If I can't have her, then no one will." He glanced at Fox, then back at the soldier. "If he wins, kill her."

Complete and utter dread washed over Jordan.

The soldier swung his gaze to Jordan, then back to Evan. "Yes, my lord."

Evan locked gazes with Jordan. His eyes looked cold and dark and sinister. In that instant, she realized everything she had heard about him was true. Everything Michael had tried to warn her about was true. He was heartless and selfish. He would do everything he could to win. And if he couldn't, he would make sure Fox didn't, either.

Jordan looked desperately at Fox. He was already

mounting his steed, preparing for the battle. She couldn't even warn him!

Evan swung himself up onto his horse, then turned to face Fox. Fox was already fully mounted, facing him. Each man grabbed a lance.

The field became very quiet, very still. The sun continued to slowly inch its way into the sky, heralding the middle of the day. Jordan wasn't certain if the day would be a new beginning for her, or the beginning of the end. She stood nervously on the platform that bordered the center of the field, praying for a new beginning.

Then Fox spurred his horse forward. Evan immediately did the same. The two horses galloped toward each other, their hooves pounding the ground. Mud splattered up behind them. Fox leveled his lance at Evan, gripping the long pole steadily. Evan mirrored his move, lowering his pole.

Suddenly, Fox's steed slipped on the slick earth and Fox yanked on the reins, steering his steed away from Vaughn. Jordan gasped as Evan's lance struck a glancing blow to Fox's arm.

Jordan watched in horror as Fox teetered in the saddle, favoring his arm, grimacing in pain. She gripped the wooden railings on the platform tightly, dreading the worst. But then he quickly righted himself, staying tall in the saddle. Jordan forced her fingers to relax as Fox spurred his horse across the field again. He reached for another lance leaning against the wooden fence.

As Fox turned, Evan was already charging. Fox charged forward, lowering his lance, whether because of some plan or because of the pain in his clenched jaw, Jordan couldn't tell.

Evan had gotten the jump on him and his lance was

leveled at Fox. Fox lifted his lance at the last moment, knocking Evan's away.

Fox rode his horse past where Jordan stood, moving quickly for another lance. As he passed her, Jordan saw blood on Fox's left arm, the dark red liquid dripping to the muddy ground below him. It was his old wound, the one she had inflicted with her own dagger. Evan's blow had reopened it. She instinctively jerked toward Fox, but the soldier beside her put a restraining hand on her arm. Jordan glared hotly at the soldier and jerked her arm free.

She turned back to face the field. The two men were already turning for another round. Both of them reined in their horses, pausing for a moment.

Fox drew his sword.

Evan flipped up his visor, and a grin stretched across his lips before he slammed his faceplate back into place.

They began again, charging across the field toward each other. Evan hunched low in his saddle, readying himself for the finishing blow.

Fox leaned forward, but not to the degree Evan did. He held the lance in one hand, his sword at the ready beside him.

The horses drew closer, their speed increasing.

Jordan's heart pounded.

Suddenly, just before the lances struck, Fox whirled his sword, smashing it against Evan's lance. The lance spun away, jarring Evan. At the same time, Fox leaned forward and his lance struck Evan's shield, hard, knocking him backward. Evan tried to hold on to the reins, but the combined impacts were brutal, pushing him back and off of his horse.

Evan landed in the mud of the field with a dull thud.

Joy filled Jordan and she turned her gaze to Fox. Fox staggered in his saddle, slowing his animal to a stop. He swung one leg from his horse to clumsily dismount. His sword dragged in the mud as he approached Evan. He held his other arm tightly to his side.

His face was twisted in pain. Fox was hurt! Jordan wanted to run to him, to help him. But she could not interfere.

Evan pushed himself to his feet, drawing his sword as Fox approached. "Surrender to me now, Mercer, and I will make your death quick," Evan called.

Fox answered with a silent, swift attack, his strength seemingly renewed. He swung his sword with two hands, driving the blade at Evan's head. Evan blocked the blow and countered with a thrust.

Fox sidestepped the strike, whirling to attack again and again.

Evan blocked the strikes and then they separated, pushing off each other's blades. "You'll never win," Evan taunted. Blood continued to trickle from Fox's wound. Evan eyed it with a grimly vicious smile. "You're hurt too badly."

"You talk too much," Fox said and feinted right, then left, and lunged.

Evan barely had time to block the surprisingly quick move, almost losing his sword when he did block it. He grimaced, trying to push Fox's blade away.

But even wounded, Fox was stronger. The blade drew closer and closer to Evan's breastplate. Suddenly, Evan stepped away from Fox and Fox's sword bounced off Evan's armor. He pursued Fox relentlessly, attacking with a volley of arcs and side swings.

They were skilled warriors. In any other battle, Fox

would have defeated Evan. But he was wounded and now they were evenly matched. Jordan felt her heart stopping each time Evan swung at Fox, each time his blade whistled through the air.

Fox backed away from Evan. He looked defeated. His shoulders sagged. His sword drooped.

Jordan felt agony spear through her. She started to step forward to call a halt to the battle.

But then Evan suddenly charged, raging like a wild bull. "You are mine!" Evan snorted as he rushed forward, his sword held high over his head for the finishing blow.

Suddenly, Fox came to life, swinging his sword to knock Evan's attack aside. He continued forward, stepping into Evan's charge, slamming his shoulder into Evan's stomach. Evan buckled under the blow, and Fox added a solid blow to Evan's helmet that sent Evan toppling like a tree.

Fox stepped forward, placing a foot on Evan's sword arm and pressed his blade into Evan's throat, the hard metal just touching his soft neck. "Once again, the day is mine. And this time I will collect what is mine."

"We'll see about that," Evan spat. "You may have won this battle, but I will win the war."

Fox glared at Evan. He did not like the threat behind his words. There was something else happening that he was not aware of. "Yield," he commanded through clenched teeth. "I prefer that you don't, but I will give you this one last chance to keep your head attached to your neck."

Evan raised his hands. "I yield," he grumbled.

Fox rose slowly and stood towering over Evan for a long moment. Finally, he sheathed his sword.

"Fox!" Jordan's cry rang out through the clearing.

Fox whirled and saw Jordan running toward him, a soldier directly behind her, his sword raised above his head to cut her down.

"Jordan!!"

CHAPTER THIRTY-EIGHT

Jordan raced forward. She felt like she was running through water, her legs refusing to move any faster. She could hear the guard's heavy boots crunching the ground behind her, could hear his ragged breath as he charged after her.

She looked up to see Fox running toward her, crushing the blades of grass at the edge of the jousting field beneath his booted feet. It seemed as if he, too, was running in a macabre slowed-down motion. His blue eyes grew wider in terror as he neared her; his teeth gritted in agony. She could see him mouth her name, but for some reason she could not hear the word.

Behind her, she thought she felt the hot breath of the soldier splatter across the back of her neck.

Instinctively, Jordan stepped to her right, trying to avoid the sharp blade she knew was coming at her. But her movement wasn't enough to save her from harm. She felt a strange biting sting in her right arm.

Suddenly, Fox was before her, grabbing her arm and pulling her behind him to safety just as he met the next swing of the soldier. Fox easily intercepted one and then another of the soldier's arcs, countering with a hard thrust and then another, driving the soldier back from Jordan.

Jordan took a few steps back, moving away from the fight.

Fox swung again and again, then deflected a thrust. He swung his arm around hard, knocking the soldier's blade aside. Then he swung the hilt of his sword upward, striking the solder solidly on his exposed chin. The man staggered back a step and Fox moved in, delivering another solid strike with the handle of his weapon, crunching the leather-wrapped metal into the guard's chin, then into his cheek. The force of the final hit spun the soldier completely around, and he collapsed unconscious to the grass.

Jordan raced to Fox, throwing her arms around him. She trembled with relief as she clung tightly to him. "Fox, Fox," she gasped. "Take me with you. Don't leave me here. Please, take me with you."

Fox put one arm around Jordan, the other clutching tightly to his side. "You are coming with me." His hand squeezed her arm and a bright flare of pain erupted. She groaned and pulled back to look down at her arm.

"You're hurt," Fox whispered as he looked at her arm.

Jordan glanced down at her arm to see a cut and a thin red line trickling from it. The soldier's sword had just barely nicked her. She pulled Fox against her, never wanting to let go. Never wanting to relinquish him again. She pressed her face against his shoulder and noticed Fox had his own trail of blood to deal with. "So are you," she whispered back.

"It's the old wound," he said. And then he smiled a most wondrous smile at her. "I guess we will have to tend to each other."

Jordan smiled back. "Yes. For a long, long time."

They stared at each other for a long, lingering moment. Fox moved his face closer to hers, and she parted her lips in anticipation of his kiss.

Suddenly, a hulking shadow fell over them, blocking the sun. Fox quickly moved in front of Jordan, his body shielding her against any would-be attacker. He looked up to see his old friend.

Evan sat atop his horse, glaring down at them. Fox held his sword ready, lifting it slightly, the sharp tip pointing directly at Evan.

"You may have won your love," Evan snarled at Jordan, "but who will save your children?" With those dark words, he abruptly whirled around and spurred his horse brutally hard, driving the animal toward the gates of Castle Vaughn.

Jordan instinctively reached for the dagger at her thigh, her sheath was empty. She couldn't even remember when she had seen the dagger last. Fear and desperation seized her as she watched Evan ride off toward Castle Vaughn. The children!

Desperate, despondent, Jordan began to race after Evan, running as fast as her legs would carry her. Fear tightened its hold around her heart.

Suddenly, Fox was beside her on his horse, his hand outstretched to her. "Here, Jordan," Fox called.

She grabbed his hand and he pulled her up before him, seating her in front of him. He spurred the horse forward.

Evan was so far in front of them! The horse had to go faster, but the poor animal was already panting hard, worn out from the joust.

Jordan's hands clutched the pommel as Fox maneuvered the horse over a fallen tree. She lost her balance and teetered for a second, but Fox held her firmly against him. "Hold on," he urged.

His tone somehow calmed her, taking some of her fear away. Evan was too far ahead for them to catch up to him. He was going to reach the castle first. *Faster,* her mind urged. *Faster.* But they had two people on their horse where he had only one. They would never stop him in time. A sob welled up in her throat and tears blurred her eyes. What horrible things would he do to the children just to get back at her? She couldn't even bear to imagine, but Evan was capable of just about anything. "Fox," Jordan pleaded, her voice fading in the wind that rushed by them.

"Here."

Jordan looked down. Fox held a dagger in his hand, holding it before her. She took it from him as the horse lurched forward.

"You have to do it," Fox said.

Jordan looked up at Evan. She could see his back just ahead of her. "I can't. He's too far. We're moving too fast."

"You have to! It's our only hope. If he reaches Castle Vaughn before us, the children don't have a chance!"

"He's wearing chain mail. It will do no good."

The horse leaped over a scattered pile of rocks.

"I'll get in as close as I can. You have to aim for his head or his neck."

Horror speared through Jordan as Fox urged his horse faster with a slight kick. How could she throw a dagger at Evan's neck? It would kill him! How could she kill him?

How can I not? she wondered. *He'll kill the children if I don't stop him. Or worse.* Jordan glanced down at the dagger in her hand. Her fist was trembling. What if she missed?

Jordan lifted her gaze to see Evan moving fast down the dirt road toward Castle Vaughn. She had to stop him. It was all up to her. Resolve filled her. She clutched the dagger tightly.

Evan would not beat them back to Castle Vaughn.

"He's getting too close to the gates!" Fox declared.

Jordan watched Evan ride. She had certainly hit a target as far as that before, but she had been standing still, not riding a moving animal, and the target had been still. "Fox," Jordan whispered in doubt.

"You have to do it," Fox said.

Jordan saw Evan's bare neck moving up and down as he galloped hard on his horse. She knew she couldn't hit it. It was too small a target, moving too fast and too far away.

"You're the only chance the children have," he said.

Jordan's gaze dropped to the dagger.

"Do it now!" Fox ordered.

Evan erupted through the thin trees, racing hard for the drawbridge. They followed, moving quickly behind him.

Castle Vaughn rose before them, its tall towers reaching skyward. Where the castle had once appeared warm and beautiful and inviting to Jordan, it now looked as grim and ugly as she knew Evan's soul to be. In her mind, the crumbling ruins of Castle Mercer held more grandeur and majesty than the starkly foreboding, perfectly maintained fortress of Castle Vaughn.

Evan reached the drawbridge and started across.

"Do it now, Jordan!"

She brought her arm back and flung the dagger with all her strength, praying for her throw to be true to its mark.

CHAPTER THIRTY-NINE

The dagger flew straight and hard, zeroing in on its target, the blade heading directly for the exposed flesh on Evan's neck. But at the last moment, Evan's horse made a small leap onto the lowered drawbridge, and the metal blade struck Evan in the shoulder, clanging loudly as it struck his armor. The dagger careened off his chain mail and hit the castle wall in front of them, smashing into a torch burning on the wall, sending sparks and flames flying into the air.

Spooked by the sudden burst of fire, Evan's horse whinnied in fear and reared back, then bucked wildly. Evan tugged at the reins, trying to get the frightened animal under control, but his horse kept snorting in terror and bucking so frantically that Evan lost his grip on the reins and fell out of the saddle. Evan hit the edge of the drawbridge hard with a tremendous thud.

Then he tumbled over the side and fell into the brackish moat below.

Jordan and Fox reached the drawbridge, moving to the spot where Evan had entered the water. Jordan waited for Evan to resurface. Fox reined in his horse to gaze down at the moat. Bubbles emerged from the brown water, but Evan did not surface.

A cry of alarm echoed from the walkways of the castle.

Fox cursed silently from behind Jordan and dismounted. He moved quickly to the edge of the drawbridge.

"No, Fox," Jordan whispered, unable to move from the saddle for a long moment, fearful of what he meant to do.

But Fox ignored her and launched forward, diving into the moat waters. His body pierced the muddy waters like a knife.

Frantic, fearful, Jordan dismounted. She stared at the waters below. Jordan felt bodies press close around her, and without looking knew they were all staring as raptly into the water as she was.

The dirt and mud churned up from the moat's bottom made it impossible to see what was happening beneath its dark surface. Jordan's mind and heart screamed as the minutes passed. Where was he? She silently begged Fox to resurface.

But the water remained still.

Someone beside her jumped into the moat water. And then another.

Suddenly, the water erupted and Fox emerged, gasping for air. He had an arm around Evan's neck, straining to keep his head out of the water. Evan was slumped over, unmoving.

The two men who had jumped into the water moved quickly to Fox's side. They took Evan from his arms and swam to the drawbridge, pulling Evan along with them. Several farmers and knights helped to lift Evan out of the moat and onto the drawbridge.

Jordan watched as Fox swam to the drawbridge. She leaned over, reaching down for him. Fox grabbed her outstretched hand. The soldier beside her reached down to help Fox up, and together they helped him onto the drawbridge. Jordan wrapped her arms around him, relief coursing through her body. They sat for a long moment, entwined in each other's embrace.

Jordan pulled back to look into his eyes. She couldn't understand why he would dive in after Evan. Why, after everything Evan had done to keep them apart?

Fox smiled wearily at her and cupped her cheek.

Silence settled around them. Fox glanced over his shoulder.

Evan lay very still in the middle of a group of soldiers and villagers.

Fox glanced at Jordan. Anxiety lit his eyes. She knew he wanted to leave, to flee before Evan could charge them with trying to kill him. He stood, drawing Jordan up with him, his arm tight about her shoulders.

One of the villagers turned to look at him. Jordan thought for a moment there would be a cry of alarm. The villager opened his mouth. "You're very noble and honorable to rescue m'lord."

Fox shared a startled gaze with Jordan.

"You dived in to save Lord Vaughn."

Fox's surprise faded and a darkness settled over his face.

"Yes," Jordan supplied quickly before Fox could respond. "He is very noble."

Fox turned a startled gaze on Jordan, and she realized

for the first time he was as much a noble in deed as she was in name.

As they approached Evan, the villagers and soldiers parted, making a path for them. Jordan's arm tightened around Fox's waist. When Evan saw them, would he shout orders for their imprisonment? Would he threaten Fox's life again?

Jordan faltered just as the last man standing near Evan stepped aside. Evan lay on the drawbridge, unmoving. His eyes did not open. His chest did not rise and fall.

"It was the weight of his armor," one of the soldiers whispered. "He drowned."

Evan was dead.

Jordan almost collapsed at the realization, but Fox held her up. Evan was dead. The monster he was would torment her no more. The children were safe, and Fox was the true victor. Tears filled Jordan's eyes. Tears of happiness, tears of joy. She threw her arms around Fox, sobbing against his shoulder.

Fox embraced her tightly.

Relief swept through her, and she knew that the future was bright. Somehow, they had overcome incredible odds and they were still together. She looked up at Fox, but there was something sad in his eyes. He took her hand and led her away from the crowd of people, off the drawbridge. The soldiers let them pass. They seemed disoriented and lost, bewildered at what to do next after the loss of their lord and leader.

Fox stopped just at the base of the drawbridge and turned to Jordan. He looked down at his feet.

He was leaving her. The realization hit like lightning. "No," she whispered.

Fox looked over her shoulder at the crowd of villagers

and soldiers that were now lifting Evan's body to carry him into the castle. "I don't belong here," he said.

Jordan stared at him in disbelief. She didn't know what to say to him.

"I'm an outlaw," he told her quietly, his eyes finally coming to rest on her.

Tears filled her eyes. "After all this, you're still going?"

"Don't make this harder than it is," Fox said softly. He took her face into his hands. "If there's anything you need, anything you want, I'll always be here."

Anguish ripped Jordan's heart. He pressed his lips to hers in a tender, warm kiss. A promise. Then he turned, took the reins of his horse, and began to lead it away, walking into the grassy field.

Jordan watched him, the proud gait of his steps, the straight back. He was a powerful, proud man. No longer the boy she had left. Now a man—a man who was leaving her, a man she loved more than anything in the world.

He was moving away from her, moving out of her life again. "No," she whispered and stepped forward. *Not again. This can't be happening.* She was sobbing now, tears streaking her face, blurring her vision. *He's just giving up. Just walking away.*

Jordan ran after him, calling his name. "Fox!"

He paused and turned to her.

Jordan slowed as she approached him. "I need something."

"What?" he asked, confused.

"You," she told him. "You can't just walk away from me. I left you ten years ago, and I won't let you make the same mistake now."

"What would you have me do, Jordan?"

"Carry through on your threat."

Fox lifted startled eyes to her.

"Marry me," she dared.

He studied her face for a long moment. "Do you know what you ask?"

Jordan stared at him in disbelief. "Yes!" She took a step toward him. "To be with you for the rest of my life."

"In a run-down castle. Titleless, denounced by your father, always scrabbling for food."

Jordan moved forward, her hands reaching out to him. She clenched them in his tunic. "We can find a way to change this. We can do it together, Fox. I can talk to my father with you by my side. We can petition the king. It's not impossible—not if we do it together."

Fox gazed down at Jordan. His eyes were hard and unrelenting. But the longer he stared, the softer his gaze and his features became. "I cannot fight against you. I just don't want to." He clenched her hands in his, holding them against his chest. "With you, I believe anything is possible." He brushed a strand of hair from her cheek. "My love," he whispered and cupped her face, drawing her closer to him. "I will fight for you."

He kissed her, tenderly caressing her soft lips. Jordan's body tingled with his kiss, igniting an inferno of possibilities. She knew as their kiss deepened that their love could overcome any evil.

EPILOGUE

"... it was how I won Jordan's mother."

Fox watched Lord James of Ruvane speak to the assemblage of gathered dukes and barons and earls and their ladies. The room was silent now. Even the boisterous, blubbering soldier who'd had much too much to drink was sitting quietly listening to Lord Ruvane. The guests had come from all across the lands at the bequest of Jordan's father. They had been invited to join in the celebration and now had all gathered in the Great Hall of Castle Ruvane to listen to Lord Ruvane speak of carrying on the Ruvane tradition.

Lord Ruvane turned his attention to Fox, who sat beside him. "I was wrong to question the outcome."

Fox glanced at Jordan. Her elaborate blue velvet dress was fringed with expensive gold. Her hair had been combed until it shone like polished mahogany. She had pulled her hair back behind her head and curled it into a circular braid. A crown befitting a royal lady. She was the most beautiful woman Fox had ever laid eyes on.

She turned to him as if sensing his stare and cast him the most beguiling smile.

Fox set his hand on top of hers as it lay on the table. An immediate jolt shot through his body to the very bottom of his toes. Did the mere touch of her hand have to send that kind of arousal through him every time? He smiled back at her, already knowing the answer to his own silent question.

"The true winner of the tournament shall wed my daughter!" Lord Ruvane heartily proclaimed as he raised his goblet in salute. "Fox Mercer has proven himself to be a man of impeccable character. I welcome him into my family with open arms."

The hall erupted in wild shouts of approval and agreement. Fox thought he heard Pick's big voice leading the group. Of course, Fox mused, his cheerful shout could have been because Lord Ruvane's speech was over and the drinking and revelry could commence once again.

Jordan turned to Fox as the talking resumed throughout the Great Hall, happiness shining in her eyes. "Betrothed," she said, the word rolling sensually from her lips. "What do you think of that?"

Fox chuckled low in his throat. "I think I can't wait until the wedding night."

Jordan smiled in agreement, giving Fox a half-lidded look that promised pleasures beyond his imaginings.

God help him, but Fox wanted her alone with him now, to touch her and caress her in ways only lovers understood.

Suddenly, a loud gasp of awe filled the room. Fox glanced up to see a man lowering a sword down his throat. Another man was juggling hot pokers. A third was cuffing a large bear, mock wrestling with the animal. The room was suddenly, almost magically, full of exotic performers. Jugglers tossed bags of beans in the air and caught them with their teeth. Soft harp music filtered over the entire assembly.

Fox's gaze moved past the entertainment and over the crowd. Farmers and their families feasted on mutton and veal. Merchants sipped ale and gorged themselves on spiced potatoes. He spotted Beau and Pick seated in the middle of a dozen men. Pick swept his arm before him in a grand gesture and Fox knew he was retelling some tale, exaggerating his skill and prowess, no doubt. Beau shook his head, smiling slightly.

Fox grinned warmly at the sight. He was grateful all of his friends had been unharmed in Evan's schemes.

"Fox."

Fox lifted his gaze to find Lord Ruvane standing before him. "I do hope you can forgive me for everything. I can be a pompous old goat at times."

Fox nodded at him. "If you are willing to entrust your most valued treasure to me, then I can do no less." His eyes again lighted on Jordan, who gave him a vibrant, glowing smile. Fox lifted her hand to his lips and bestowed a kiss to her knuckles.

"I would entrust her to no one else," Lord Ruvane whispered and bent to kiss Jordan's cheek. He looked back over at Fox. "I can see in her eyes that you are the true champion of her heart."

Kara suddenly emerged from beneath the wooden table, giggling. She raced past Jordan, followed by Mary Kate, who was screeching with glee. The two children raced off and little Jason poked his head out from beneath the table.

Jordan waved him out. The boy paused before her,

panting. "Did Kara and Mary Kate come this way?" he wondered.

Jordan nodded and pointed toward the kitchens. Jason scampered away from them. Jordan looked up at Fox.

"Do you think our children will be as precocious?" Fox wondered.

"Without a doubt," Jordan said, watching the children weave through the crowded hall until they disappeared behind a group of soldiers.

Fox seized Jordan's hand, pulling her to her feet. Jordan let out a startled cry, but she let Fox lead her out through the crowded kitchens and across the hall. He stopped in a secluded corridor and stepped closer to her, moving her back to the wall, then bent his head, claiming her lips.

When they separated, Jordan whispered, "My lord, is this the appropriate place?"

"Now that you will be my wife, there is no inappropriate place," he responded, bending his head again to hers.

"I told you we'd find him here!"

Fox groaned against Jordan's lips and slowly separated from her to turn toward Beau. Pick, Scout, and Smithy followed. Fox turned to Beau. "Just because you're now my captain of the guard doesn't mean you can disturb me at every opportunity."

Beau laughed. "Actually, Pick and I were having an argument. Pick thinks that we have to call you 'm'lord Fox' now."

"It is my title," Fox replied.

"Are you serious?" Beau gasped. "After all my years of service?"

Fox gazed down at Jordan, a smile on his lips.

A cacophony of giggles echoed through the hallway, announcing the children as they raced down the hall toward them. Kara grabbed Jordan's skirt, circling her and Fox. "Jason won't leave me alone!"

"Is Castle Mercer going to be our home now?" John asked as he reached Jordan, looking a bit nervously at her. "Forever?"

"Forever," she assured him. "You can even help us rebuild it."

John beamed her a magnificently happy smile. "Can I be Fox's squire?"

Fox nodded. "I would have no one else."

The corridor erupted in argument.

Beau complained, "Who will be my squire?"

"I wanted to be your squire!" Jason groaned, pausing in his tormenting of Kara.

"Fox promised I could be his squire," Mary Kate called.

Fox sighed and lifted his gaze. Through the doorway he saw his father standing proudly amidst a group of nobles, all shaking his hand and congratulating him. Fox smiled. His father would once again enjoy the company of flesh and blood friends. His dignity had been restored. He didn't have to pretend anymore.

Michael stood nearby, talking to another monk. A smile split his lips, and Fox thought it odd how he couldn't remember the last time Michael had smiled.

His brother, his father, his friends. All happy. And he, the happiest of all!

And it was all because of Jordan.

His arms tightened around her. She had been worth waiting for. Ten years of loneliness and a future of joy. It suddenly seemed fair. There would be no more loneliness. There would be no more ghosts.

There would only be love.

None of them would ever live in darkness again.